Something Twisted

by ace gray

Copyright © 2020 Ace Gray

Except the original material written by the author, all songs, song lyrics, and song titles contained in this book are the property of the respective songwriters and copyright holders. The author concedes to the trademarked status and trademark owners of the products mentioned in this fiction novel and recognizes that they have been used without permission. The use and publication of these trademarks is not authorized, associated with, or sponsored by the trademark owners.

No part of this book may be reproduced in any form or by any electronic or mechanical means, including information storage and retrieval systems, without permission in writing from the author. The only exception is by a reviewer, who may quote short excerpts in a review.

This book is a work of fiction. Names, characters, places, and incidents either are products of the author's imagination or are used fictitiously. Any resemblance to actual persons, living or dead or events is entirely coincidental.

editing by Payne Proof
formatting by J.R. Rogue
cover design by Book Cover Kingdom

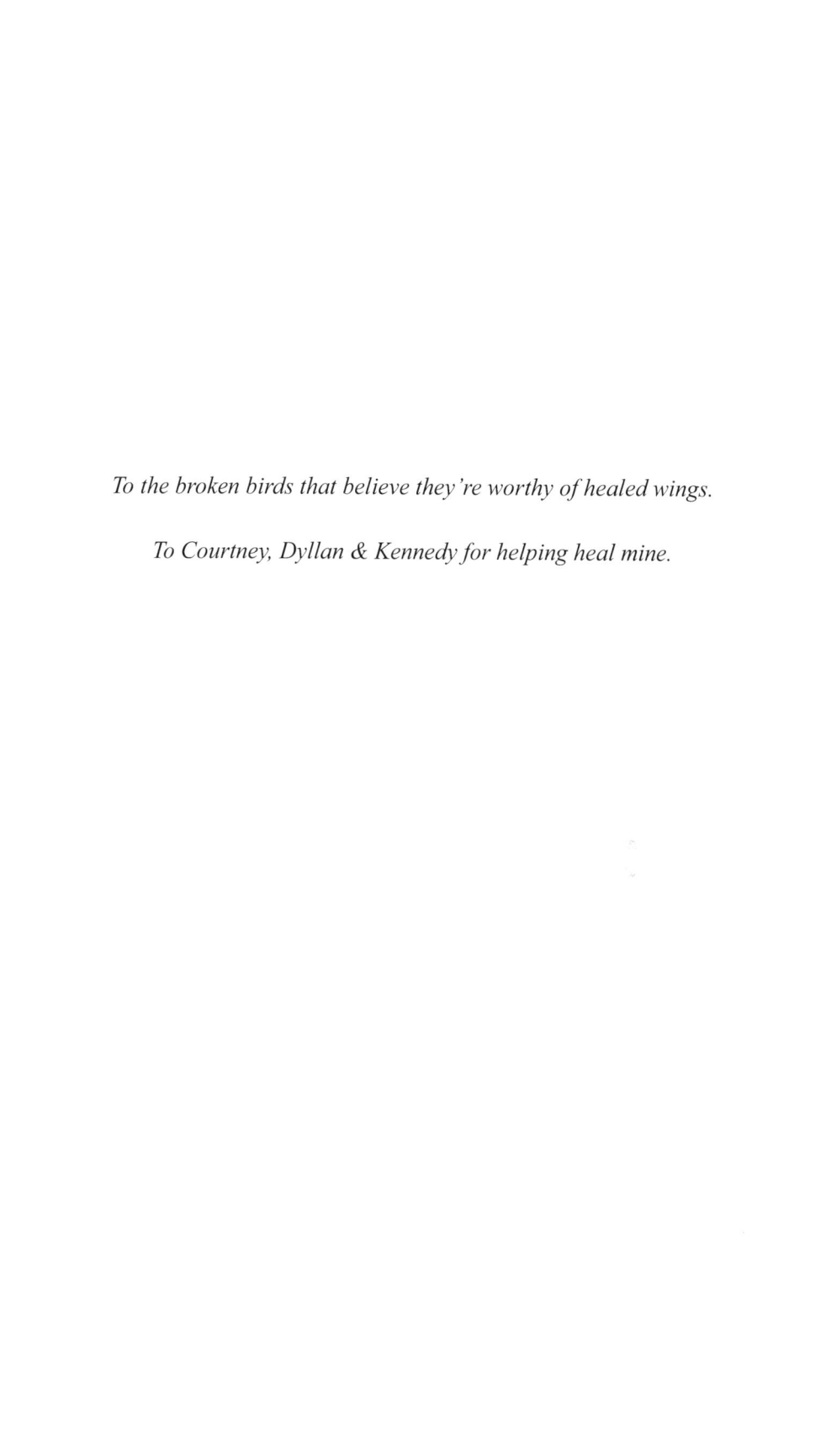

To the broken birds that believe they're worthy of healed wings.

To Courtney, Dyllan & Kennedy for helping heal mine.

PROLOGUE

I tried not to stare but one of her ears was shredded. *Shredded.* Like a cat had set razor claws to her flesh and left it in ribbons. I wanted to heave. Her other ear held a giant metal disk, the kind she'd stretched her lobe to fit. If it hadn't been for her ears, she would have been the most beautiful woman I'd ever seen.

Dark red hair was piled on top of her head so rich it was almost black. Her lips matched. Freckles were smattered across the bridge of her nose and cheek bones. Bright green eyes watched me, tracking my every move as I walked into the shop? Office?

What was this place…?

Rich silks hung haphazardly from the ceiling and were pinned to the walls. There were three different tables, all of varying heights and all in different spots within the room. The tallest had a mosaic tabletop, one that seemed to depict a Celtic knot. The regular one seemed more ancient than the symbol itself and each chair sitting around it was different.

She guided me to the last. The one that sat close the ground and had plush silken pillows in rich jewel tones surrounding it. Swirls of incense churned in my wake, thick and cloying.

"Deirdre?" she asked even though I couldn't recall giving her my name. "Tragic name for an Irish girl."

"My friends call me Drea."

"Have you heard the legend of Deirdre of the Sorrows?" she asked as she opened a drawer and pulled out a velvet sack.

"No."

"You'd do well to know your history." She eyed me.

I shuddered at my own personal history. Nothing good lay behind me. *Nothing.* And I refused to look back there.

"Look, I just want to know who to choose."

"Oh matters of the heart." She clucked as she walked toward a cabinet of curios and vials.

"I love Niall." My fists balled at my sides.

She chuckled. "You *want* to love Niall."

The incense seemed to thicken, tickling my nose, scratching my throat. I waved at it wildly only to swallow some and begin to choke.

"Did you know Naoise dies in the legend?"

A candle sparked beside me, though I didn't see her reach for it, let alone strike a match. Another thick fragrance swelled up with the smoke. I coughed until my eyes watered.

"His name is Niall," I squeaked out.

"Drink this." She shoved a mug toward me that I hadn't seen her holding a minute ago.

"No." I wheezed. "I don't..." My protest cut off, my throat too tight to speak. To breathe.

"Drink." She offered again.

This time I took the porcelain cup and tipped it up. Whatever thick mulch was in there tasted like tar.

"Fucking gross." I almost spat it out as I slammed the cup back down. It teetered on the rim of the saucer she'd set down then spilled across the table. "Sorry." I winced. "But that was disgusting..." My tongue was suddenly heavy in my mouth; my vision whomped in and out.

"Now I will read your bones." She sat calmly, her long legs folding beneath her.

"What in the actual fuck?" I asked though it sounded muddled.

She shook the bag then rolled the velvet in her hand, whispering something that sounded Gaelic before dumping fragments of spine onto the table and into the spilled tea. The tar coated the ivory and even though my vision pulsed in and out, I realized they'd turned the color red.

Blood red.

I almost lost it there on the table but a cool and clearing breeze materialized from nowhere. It soothed me every bit as much as it sent a shiver down my spine.

"My, my, this is interesting. Perhaps Deirdre is an appropriate name after all."

"What the shit is going on here?" My mind was clearing. Sort of.

"I'm reading your future, darling. Your dismal and sorrowful future."

I felt like I'd been hit. Hard. And I knew what it was like to be punched, slapped, kicked… I tried to shake off the list.

"What does it say?" My words were shaky, no matter how I tried to steady them.

"You will cause much unrest in this little corner of the world."

The hair on the back of my neck stood up. *No,* was on the tip of my tongue. My mom had gotten me out of a life of mobsters and murderers. I wasn't an Ulster anymore. I wouldn't be. I was just another teenaged girl wondering about her future.

"Rivers of blood. Chaos and pain. Betrayal all at your hand," she mused in partial phrases. "You will need a soldier at your side if you wish to be free of it all."

"A soldier?" I swallowed, sorrow swelling in my heart.

"Someone to wage war. Someone ruthless and brutal and savage." She arched her eyebrow. "If you don't find him, you both end up dead. Just like the legend."

I rolled my eyes with a wild grunt and shoved up from the table. "Convenient legend," I snarked under my breath.

"Heed my words or don't, it makes no matter to me. It's your fate and your fate alone that you have to face." She shrugged before unwinding to stand. Incense swirled around her again as she walked toward the back corner of the room.

I shoved up from the stupid pillows on the stupid floor of the stupid Irish gypsy and started to stomp off.

"Today, lightning will strike, Deirdre of the sorrows." Her voice seemed far away, too far away. "Take that as a sign of what's been set in motion."

As if on cue, the door I'd used to come in snapped open.

"Don't need to tell me twice," I muttered, as I scuttled out the door, my mind muddy, thoughts barely formed but racing.

It wasn't until the bright sun and fresh air of the street outside rushed in that I could see straight or breathe right again. I had to steady myself on the steps until my knees straightened.

"Well?"

I couldn't help but smile at that deep, albeit cold, silken voice.

"That was stupid." I rolled my eyes even though I was unsettled and couldn't explain why.

"I could have told you that. She's a fortune teller…" Niall smirked, chuckling darkly, and damn if that sound didn't make me weak at the knees all over again.

He noticed and reached around me, pulling me close even though I was a step above him. He was strong but lean, tall even compared to me, and it was easy to wrap my legs around his narrow hips.

"What do you want to be when you grow up, Niall?" I leaned my forehead to his.

"What?" He cocked his head, his piercing eyes evaluating me.

"What are you going to do after Northwestern? After lacrosse?" I tuck the unruly dark curls of his hair behind his ears.

"Besides be with you?" he asked. I playfully smacked his chest, his answer made my heart flutter. "I'm thinking that I want to be a non-profit lawyer. Help people who can't help themselves, ya know. Or the earth. I dunno."

"You always have an answer, huh?"

"Is that what this is about?" He shifted just enough to kiss the tip of my nose. "Answers?" He arched his eyebrow up under his shaggy hair. "You're still freaking out about what to do after you leave St. Mary's?"

"No." I wasn't. Not really. Not completely. "I mean they want me to start applying for colleges, and how am I even going to afford that? Do I want to afford that? I don't know what I want to be or do or anything." I threw my arms up, and damn if Niall didn't catch me, keep me steady.

"Go to college, Drea. Become anything you want to be." He spun me around before gently setting me on my toes.

"The money…"

"There's grants and scholarships and financial aid." He shoved his hands up into my hair and pulled me close. His dark curl that hung in his eyes danced against my eyelashes; his green eyes bored into mine. Mine cast downward when he wet the perfect pink of his lips, the tip of his tongue barely visible. "And besides, whatever they don't cover, I'll pay for," he added softly. "I'll work ten jobs if I have to."

My lips crashed to his as they'd done a thousand times before, but something was different. This kiss, his lips against mine, lit me up. Everything in me was alive and electric. Our tongues tumbled and the world seemed to stop.

He pulled back but just enough to whisper against my mouth. "I love you, Drea."

And just like that, lightning struck.

TWELVE YEARS LATER

I HAD BEEN A GOOD KID. VALEDICTORIAN IN HIGH SCHOOL, AND captain of the lacrosse team in college. Then I'd been framed for murder, sent to jail, and sold my soul to be released. Needless to say, I'd seen some fucked up shit in my day, but this... I crossed myself and kissed the likeness of Saint Christopher that hung around my neck. This was a blood bath.

What looked like just another elegant Chicago brownstone from the street was actually the former lair of Connor MacCowan. One of five heads of house. Irish. Brutal. Blood thirsty. He'd taken over as head of the Maloney family years ago, every bit as dark and devious as Mickey Maloney had been before him.

Or as Mac Ulster was now. And I worked for Mac.

"Getting squeamish in your old age, Niall?" Ailee asked, her warm and wicked chuckle trailing behind her as she crouched down and studied one of the bodies on the floor.

"Just surprised someone pulled this off." I shrugged, supposing the MacCowans deserved it more than anyone else, and considering the company I kept, that said a lot.

No less than twelve men laid in the twisted shapes of death between the living room and dining room on the first floor. Blood puddled everywhere, thick and sticky. Brains and organs stuck in spray patterns to the walls. Thank God I'd skipped the raspberry jam tart this morning.

"Connor is dead as a fucking doornail." Ardan ducked in front of the old man slumped in a chair and waved even though the bullet hole he wore clearly said he was dead. Ardan's crazed, off kilter laugh filled the room. Ailee and I were used to it by now, shaking it off as we went about our inspection. I adjusted my gloves and looked at the hulk of a man at my feet.

"Emmett too." I couldn't help but smile as I turned him over. Fucking Emmett. The good little *soldier*. I only wish he'd suffered far worse than a gunshot. He deserved to be disemboweled and degraded. "Maybe God has a sense of humor after all."

Ardan's laugh filled the room again, so wild, so unhinged that the hairs on the back of my neck stood up. "This is Satan. Can't you see him in the artistry."

"Your brother is fucked up," I said to Ailee as I stood and continued my survey of the MacCowan house.

"So are you." She shrugged as she walked over to her brother.

The twins were my favorite of Mac Ulster's goons. I dared to call them friends, they were as close as soulless monsters got to having friends anyhow. We were loyal to each other and that said something. The last time I'd let someone in beyond that… I shook my head. I wouldn't think about her now except to wonder if *she* was among the bodies.

Or to wonder whether I wanted her to be among them.

Shit.

Deirdre Ulster had been my world when I was twenty-one. I was building my life up piece by piece on the foundation of us. But then she up and left. And with no explanation. To make matters worse, she took up with the MacCowans, when I thought all she wanted was out. None of it made sense. All that shit should have made the answer to my question easy. That second question shouldn't even cross my mind.

Fucking Drea.

I stepped over a few more bodies on my way to the stairs.

"Ardan, take pictures. Catalog the dead. Ailee, downstairs." I gestured opposite of the way I was going when I gave my orders.

I pulled my gun from my shoulder holster as I moved slowly and swiftly up the stairs. Whoever was left in this building—*if* anyone was left—was a threat.

The floorboards creaked as I worked my way up, sun shone in through the Tiffany glass windows. The carpet was rich and plush, the mahogany bannister smooth up to the golden angel statues that adorned them. I couldn't picture Drea living in a place like this.

Until I found her room.

It smelled like her. Cocoa butter and vanilla. I took a deep breath and slipped into the past. I always liked the way she smelled in fall most, somehow apple pie and deep orange and red colored leaves made her that much better. I'd bury myself in her neck to smell it on her thick, chunky scarves or long, dark wavy hair.

Then again, she left me for Emmett in the fall.

Fucking whore.

I let my fingers run over the clothes hanging in her closet, the few small things she kept on a bookshelf. Nothing but text books filled the shelf. For a moment, I caught myself wondering why? What had she decided to study in the end? What had she become when she grew up?

Well, besides the MacCowan family whore. I'd meant it quite literally when I called her one. I'd heard how they used her. How they trotted her out at parties for Connor or his son Brye to use.

This room didn't say whore though. The walls were bare except for one massive tropical beach photo, and the muted colors of the room seemed spun from the sand. They weren't the deep jewels she had loved when we... What in the fuck was wrong with me?

I rubbed the Saint Christopher necklace hanging beneath my shirt. Out of nowhere she had left me. *Me.* I was safe and secure, and I was going to offer her the world. A world away from all this. But she left me for *Emmett*. Emmett who was the right hand man of an Irish family heir that did the same fucked up shit her stepfather did. The same shit she was running from. I'd fought for her, tried to get her back, but then...

Then this fucking life happened. As a way to lure his stepdaughter back, Mac Ulster offered me freedom. I hadn't known I was trading a prison cell for invisible handcuffs soaked in blood and locked with steely threats. She never came back.

Fuck her. Fuck her for leaving me. Fuck her for choosing the MacCowans. Fuck her for ever loving me.

I turned and left the room, clearing the others one by one. There was the one with guns hanging on the walls. There was the one with a bloody towel laying on a bed. And last, one with all the artwork. I looked at the floor to ceiling paintings wondering who in this house still found beauty in art.

Who still found beauty in anything for that matter?

I turned for the stairs and skipped down them.

"Anything?" I asked when I found Ailee sitting at the table with her heels kicked up.

"Not a soul." She shook her head.

"It's fucking weird, right?" I asked, looking around again.

"Yup." She popped her P at the end of her word.

"Even I think it's weird." Ardan pointed to himself and shrugged.

"That should say it all." Ailee arched an eyebrow and laughed.

I couldn't help but join her. "Remind me the last thing you thought was weird?"

"Well, it was really fuckin' weird when that little kid who isn't very good at playing violin made it to the finals of that gameshow last summer." He shook his head. "I mean, I can play the violin better than that."

"You can't play the violin." Ailee cocked her head.

"My point exactly."

"It's not about the violin, it's about the kid. His story. Pulls on America's heartstrings," I said still looking around the room.

"Oh…" He drug out the word. "I forget people have hearts." He clapped his palm to his forehead, and his eyes went wide in shock.

"We know." Ailee and I said it in unison.

"Man, I am *always* missing the point." He laughed again; God almighty that sound would give most people the creeps.

"What are we missing here?" My brow furrowed as I looked around again.

There wasn't anything strange about a shoot-out—not even one as bloody as this. There were coups inside the families or between them. Turf wars hadn't happened recently but they were undeniable in the Chicago history. The thing about them was, they were blatant. Obvious. There were rumblings and signatures.

No one ever left the seat of power vacant.

"What do we know about the MacCowan family?" I asked, taking a seat across from Ailee.

"One son, Brye, assumed he'd take over but now missing. At least not among the dead. Emmett, Brye's second, close range stomach bullet wound, likely punctured the lungs due to the upward tilt of the entry wound, dead on the floor." Ailee started rattling off more names. "Deirdre Ulster, longtime family *confidant*." The way she said the word made my skin crawl. "Confirmed discontent with the family, also missing."

"Confirmed discontent?" I sat up; I hadn't heard anything about that.

"She's been calling the house. Mac won't answer but every day she calls. In the last few days, it's been *numerous* times."

"Why didn't anyone tell me?" I snarled.

"Why would they?" She cocked her head to the other side, studying me. "I deal in recon, you deal in death."

I nodded, remembering just how well Ailee could read people. How she'd likely already read me.

"If you must know, I followed her a week ago. She was following Emmett. It all looked suspicious as hell. I followed her again yesterday and she'd been beat to shit."

I had to crack my neck to keep from reacting. Particularly because I didn't know how to react.

"Well if she'd been beat to shit, do we suspect her?" I asked.

"There's a set of footprints here that are much smaller. They missed most of the blood but you can see them here." Ardan crouched near Emmett's body, gesturing with his pinky. "Could explain why the shot was from a lower angle," he mused.

"So what? She gets pissed off, they rough her up, and she kills a dozen men?" I couldn't help but snort. "Not, fucking likely."

"I know chicks that would do it." Ardan pointed his wicked smile in Ailee's direction.

"Not her." I rolled my eyes at the mere thought of it.

"Did she have friends? Connections to any other families?" Ardan asked in a surprising moment of clarity.

"Not that I can tell."

A soft knock at the door made us all shoot forward, guns in hand, loaded and pointed right at the entryway.

"It's just me," Officer Daniels, a young cop on our payroll said, poking his head through the door, his hands held up in surrender. "Feds will be here in fifteen."

I nodded, and needing no other command, he slid back out the door. Ailee was smiling expectantly when I turned back to her, Ardan was jumping from one foot to another.

With a small chuckle, I looked him straight in the face. "Blow it up."

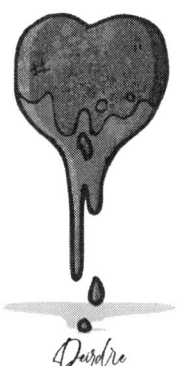

Deirdre

I stood staring at the big white mansion from my childhood. From the outside it looked the same as any other large Colonial style home on the street. A small paved horseshoe shaped driveway led up to columns flanking the front door. The lawn was perfectly green, perfectly manicured, and a line of tall oaks separated it from the house next door.

It looked so damned normal.

Standing here, staring at it, was so fucked up. Considering this was so fucked up. *I* was so fucked up. But my mom was in there and even though she wasn't up for mother of the year, when shit went sideways, I still wanted her. And for the first time in years, I was allowed to go to her. Unfortunately, she happened to share a house with my stepfather.

Fear rooted me to the spot in the drive. Bone deep exhaustion wouldn't let me leave. I had no money to my name and no access to the things I'd called mine. All I needed was somewhere safe to sleep.

Maybe one of my mom's big hugs.

I hadn't meant to, but I kind of, sort of unleashed hell in Chicago. I mean, who was I kidding, it already was hell, I just blew it wide open, so the demons had free reign. I'd only thought of them—of Filly Ryan and Brye MacCowan—when I accidentally ignited that blood feud. But if their love could conquer all this shit, maybe…maybe I had a chance.

I laughed at myself. All those years ago the fortune teller had told me to find a soldier and I'd failed. Epically. I'd tried. I'd tried to shove away what the fortune teller said, I tried to ignore the world outside Niall McDonough but then there was *that night.* The night that changed everything. Now *e*verything she said was coming true. Everything she said was real. All that was left was for both of us to die. I suppose that was coming my way. Hadn't it been for a while now?

I looked back up at the navy door that wasn't just some design feature but a portal to hell. It opened as I stared.

"Well, well, well. What have we here?" My stepfather, Mac Ulster, head of the Ulster crime family, stepped onto the stoop, arms crossed, voice slithering like Satan's snake itself. Right down my spine.

"It's, um, well, uh… Is my mom here?" I swallowed down the utter pain and agony of having to ask in the first place.

"Not at this exact moment," he answered from where he leaned casually against the column. "Interesting day to come for a visit."

"Yeah, well, it's been an interesting week."

"I can tell by your face." He jerked his chin toward the scrapes and yellowing bruises Emmett had given me before he died. "You look pretty that way, Deirdre."

Fuck off was right there—right there—but if he told me to leave, I had nowhere to go. Absolutely nowhere. And at a time where I would be caught, killed, or used by whoever found me first. Likely all three. What was the saying? Better the devil I know…

And, oh God, my stepfather was the devil.

Why was I here?

I started to back away. I'd been stupid. So, so stupid.

A hand grabbed at my elbow and I yanked away on instinct. It only tightened. I looked over to find a man dressed like a gardener except for the pistol shoved into my ribs.

"Do come inside, darling daughter." He started to laugh as the man beside me pulled me toward the front door. Toward hell.

"I just want to see my mom." I tried to rip out of his grip as the door snapped shut behind me.

"Oh, but you came to *my* house, stood on *my* lawn, so it seems your business is with *me*." His smile curled into something wicked but otherwise he didn't flinch.

This time when I tried to swallow down the fear that leeched from these walls, my throat was sandpaper and I couldn't. I looked back at the two men holding semi-automatics, flanking the door. Was it too late to run?

"Come into the living room. Sit with me." A fleck of crazy glinted in my stepfather's eye, and his smile somehow spread wider as he gestured toward the room, unchanged in the years I'd been gone. "Tell me about your troubles, little iníon."

I flinched at the exact words he used to use before... I tried not to think about that time, about how I'd been taken advantage of. About how my life was really just that story on repeat. A different man. A different house. A different day.

This was all I ever would be.

"I just want to talk to my mom." I tried to steel my voice. I'd seen so many depraved things, I'd done so many more, I couldn't let him shake me.

"Do you remember when you resisted me?" he asked coolly, as he crossed the distance between us.

Despite time, I still didn't measure up to my stepfather. Mac Ulster's reputation was larger than life, but then again, so was he. He was tall enough that I had to arch back and look upward. His almost coal colored eyes held me pinned precisely, his shoulders slumped, and his head angled to almost meet mine. He was strong, he always had been, but he was wiry and lithe like a boxer. One look at the lines of his face, the set of his jaw, betrayed his ruthless nature.

"Get in the fucking living room, Deirdre, or I'll give you a matching scar." He raised his hand and traced the one that curved along the line of my jaw. I prayed to all the saints he didn't get close to my bottom lip, that he didn't find the scars there. "And I haven't decided just how you'll get it yet." He bit his lip and grabbed his crotch. "Go."

I broke away from him before the bile rising in my chest spilled into my mouth. The echo of each of my steps into the living room was a sound I knew too well. It haunted my nightmares. *Echo, echo, echo, scream.* I wouldn't give him the satisfaction of a scream even if it was already crawling upward.

"Why are you here, Deirdre?" he asked, his voice betraying how close he stood behind me. "And don't give me that shit about your mother."

"I... I had..." My voice trembled, I couldn't tame it now. Not as I walked into the room that looked the same. The sleek mid-century furniture hadn't changed. Nor the white, gray and silver design of the room.

When I closed my eyes, I could still see red seeping across the floor, I could hear him explaining to my mother why she wasn't allowed to buy rugs. *This is where I kill them, Lea. Where we live, they shall die so I can see it always.*

I could still see it. It just didn't terrify me the way it used to.

Without warning, he shoved me forward, bending me over the back of the chair closest to us. My hands shot out to stop me, but he shoved all the harder. The texture of the thick upholstery pressed into my cheek.

His other hand caressed the curve of my ass then slid between my thighs.

I closed my eyes and thought about all the times I'd been here. Bent over for someone to take advantage of. I'd fought back only once—against Emmett and Connor—and look at where it had gotten me. I wanted to do it again, I wanted to stand up for myself but—

His hand slid up my back for just a moment before sinking back down. Beneath my jeans.

"You know why I think you're here?" He leaned down and purred in my ear as his finger grazed my backside before rubbing in my slit. A single tear fell from my eyes. "Because there's no one left to protect you."

I started to protest when he slipped his finger into me.

"Did you think your mother would?" He pulled out and slid his finger in the slickness of my slit. I couldn't help but twitch. "Did you think I would?"

The well of sorrow that always filled my chest when men used me like this built up pressure. Wild sobs were right there, streams of cascading tears too, but I dammed them up. I always did. It was the fifth or sixth time Mac had touched me, here in this living room, that I decided not to let them see me cry.

I made myself think about Niall. As my stepfather continued to fondle me, I tried to pull up memories of Niall and I fooling around. For years I'd tried to put him in place of the man taking me. It was his fingers. His kiss. Caress.

It was my choice.

"Pray tell, little iníon, are you the reason Connor MacCowan is dead?" He pinched my clit. "Emmett too? Are you, my daughter, the reason no heir remains?" He drug his finger up and pressed it against the gentle pucker of my backside.

"Ailee'd put money on it." A new voice answered, and it made everything below my belly button clench. It was a voice that I knew all too well.

No!

My body tensed as I wondered how? How was Niall here? And why? Why would he come anywhere near Mac? What in the actual fuck? My heart slammed against my chest echoing the sentiment.

Mac started laughing, each note insinuating pure evil as he pressed against my ass again. I bit the inside of my cheek, hoping it would quell the physical pain. I knew the emotional would never go away.

"Niall," he said with another laugh. "I think she remembered you." He pushed harder. The deep, sinfully honied voice laughed along with Mac.

"No." I gasped.

"What did you say?" Mac fisted into my hair and yanked my head up.

Niall—my Niall—sat on the couch across from me, cleaning

his nails with a far too large blade. Only he wasn't my Niall anymore. He hadn't been since I walked away from him without a word. Without an explanation. The shame had hung too heavy on my heart to let him see it.

He had the same searing green eyes but everything else had changed. Hardened. His hair was cut tight on the sides, almost shaved, and the dark locks that were left waved ever so slightly. Only one singular curl hung in his eyes. Every muscle I'd known intimately was bigger, threatening to rip out of his perfectly tailored white button-up shirt and fitted slacks. He wore a shoulder holster that matched his rich leather belt, the matching silver guns it contained accented the silver buckle at his waist.

When he thinned his lips in disappointment, he scraped his teeth across his bottom one and a lip ring glinted in the light.

Good Christ.

He flicked his frigid eyes up at me as if I was a fly buzzing at the windowsill only to look back down and continue his work with the knife. There was no warmth about him, no life left in his eyes. He didn't stop my stepfather; he didn't even flinch at what Mac was doing.

What had happened to him?

"Answer me, girl," Mac commanded, before shoving at my jeans and landing a solid, stinging swat across the bare skin of my ass. "What did you say?"

"Nothing," I bit out, trying to keep the shame, the fury, the agony from my voice. "I said nothing."

"I think she's shocked to see you, Niall." Mac chuckled as he pressed into my backside.

"Shocked to see me period? Or just shocked to see me out of the cell her boyfriend put me in?" He propped his feet up one at a time on the coffee table.

"I'll shock her," Mac said just before he shoved into me again. Harder this time.

I screamed. I couldn't help it.

"I remember when I used to hate that sound." Niall shoved his knife back into his boot and crossed his arms.

"Hate it?" Mac asked just before gathering up his spit and hawking it on my ass. "How could you?"

Even without my permission a sob shook my shoulders and true tears started to fall. This wasn't the worst I'd taken in my years of... *service* but this time it was in front of Niall. A Niall that didn't give a fuck. A Niall I couldn't hide behind.

"Make her do it again," Niall urged, and I looked up to find his smile the mirror of Mac's.

Mac pulled his finger out, glazed it through the saliva coating my skin, then pressed in again. This time with two fingers. My sob was mangled and mean just like Mac Ulster.

When I finally opened my eyes, Niall was crouching in front of me. Nothing of the boy I loved was still there. Not even a ghost looked out from behind his eyes.

"Hello, *Deirdre*." He spat out my name like it tasted awful. "Long time, no see." He reached over and clamped his hand down on my neck, squeezing hard. Tattoos I hadn't seen before peeked at the edges of his sleeves. "You ruined me," he murmured as he reached out and wiped my tears away. "I was going to be a good kid." He licked the salt from his fingers. "But you showed me that good guys go nowhere."

"And I let him go bad." Mac pulled out and spanked me again.

"I didn't—" I choked on my words, my tears.

"You did," Niall said simply.

"He's my little soldier now, Deirdre." Mac reached for my hair and yanked me back to standing only to turn me. "You wanted protection iníon? You'll get it but only on my terms."

I wanted to scream that I didn't want it—that they could go fuck themselves—but I couldn't find my words. My tears seemed to sear my skin.

"Thank you," I muttered, knowing it was the only thing I could say.

"Say it again." He grabbed my cheeks and chin and squeezed.

"Thank you," I shouted.

"Take her downstairs, Niall." He dropped my face and commanded Niall with a simple wave of her hand.

"No." I tried to shuffle away but my pants shoved around my thighs kept me from being able to get very far. Niall stood and swiftly moved around the chair, grabbing me before I could go anywhere. "Don't touch me." I shoved at his hands, but he didn't answer, he didn't even waver. He was too big, too strong. Instead he grabbed me and slung me over his shoulder, my ass still exposed. "Please," I screamed, again letting the tears fall freely now. "Please." I writhed on his shoulder and he just clamped down harder. "I can't…" I screeched, letting tears flow freely.

"Don't take me downstairs!"

Shit. Shitfuckpisscuntdamnhellfuckshit. Did I leave anything out?

Seeing Drea was a shot to my gut. I knew she'd made it out of the MacCowan house, I'd almost been glad of it, but not in my wildest dreams did I think the bitch would come here. This was hell on earth. Her being more beautiful than I remembered made it even worse.

Luckily I'd learned the hard way that I was one of the devil's favorite minions, and her beauty was skin-deep. I could keep my shit together.

I tried to shove our past—our past that she so fucking callously threw away—down as I let my hand rove over her bare skin as I carried her through the kitchen to the stairs that led to the basement. Her bare skin that was so beautifully pale and creamy. The skin that was a beacon to me in the night. I would *not* think about tentative touches, kisses, caresses from when we were innocent and in the dark. From when we were in love. That time was dead and gone.

Like she should have stayed.

She was right to kick and scream as I carried her, the stairs to The Pit were the slow descent into hell itself for a woman.

"Please, Niall, please," she begged.

Sure, her voice still strummed at some dark place inside me, but I'd be damned if I let that part of me gain any foothold. After what she'd done…

"Shut the fuck up, Drea."

She froze when I called her by her nickname. It made my trip down the stairs infinitely easier but she only stayed still and quiet for a moment.

"No, stop," she screamed as she reached for the doorframe and fought to wrench against me. "Please, please don't. If you ever loved me—"

"Keep that word out of your mouth. You don't know the meaning of it," I growled.

My jaw went rigid as I yanked her, first from the doorframe then from my shoulder to stand her in front of me. My teeth grit as I lifted my hand ready to let it fly. She tensed and turned away.

It gave me a moment to really look her over.

She looked like hell. Bruises colored her face in varying shades of purple, blue, green and yellow. Scabs and scars hash-marked the left side of her face—lips, cheekbone, the arch of her eyebrow. Her hair had been piled on her head but now it fell in disarray. I still wanted to cup her cheek and run those luxe, silken strands through my fingertips. Her body was built for sin—big beautiful tits, a toned stomach, a perfectly curved ass—but I could only see how it would fit in my arms.

I was a fucking idiot.

"Niall, please…" She tried to steady herself and her words. "I can explain. I can explain everything. Why I wouldn't call you back. What actually happened. Even Emmett."

Mercifully her words snapped the spell. Her begging, pleading, grated on my nerves, on my ragged heart. *How dare she?* How dare she think that *she* could beg of *me*.

"I bet you can." I lifted my foot up and stuck the toe of my boot in the crotch of her pants and shoved the fabric down to her ankles. She collapsed to cover herself. "I just don't give a shit what that explanation is."

"Emmett framed—"

"I fucking know Emmett framed me." The fuse of my temper was lit, hissing as flame devoured it. "But you let it happen." I reached for the hem of her shirt and ripped it upward. She tried to fight me, her hands leaving her body to yank at the hem, but she wasn't strong enough to keep me from ripping. "You let me get arrested." I tossed the top to the floor then tore at her bra. She disintegrated into sobs. "*You left me!*"

"I didn't want to." She curled in on her now-naked body even as she reached for my shirt, balling it in her fists as tears started to fall down her cheeks again. She was even more beautiful in her pain.

"Stop lying to me." I raised my forearm up and crashed it down on hers, freeing my shirt from her claws. "And more than that, stop lying to your fucking self." I shoved her back against one of the last open cages.

"No." She tried to brace herself against the metal bars. "I'm not."

She tensed and bowed. I held her firm as I let my eyes rove from head to toe and back again. God she was gorgeous. I pinned her arms and shoved her in the small opening all the same. She screamed as I shut the door of the cage and locked it.

"Niall!" She wrapped her hands around the bars and shook wildly. "You can't do this to me. *He* can't do this to me. Help me. Please!" Her words were rushed, panicked, echoing off the walls.

The other girls watched her with wide eyes and shut mouths as she went insane.

I looked around at those docile pets, all knowing their place in this world. Drea should have known her place too. She grew up here. My hand shot between the bars and grabbed her by the throat, pulling her face so it was close to mine.

"Shut the fuck up," I hissed at her. "Even if all of that were true, I wouldn't help you. I won't do anything but watch as Mac fucks you." I shoved her when I let her go, watching her tumble back in the cage. "Because no matter how you phrase it, you picked him over me."

I turned and walked away even as she started to rattle her cage that much harder, and her tears spilled fresh down her cheeks. She could burn in hell.

If she was in The Pit, she probably would.

"She go quietly?" Mac asked when I resurfaced. I gestured toward the staircase, her wails still echoing up in my wake. "She was a whore for Connor. Did you know that? One of his branded slaves. I watched her at a dinner party once. She'll settle into it eventually."

I clenched my jaw as I nodded. No matter the monster I was—that she'd been branded—knifed at me. That the man laughing about it was her stepfather turned my stomach.

The memory of her confessing her stepfather had molested her resurfaced. That was a different life. We were different people. She was so fragile when she found the courage to say those words to me. An explanation of why I needed to be gentle, go slow. Only streetlights had warmed my dorm room, casting shadows across the sheets when she whispered those words to me. Into my chest where she laid, almost in tears. I would have ripped the world apart at the seams for her that day. I'd vowed to protect her, no matter the cost to my body or my soul.

Fuck my body. Fuck my soul, and for the love of God, fuck her.

Look at where we were now. I'd watched him do it today. I'd watch him do it again soon. Part of me wanted to ask how we'd gotten here. Part of me knew Drea had done it.

"Tell me about the MacCowans," Mac prompted, pulling me back to myself. To who and what I was now. Thanks to her.

"Jesus." I thought back to the house we'd blown up yesterday. The house coated in blood. "It was a mess. A fucking mess. Twelve dead bodies. One of which was Connor himself, the other Emmett."

Deirdre still screamed downstairs. Her cries were still feral and fierce.

"No one was there? No one filled the seat?" Mac arched an eyebrow.

"No." I shook my head, hoping it would drown out Drea. "But Ardan left our signature."

He chuckled, no doubt envisioning Ardan doing what Ardan did best. Besides being batshit.

"Any sign of who might come?"

My eyes darted toward the stairs to Drea. Mac followed my eyesight.

"Really? The shrieking cat in heat downstairs." Mac reached for a decanter of scotch with an arched eyebrow. "I don't buy it."

"There were chick footprints at the scene." I could vividly picture those tiny little diamond, Chuck Taylor prints. "Facing Emmett, everything indicates she took a close range shot."

"That shortens the list," Mac mused.

"Considerably." The women that held positions of power in Chicago were few and far between. They'd clawed their way into those positions and each one I could think of was more ruthless than the last.

"If it was one of the five…" Mac trailed off.

"They would have been sitting at the head of that table, smug as shit, waiting for someone else to show up and see," I finished for him.

"Hence the theory, my darling daughter did it." His eyes flicked toward the stairwell, and I didn't let myself follow this time. It didn't fit her—power wasn't her motive. Drea was a fighter but she only did it to survive. She wanted to be free of all this.

Or at least she had.

"Could she have found someone to help?"

"It'd be a bit more believable that way. But what did she give them if it wasn't the head of the family?" I asked as I declined his offered scotch, not trusting myself here. Now. With her. "We need her to talk."

Mac smiled and chuckled before he took a sip. "Wouldn't you enjoy making her more than me?"

"Nope." And that was the truth.

I hated her for choosing Emmet over me. She knew I loved her. She knew I was going to take her far away from this shit place and these shit people. But she chose to dive back in. Emmet wasn't an Ulster but he was just as bad. Bad like I'd become when I got pulled into this stupid fucking game.

Using her wouldn't fix all that. Or make me feel better.

"I'm going to use her. Ruin her if I can." Mac watched me expectantly. "You know I've always wanted to watch her break at my feet."

I looked him dead in the face. "Should I bring her back up?"

He smiled and took another sip of scotch. "Not yet." He smirked. "Take the twins, twenty-four hours to find out who. I want that seat. Figure out who I'm competing against, how to get it."

I nodded and turned, knowing exactly where Ardan and Ailee had ducked off to.

The second I left the house, I took a deep breath. I hadn't lied—I wanted nothing to do with Drea—but I needed to clear my lungs of her. Let her screams fall from my ears. A walk through the neighborhood to the pub would do me good.

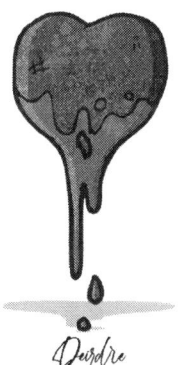

Deirdre

THE FLOORBOARDS SQUEAKED BENEATH MY SPARKLY PINK TOENAILS, and I winced, tensing beside the basement door. My mom and I had lived with my new stepfather for only three months when I started to hear noises coming from that stairwell.

No one would let me near the door. I'd been slapped just for touching the handle, but it hadn't stifled my curiosity. Two years. I waited two years before I couldn't take the not knowing anymore.

"Hello little inion. What are you doing down here?" Mac had always made my hair stand on end, from the very first time I'd met him. But that night, that night was worse. He was nice to me, too nice. "Were you trying to go downstairs?"

I swallowed but I didn't answer him.

"I'll take that as a yes." He reached over and opened the door.

I looked up at him with wide eyes, knowing it was a trap but also, oddly, not able to run away. The temptation was too much. I stepped toward the stairwell that seemed to open as a widening maw. Mac pushed me down the first step.

"You know what they say about curiosity, inion?" He was close behind me. Too close.

"Nah... No."

"It killed the cat." He chuckled in the dark as we both moved another step or two.

I gasped.

"But me? I like to keep my cats," he said as he flipped on the light.

I pissed myself.

IN HINDSIGHT, twelve-year-old me was far smarter than twenty-nine-year-old me. I'd given up screaming an hour ago when I realized none of them cared. Mac wasn't going to let my mom come down here. He wasn't even going to tell her it was me. I tried to shift in my cage but barely could. The thin metal bars of the dog kennel dug into me no matter how I sat or curled. They bit into my skin and made my skeleton crunch and ache. My legs couldn't tuck up tight enough, my shoulders seemed boney.

I had known this was what Mac did to girls. I'd known since that night when I was twelve, when he showed me kennels stacked two high around the perimeter of our basement, all housing naked women. But he'd never done it to me.

He touched me, tormented me, for three years after that night but always in the living room. I always slept in my bed. I'd been naive enough to think he'd extend the same *courtesy* again.

Wrong. So fucking stupid and wrong.

That really should have been what the fortune teller told me. *Deirdre, you're meant to make every mistake available to you. In this life and in the next.* That sure as shit had come true.

"I'm usually most comfortable slouched in the corner," the girl next to me said.

I almost snapped at her before taking in a deep breath and mimicking her pose. What I could see of it anyway. Her bright eyes and little else was visible in the darkness.

"Thanks," I muttered.

"That was quite the show before," she said, and I heard the shift of the cages as girls moved to listen. "You know Niall McDonough?"

I bristled at his name. Did I know him? Of course I knew him. He was my one true love that I couldn't look in the face after what had happened to me. But this version? The man I'd just seen was awful. Horrible. I hated him.

And I was entirely too jealous at the way she said his name.

"He and I used to date." I don't know why I said it.

"Seems like things ended well." She laughed even louder, my fists balled. "Sorry. I wasn't good with tact before... all this." I could imagine her waving her hand around. "Always the one to put my foot in my mouth."

"Good trick in this situation," I grumbled.

"Oh I like you." She ticked her nail on the bars of the cage. "I hope you kneed him in the balls."

I blew out a deep breath.

"I should have." God that would have been a good move.

"Next time perhaps."

"How long until next time?" I needed to start steeling myself now.

"Honestly, life's usually pretty boring around here."

"Until it's not," another girl added with a sniffle.

"Well, there's that." The girl who'd first spoken to me sounded like she was rolling her eyes.

"How can you say that, Saoirse?" the second bit out.

"It's just sex." She chuckled darkly. I couldn't help but join in. "See, the new girl gets it." She pushed her fingers through the side of cage. "I'm Saoirse."

I brushed her fingers as best as I could. "Deirdre."

"Thought it would be something like that based on your accent. Us Irish girls gotta stick together."

"Been here long?" I asked.

"Is that the sex slave equivalent to come here often?" She laughed again, and a few of the girls chided her.

"I've had women. Many of them. Doesn't do it for me." I shrugged and smiled even though she couldn't see.

"You're in a fucking cage, it's not about you anymore," the girl below us screeched.

"I'm well aware, princess." I sighed. "This isn't my first rodeo."

"Or second, or third, or fourth, or fifth…" Saoirse rattled off.

I sent a prayer of thanks to whatever saint protected sarcastic whores for giving me Saoirse. "You sound like me."

"I am like you. A daughter from one of the families, treated like trash, traded for a debt. Before they metaphorically fucked me every single day, now they just literally fuck me whenever they feel like it."

I closed my eyes and the memories swarmed in.

When I met Emmett, he pursued me. Relentlessly. I knew he was part of the MacCowan family, and I didn't give him the time of day. Not until that night… My head rolled back against the cage.

I'd needed a soldier.

And he was one. After that night—that last night I'd seen Mac Ulster—I made a choice. Not just for me, but for Niall too. I was damaged, broken, and pain did in fact follow in my wake, so I chose someone who was brutal and savage. Someone who would fight Mac. I chose Emmett.

Then it all went so bad. Worse than bad.

I raised my hand to rub beneath my bottom lip. The lines of scar tissue noticeably shifted under my hand. What Emmett had done should have made me cry but it didn't. I remembered the sear of the brand as it tore into my skin, but it was the fact that the man who I thought would save me had held the iron that tore at my soul. It was easy to let them use me after that. Hell, it was a distraction from what really hurt.

Sometimes I could convince myself they cared.

I blew out a deep breath and settled against the cold bars. Goose bumps blanketed my skin as I accepted how entirely shit this situation was. Here, in this house, and with this family, things were going to be worse. Hurt more. I knew, I knew in the very depths of my soul. But I didn't have a choice.

And I didn't feel worthy of making one.

I KNEW WHERE THE TWINS WOULD BE SITTING BEFORE I EVEN looked. Front right, corner table. It was tucked back past the windows, protected from the street by brick. It gave a perfect view of the front door but was dark enough that patron's eyes seemed to glaze over it. The swinging door to the kitchen was right beside it and more than once, we'd silently risen, pushed in, walked through the kitchen like we owned it, and left by the back door.

I knew they'd be there, watching as I walked in without a single glance, headed straight for the bar, and ordered not one but two shots. Jameson. Hot and sweet as it burned.

Just like Drea.

I signaled for another drink—well, just Jameson in a taller glass so it wasn't a pain in the ass to carry—before turning for Ardan and Ailee. They didn't say a word as I slid into the chair with the best view. Or as I sipped on the whiskey.

As we sat in silence, my third gun, the one tucked into my waistband at my back, got uncomfortable so I pulled it out and put it on the table without giving a single damn who saw. My fingers itched to light a cigarette. Why did they make smoking illegal in bars? Something about a health risk?

For fucks sake.

"Well this is fun," Ailee said, ordering another round with a single finger.

"Can I play with my toys at the table?" Ardan chuckled.

"No," I said soft but deadly, polishing off my whiskey.

He sat back, pouting with his hands crossed on his chest. Ailee just watched. Unmoving. I knew she was going to tell me to spill it, so I gestured for another and started talking.

"I met her in boarding school. All girls." Even if it was halls and halls of cute girls it hurt to think about. Ardan giggled manically and held out his fist for a bump. I shot him a look. "I wasn't this. The most trouble I got into was sneaking booze into their dorms." I smiled at the memories. "When I met her, Christ, it wasn't just that she was beautiful." My fingers were jonesing for something.

Ailee just cocked her head to the other side, a prompt to continue. Mercifully, my drink arrived.

"She was... she was someone who needed saving."

"Ooooo the white knight," Ardan taunted again, Ailee softened.

"Better than the angel of death." I took another sip, finally feeling the tension melt from my shoulder.

"Is it?" My throat still burned. "She told me about all this back then. About her family, about Mac." I shook my head. "She even told me about him touching her and The Pit. I was horrified. I was going to take her away."

"Why didn't you?" Ailee finally spoke.

"You got a smoke?" I bit my lip, fiddling with the ring front and center, rubbing my palms down my pants.

"I thought you quit?" She arched her eyebrow.

I held my hand out and snapped, expectantly. Ardan materialized one and I snatched it. Feeling the barely-there weight of it, the soft paper and firm filter as I let it hang loosely between my lips. Ailee leaned in and lit it.

"Then came Emmett," I said as I drew in the smoke, held it, then let it billow like I was a damn dragon.

"Sir, I'm sorry but you can't smoke in here." A girl came to our table. None of us looked up. I let the smoke tendril curl as I simply readjusted the gun that sat on the table.

"Might want to ask your boss about that policy again." I knew the voice that would play her best, equal parts seduction and destruction.

"A MacCowan?" Ardan asked, continuing our conversation without acknowledging her.

"Yeah, a fucking MacCowan." I drew another long drag on my cigarette.

"Spit on their graves," Ardan gathered it up like he was going to. I waved him off.

"You have no idea." I downed the fourth bit of whiskey in less than thirty minutes. "She snapped. I still don't know why. One day we were perfect, the next day she was with *him*," I snarled. "I fought for her. All sorts of shit you two would mock me for now—"

"Stand outside her window with a boombox?" Ailee reached over and took my cigarette from between my finger and drug once herself.

"Twice."

"And she didn't take you back?" she asked, choked, smoke still in her lungs. "Fucking bitch."

"One better." I took the tobacco back. "Emmett framed me for murder. Made it almost undeniable then paid off people to make sure."

"You didn't even get the pleasure of actually offing the bitch you went to jail for?" Ardan was disgusted. "That's bullshit."

"Well, if you really think about it, the bitch I went to jail for is sitting in a cage in The Pit."

"You going to make her pay?" Ailee reached her hand out for her own cigarette.

"Not for the next twenty-four." I raised my hand up and rubbed my temple. "We have a job."

"I'm bored," Ardan complained from where he was sprawled in the backseat. "Why didn't anyone bring toys?"

"Because you're not a child," I grumbled, desperate for another cigarette.

"Not true, the male brain doesn't reach maturity until age twenty-five."

Ailee and I shot each other a look across the front seat. "Two months hardly counts, Danny."

"I hate it when you call me Danny." Ardan went quiet. Ailee just started a gentle hum of *Oh, Danny Boy*; she knew exactly how to manipulate him. How to manipulate most men in fact.

"Knock it off guys." I leaned back against the headrest and rolled my eyes.

"What are we even looking for?" Ardan threw his burger wrapper in the air like it was a baseball.

"Anything out of the ordinary." Ailee sharpened her gaze toward the front door we were watching.

"Are we worried about the feds?" They'd been *right there* at the MacCowans.

Ailee's face folded but she didn't answer. "Let's focus on the matter at hand."

"This is the third fucking family…" Ardan whined.

"Two more," I said out habit.

"One," Ailee corrected.

I laughed. "Tou-fucking-che, Ailee."

"None of them know anything, two of them didn't even know the MacCowans were dead." Ailee snuggled down into her seat, letting her eyes close. "This is bullshit."

"Let's bugger off," Ardan groaned.

"You wanna tell Mac why we disobeyed? I sure as hell am not taking that bullet." I fidgeted with my fingers again. Fuck did I want to ask Ardan for another smoke.

"You will sleep in this damn car and you will like it. I need to get laid," Ailee grumbled.

"Jack off into a lotion bottle and be done with it," Ardan scoffed.

"Jilling off doesn't work like that, fuck head."

"Jilling off?" I asked with an arched eyebrow.

"Not okay with me taking back a word for masturbation?" She shot me a look over the side of her collar.

"Isn't it about equality? Wouldn't something gender neutral be better?" I couldn't help the smirk.

"Fine." She sat up and gripped the seats smoothly, shoving her head into the back seat. "Ardan, I have a vagina, so I fuck it with my fingers." She plopped back down in her seat. "Happy?"

"Dudes cannot put fingers in their sweet, hot cunts." I started laughing, Ardan echoed it.

"Fuck you two."

"Only if it's with fingers in our vaginas." Ardan unhinged a little more. Without a word Ailee shoved out of the Range Rover and started walking down the sidewalk. "Nothing like a little feminism to get everybody all riled up."

I chuckled. "We're assholes."

"See, now that's gender neutral." Ardan finally sat up as I watched Ailee jog across the street to the house we'd been watching and start stomping up the stairs to the front door.

"Shit," I swore as I shoved out of the car after her.

"Exactly, everybody shits."

"No, you fuck stain." I jerked my head toward the Murphy's house. "Get out here." I held my hand out to stop oncoming traffic as I bolted after her. "Ailee, what the fuck are you doing?"

She ignored me and knocked. Two gun barrels flashed at her forehead. I had the presence of mind to hold up my hands in surrender.

"What the fuck do three Ulsters want?" one of the goons asked.

"Nothing," I said as quickly as I could.

"You guys know anything about the twelve dead MacCowans?" Ailee spoke over me, calm and cool with her hands crossed on her chest.

"What?" they answered in unison, and we both saw them falter. I stepped up, shoulder to shoulder with Ailee.

"We've been watching you for hours. You've been watching

us, watching you. It's exhausting." She waved her hand. "Just tell us if you did it."

"No," the both shot back, firm and faultless.

"Great. Thanks." She turned and started walking down the stairs, grabbing Ardan on the way.

I nodded once before following her. The second Ardan opened the backdoor, I shoved Ailee against the hood of the Range Rover. My gun was pulled and pressed to her temple without me thinking about it.

"What the fuck is wrong with you?" I shoved her, making her thud against the car.

"Do it," she challenged, not fighting back in the least.

My hands dropped away as I shook my head and pinched the bridge of my nose. She was always reckless when she had an itch to scratch, I should have known. "That's what this is about?"

"Yeah." She turned to face me, rubbing her knee up the outside of my thigh. "Do it. Fuck me."

I rolled my eyes even though she was great in bed and better at detaching herself. "Get in the car, Ailee."

"Fuck you." She stomped her foot.

I pushed the barrel of my gun to the bottom of her chin, lifting it up so she met my eyes. "One more family then maybe."

Deirdre

I HADN'T MEANT TO KEEP TRACK OF THE HOURS. I REALLY HADN'T. I'd learned the hard way at the MacCowan house that counting the minutes only made them move slower. It was like I was waiting for something. For something that would never come. All while reminding myself that something else entirely would.

It had been over a day.

The only person that had come down was a man that had given me a Pop-Tart and a Go-Gurt. It wasn't exactly what I wanted but it was better than nothing. Better than starving. Wasn't it?

I leaned back against the bars of my cage.

But then I heard the footsteps, the collective gasp and tense of the girls in the basement with me. The shuffle of skin and the creak of cages barely proceeded light flooding down from the stairs. I blew out a deep breath, ready. Watching. A shadow filled it up before he clipped down the stairs.

I held my breath. If it was Niall... Christ, I had no idea how I would feel if it was Niall.

Bright red hair was noticeable in the light coming from upstairs. I blew out the deep breath. I was grateful it wasn't Niall even if it broke my heart too.

"Hello, poppet," he said with an unhinged voice as he stepped in front of me.

"Be careful with that one," Saoirse muttered.

"You think I'm going to go quietly?" I asked.

"God, I hope not." His laugh sent shivers down my spine, so clearly wicked, a little bit deranged. "I always enjoy a good fight."

"He means it," one of the other girls whispered.

With a single finger he gestured to me to move forward. I hesitated for a moment and his smile somehow grew, seemingly toying with the edges of his face. That's all it took for me to shift onto my hands and knees and crawl forward. He held out a hand, which I took to help squeeze out of the small opening, then he looked me over head to toe. He let his eyes linger where he wanted, drift anywhere he pleased, and despite the amount of times I'd been here, this time felt different. I felt... *exposed.*

I shrunk in on myself as he pulled me up the stairs. The wood of each rotted board dug into my feet. The way he grabbed me turned me just enough to hit my elbow on the railing. I winced.

"I can kiss it and make it all better," the man said, biting his bottom lip and arching his eyebrows.

I looked over and got a good view of the man for the first time. He had fire red hair, and the bridge of his nose was blanketed in freckles that made his blue eyes seem even brighter. He had a cut jaw and muscles to match. Under different circumstances, I would have been relieved that it was him. That he was attractive and a little wild. It might have been fun.

But something was different now.

Maybe it was me. Maybe it was because I'd thought for a few glorious days that I'd left this stuff behind. Maybe it was Mac. Maybe because Niall was here and had reminded me of my soul.

Fuck.

"She's really not the friendliest, Mac." The redheaded boy shrugged.

"Whores don't have friends, Ardan," Mac sneered. "That's why we can make them feel loved."

He reached for my face, trapping both cheeks and squeezing, puckering my lips. I tensed just before he kissed me. He didn't care that I couldn't move, couldn't kiss back. He just licked at my face, my mouth. I tried to bite back the bile rushing up my throat.

Just when I didn't think I could keep it together anymore, he pulled back and sucker punched me in the stomach. That acid turned to puke, and I lost it on the floor. My knees crumbled in pain and shock, landing in the contents of my stomach. Ardan still held my elbow or I might have collapsed face first based on the force of the hit.

I sucked in a deep breath and steeled myself the only way I knew how. "Enough of the foreplay, Mac, what do you want?"

Ardan laughed and for a moment I thought I'd said the right thing. Then I got a boot to ribs. I tried to scream but I couldn't catch my breath. I couldn't make my lungs expand. Not through the blinding pain. The edges of my vision darkened and the rest of it was speckled with stars.

I didn't see Mac coming for me. His hand threaded into my hair and fisted in it to start dragging me. I scrambled to get my arms and legs under me as we moved from the kitchen, past the dining room, where I'd eaten pancakes as a kid, to the living room. The damned living room.

He threw me when he let me go and my head hit against the edge of the coffee table. Heat bloomed above my eyebrow that I knew came from blood. I rolled on my back, hoping it was a sign of surrender.

A girl sat in the chair closest to my head, peering over as if she was studying me. I knew immediately she was related to Ardan. She had the same beautiful brilliant hair and the freckles as thick as the Milky Way across her nose and cheeks. Her eyes were likewise dazzling, a shade so vibrant, they were eerily similar to Ardan's even if they were green instead of blue. But where Ardan seemed unhinged and wild, she seemed calm and calculating.

Both of them seemed ruthless.

A toilet flushed from the downstairs bathroom across the foyer, and I flicked my gaze to find Niall. He wore the same clothes as yesterday but they were a little rumpled to match his mussed hair. If possible he was more gorgeous than yesterday. Less the crafted killer and more like the version only I used to see.

"Well this looks fun, but I think we'll be going." He eyed me for a second before jerking his head toward the door. The beautiful redhead stood from the chair, stepping over my body as if I were nothing.

"Don't want in on it?"

"Not really." Niall sighed, and I flinched, waiting for him to be on the receiving end of Mac's discipline. "I want to go home. I want to take a shower and fuck Ailee like a normal chick."

The girl snorted and Mac chuckled. "Normal?"

"I mean we'll probably show up with a couple of scrapes and bruises tomorrow—I can't count how many lamps we've broken—but that's normal enough, right?" Niall's dark chuckle was a sound I'd never heard, a sound that curled in the pit of my stomach.

"I could make you." Mac arched his eyebrow.

"I know. Just say the word." Niall shrugged.

"I'm gonna get answers. That's a different kind of fun." Mac toed at my ribs again. Even though it was soft, I cried out.

"Again, say the word Mac and I'll kiss the ring and rip her teeth out myself." He shoved his hands through his hair, and I pictured ripping it from his head. "But if it's all the same to you, let Ardan out of his cage for a little while."

"I knew I picked you for a reason, my boy." Mac walked over and clapped Niall on the shoulder. "Go home and destroy her. Maybe we'll both manage tonight."

I couldn't focus on the words, on what they meant. Not when Niall slid his hand to the small of the girl's back. And he guided her out the door. They were going to… Christ. And the way Niall had talked about it. It was going to be… I couldn't breathe again but it had nothing to do with my ribs likely being broken.

It was the sound of the door snapping shut behind them that finally, truly hurt. Silence settled in around me, silence except for the steadied, measured breaths of the men as compared to the rising, haggard nature of mine.

"I want answers little iníon." Mac made his way to the seat that the girl had been in. He leaned over me, just as she had. Something totally different colored his face than hers.

"3.1415926. The War of 1812. The Mauritania. The Beatles," I snapped before I could stop myself.

Mac nodded once before resting his forearms on his thighs. My eyes stayed on his as Ardan pulled me by the ankle. The tile scraped along my back until I was away from the coffee table. Ardan dropped to his knees, pinning my arms to my hips and sitting heavy on my already aching ribs.

"Hello, poppet," he repeated his words from earlier.

"Hi, Ardan." I rolled my eyes.

"I like this one." He ran his fingers down my face, letting my lips hang on them for a moment. There was something incredibly creepy about it. About how he seemed to watch my skin rather than *me*.

"Iníon, I need to know what happened in the MacCowan house," Mac asked pulling my attention from Ardan.

"They all died," I answered, and Ardan's thighs pinched tighter on my body.

"How?" Mac's voice got colder.

"Gunshot I'd imagine."

As soon as I said it, Ardan's knees dug into my sides making me scream. My voice cut off mid-sentence when his hands clamped down on my throat. I thrashed just once below him before I realized that my side hurt worse and breathing got even harder if I jerked. As quickly as he'd gripped me, he let me go.

I gasped and tried to wiggle but Mac stood and grabbed my face again. "Playing the idiot doesn't suit you my sweet. I happen to know better. I've always known better." He shoved me as he let me go. "Now tell me, *who* shot them?"

"What makes you think I was there? That I know?" I honestly needed to know.

Ardan reached again for my lip and yanked it out and down. "That."

"A prized possession." Mac ran his finger along the lines of the brand that Emmett had given me, marking me as property of the MacCowans. "You wouldn't have gone *anywhere* if you knew they were alive. You would have known you'd end up dead."

"Why do you think I'm here?" I tried to wrest my lip away from him.

"Your footprints were at the scene."

"Fuck that." The vehemence I swore at him ripped my lip from their hands. "There's no way they're mine." And that was the goddamned truth.

They were Filly's. Filly Ryan's.

And admitting that, that the Ryans had come back to town—even if it was just long enough to destroy that family—would send everything sideways. Everything. The families barely stayed in balance, the fact that the Ryans stayed gone, helped.

Besides I'd chose to help them. I'd chose to believe in what Brye MacCowan and Filly Ryan had. I'd chose to believe love mattered in this stupid, twisted, fucked up world. And I wouldn't let Mac take that choice away from me.

It was maybe the only one, ever, that was actually mine.

"Who's were they?" he snarled.

"I don't—" My words cut off when Ardan ripped at my nipple, my words switching to screams.

"Who, Deirdre?" Mac's voice got a bit more forceful, anger vibrated on the edges.

"I wasn't there."

Ardan dug his knees in again. When I screamed, he reached backward and dug his fingernails into my clit. I screamed.

"You didn't answer me, Deirdre," Mac said, fury bubbling up in his voice.

"Please!" I felt the dam inside me about to break.

"Who fucking murdered Connor MacCowan?"

"*I don't know!*"

Mac stilled and his lips flattened. He watched me as he folded back onto the seat above my head.

"You're lying iníon. And liars get punished," he said softly. And soft was scary.

He jerked his chin again and Ardan understood his wordless command. His hands left my body and moved to his button. The sound of his zipper was the only one in the room.

I knew what was coming next.

My life had revolved around what was coming next for the past twelve years.

I laid there, still, and barely breathing as Ardan shoved down his pants and shoved into me. I focused on the grout lines of the tiles where they scratched my back as my body moved limp with each of his thrusts. When he picked up pace, I couldn't help but escape to that place I'd retreated for years. To Niall. To us. To then.

It was the first time I cried since *that* night.

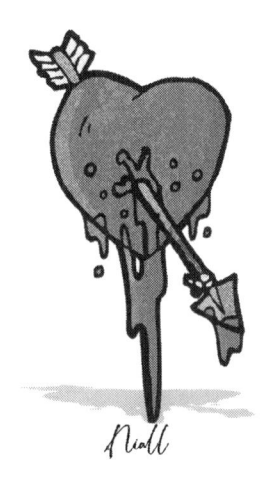

"No kissing on the mouth," Ailee said with a smile as she leaned up against my front door and ran her fingers along the edges of my holsters.

"No problem, Julia Roberts. I plan on railroading you." I rolled my eyes and reached past her to unlock the door.

"Don't make promises you can't keep." She reached down and blatantly rubbed my crotch.

"Never have. Never will."

The front door to my small townhouse swung open, and Ailee stepped in without hesitation. I flipped on the lights and scanned the room before paying her any attention. Nothing was out of place, but something still set me on edge. I refused to believe it was because of Drea.

"I bet you promised her—"

I didn't even let Ailee finish her sentence before I had the door shut, my hand around her throat, pinning her to it.

"I wouldn't if I were you." I leaned in close and let my words vibrate against her skin.

She lengthened out her neck and looked down her nose at me. "What are you gonna do about it?"

I smiled. It was a wicked one but a welcome one. Ailee knew what I needed, and she knew what she needed to say to give it to me. Fury flowed freely through my veins as I thudded Ailee against my door again. Her smile grew wide in challenge.

Fucking Christ she was a good friend.

And an even better fuck.

I kept her by the neck as I shoved my hands down her pants and cupped her sex. Each time I stroked her clit I squeezed a little harder on her neck. Her skin was slowly turning the dark red of her hair and the smallest bit of drool clung to the corner of her pale pink lips.

My grip on her relaxed at the same moment I shoved my fingers up inside her. Her gasp for air was a wild, mangled moan desperate for oxygen *and* release. I stroked her, my fingers finding the spot she loved so very much. I leaned in and kissed down her neck before biting down, hard, where my hand had been earlier.

"Fuck," she screamed, lifting her hand to take a swing at me.

The sting of her slap wasn't the only thing that I felt. Ailee wore three different rings, all with intricate settings, designed to sting. She'd spun them when I wasn't looking and now my skin was ripped open. I took my fingers out of her and rubbed them on my face. When I pulled them away, just the hint of red colored them.

"That was hot," Ailee purred just before she reached behind my neck, her rings still turned to dig into my skin, to pull my torso lower. She kneed me directly in the stomach.

All the air wooshed out of me as I instinctively reached up to cradle the ache. She used my defense to play offense. Shoving me hard backward toward the kitchen island. I bounced off the countertop and my hands shot back to try and steady me.

She wiggled her eyebrows and reached for my belt. I leaned back and let her. She undid the buckle and pulled it smoothly before working on my button. I let her do that too, watching as she knelt down and slowly pulled my dick out. Her pink lips puckered up before she remembered to go back and wet them.

"You're killing me," I murmured.

Ailee smiled and took me in her mouth at the same time she sharpened her claws down my thighs. The sting of pleasure and pain together was too good. I laced my hands into her hair, gently coaxing her up and down on the length of my dick. Each time she went further and further, I let her swallows ripple on me.

Until I pulled her off and shoved her down to the ground. She got her hands back in time to brace herself, but not in time to fend me off. I slung a leg over her torso and dropped to the floor, pining her body down and trapping her arms.

She was still writhing when I scooted forward and tried to shove my dick into her mouth. She clamped her lips shut and snapped her head away from me. With one hand below her chin, I pulled her back and held her in place. With the other I pinched her nose until she had to gulp for a breath.

I took my opening and shoved my dick in. I shifted just enough to push in. Hard. She jerked beneath me and shoved at my hold. I just shoved in until her nose touched the skin below my bellybutton. She swallowed, once, twice… then bit down.

"Fucking Christ." I skittered backward, crashing into my cabinets.

She crawled on her knees after me, holding her hands up in surrender as she stood and stripped. I sat back, picturing ripping her head from her body even as the throb of my dick started to ease. When she was naked, she stepped back and spread her legs before sliding down. Her fingers split her sex and she swallowed me whole.

Ever so slowly she started to move her hips, up and down with a gentle rock. I leaned back against the cabinet behind me and let her. My breath hitched when she started to pick up pace, and I let my hands explore.

I was so hard from our special brand of foreplay that I wasn't going to last long. Not like this, with her breasts pressing against me and her pussy holding me tight. And technically it was her turn to win so…

"In you or on you?" I grunted.

"Do you think I fucking care?" She threw her head back and shifted her hips so her clit could rub against my stomach.

Even in the muddied recesses of my brain I took the hint. I slid my hand between us and took over rubbing in the rhythm she liked best.

"Yes," she hissed, arching back and only holding on to me by the sensitive spot she'd dug into before on the back of my neck. "Fuck, yes."

I knew that tone of her voice, that tremble of her body so I let myself go, gripping her hips and pulling her down to meet me. I let out a singular grunt as I shot into her and she crumpled, her forehead falling to mine.

This was it. The only moment that Ailee Moore was ever vulnerable. A kitten without her wicked claws who just wanted to be stroked. I ran my fingers down the valley of her spine, feeling that same need for the first time in… God since…

Fucking Drea.

When I opened my eyes again, Ailee was staring directly into mine. They were soft but that didn't mean they couldn't see right through me.

"She's beautiful, Niall," she said softly and without any mocking or judgement, which only made it worse.

"Not now, Ailee. I'm still inside you." I closed my eyes again.

"You and I both know that sex between us is masturbation without the lube." She pushed her hands through my hair before hitting the cabinet. "Talk to me," she urged. "Oh shit," she giggled, "we broke the door."

I felt around behind me and finally found the splinter. "Goddamnit." I rolled my eyes as I reached my arm around her waist and pulled us up to standing. When I slipped out, cum dripped onto the floor. Ailee hissed before turning to the sink trying to find something to clean it up with.

"It's my cum." I reached out and stopped her. "I got it."

"Well now I know something's up." She cocked her eyebrow and put her hand on her hip.

"I hate her for what she did." I turned with a sigh and braced myself on the counter. Ailee was not going to see my face when I said this. "But I hate leaving her there too." The tension in my chest didn't ease at the admission. "She broke me. She fucking broke me." I banged my fist against the counter. "And when I put myself back together again, I was different. I was this."

"But…" Ailee prompted.

"But the night she first told me what Mac did to her, what The Pit was, and I heard that fear and pain in her voice… Something broke in me that night too."

"You want to go back to the house?" I knew that tone of voice, the one that told me she'd be by my side.

"No."

"Did you want to sit here and braid each other's hair or some shit?"

"Fuck you," I snapped.

"Now that we can do." A smirk tugged on her cheek. "It's your turn to win."

"It is, isn't it?" I couldn't help my dark chuckle.

Without giving her a chance to react, I shoved my forearm at her throat and used my full force to bend her backward and pin her to the kitchen counter. We studied each other for a second, a few heartbeats of calm in a wild storm, before I ducked down and bit hard enough on her nipple to leave a mark.

As she screamed, I wondered if she saw how badly I wished it was Drea pinned beneath me. Or that I wasn't sure if it was so I could fuck her or fuck her up.

Deirdre

"You hanging in there?" Saoirse asked from beside me.

I took a moment to take an inventory of my body. The near-constant pain in my ribs thudded but it hadn't gotten worse. One of my eyes was swollen shut. Cum still leaked from between my legs, I tried not to think whose it was or which hole of mine it came from.

"Are you kidding? This is better than the time I won a two weeks, all expense paid vacation," I groaned as I tried to get comfortable.

"Two weeks? You have to stop counting," Saoirse chided softly.

"I know." I winced. "What the fuck else am I supposed to do?"

"I like to recite sonnets to myself," one girl offered.

"I'm partial to writing fan fiction. Well imagining fan fic. Semantics," another said.

"I like to fantasize about orgies with some of the boys," Saoirse added.

The girls around us all had a reaction of varying degrees of horror and disgust. I laughed. "Ever think of them doing each other."

"Hell yes. I picture Ardan as a bottom. All. The. Time." She exaggerated each of her words.

"He'd never." I giggled as I tried to even imagine.

Ardan took ruthlessly. He wasn't the only man Mac set on me, but we were… *familiar* at this point. He hit hard and fast but preferred to poke the bruise after it started to turn purple. He liked it when the adrenaline had worn off but the agony remained. If I had to guess, he liked the honesty of it.

Same with passion. He always shoved in while I was still reeling from whatever pain they'd put me through. He didn't give me a chance to recover or adjust but made it a point to make me moan every single time. Like the transition from one extreme to the other was the point of the whole thing.

"That's why it's so much fun to imagine." The shadow of her hands spread in front of her face. "Picture that big mass of muscle and tight ass bent over one of those couches, all freckled and fine. That delightful dick just dangling there… *Mmmm*. You think he'd tremble or pull them wide open as he waited?" she purred.

"What exactly do you picture him waiting for?" I grimaced as I pulled myself up to rest in the corner.

"His sister. With a strap on," she said simply.

"Holy shit." I laughed even if it was so fucked up.

"Totally. She'd spit on him then shove on in. Like brother, like sister." She growled playfully. "I can just picture her hammering into him. Skin and muscle shaking. The leather tight and digging into her pale skin. In my fantasy he strokes himself until he almost comes then she pulls out and gets a really good face and tits shot."

"You have to stop…"

"Come on. Don't be a prude. She's got great tits."

Ailee was the ice to Ardan's fire. Where he watched everything with rapt fascination, she managed a cool detachment. Ardan said anything that came to mind where she spoke rarely and with an odd gravitas considering it was usually about fucking something or fucking something up. She *was* beautiful, her tits *were* great, and I hated her for it.

Particularly because Niall seemed to notice.

"I'd rather imagine her being the one that gets fucked," I grumbled. "By something very sharp and pointy."

Saoirse chuckled. "I like this side of you." She shifted in her cage. "But I don't think it's like that."

"What do you mean?"

"Niall and her."

"I don't... so... they're whatever." I stammered over my words. "I don't care about Niall." I put as much force as I could muster in my voice.

"Oh come on." Saoirse had a way of sounding like she was rolling her eyes. "The guy drives you crazy."

"Yeah because he's a complete and utter asshole."

"And he didn't use to be?" She sounded genuinely curious.

"No. Once upon a time he was perfect," I grumbled. Saoirse laughed.

"We don't get fairy tales around here, and I think you know that."

"And here I was waiting for someone to come rescue me from my luxury tower accommodations," I snarked.

"They really are high end dog kennels, aren't they?" Saoirse's sense of humor was a godsend. "I mean, this brushed metal really is far superior to the beige plastic model."

The other girls groaned but I giggled.

"I know, right?"

"Now I'm just waiting for Prince Charming."

As if on cue the door to the basement opened and a few men came down. This happened from time to time as a reward. They flipped on the lights and went cage to cage to choose.

It was the only time I got to see the other girls. They were all young and beautiful, folded into their tiny boxes. They were different than the girls that had been there when I was little but in so many ways, they were the same too.

"You." One of the guys pointed at a tiny fragile brunette backed into a corner. "And you." He chose another girl, almost matching. The evil way he smiled at the two girls half his size told me plenty about his taste.

The other two goons chose women as well. One of them fingering the girl before she got out of the cage to make sure he wanted to sink inside her.

"Niall's gonna like watching me with her," the man said as he pulled her out of the cage and slapped her on the ass to move her up the stairs.

"Bet he's gonna blow his load on my girl," the other one countered.

"You two are fucking idiots. Pain is what makes him hard. You saw the hard-on he was sporting after they beat that girl. Why do you think I chose such breakable goods." The man who had selected two women clapped the other men on the shoulders and coaxed them toward the stairs.

None of the remaining girls moved, hell, maybe even breathed until they'd turned off the light and shut the door.

It took that long for me to process what they'd said about Niall. About how watching a girl in pain had made him hard. About how watching *me* had made him hard. Was it the sex? Or the abuse? And why the fuck did I care either way?

This version of Niall wasn't worth the time or energy. He was callus and cruel. Nothing was left of the man that had threatened the universe if it didn't lay down at my feet.

I sighed and settled back into my cage. "Ya know what Saoirse?"

"Hmmm?" she answered.

"If Prince Charming exists, he's just an asshole like the rest of them."

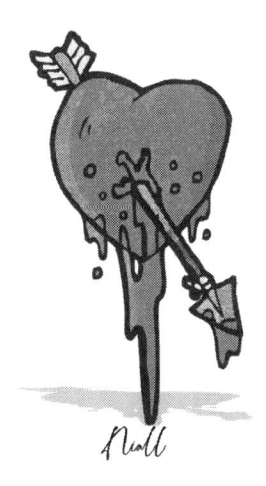

It was a fucking joke that he kept parading her out. No one was coming. No one had helped her. Or at least no one that cared. We'd figured that out a month ago and Mac had seized power anyway. But I'd still been treated to a full fucking month of watching Mac finger his stepdaughter and various men fuck my ex.

I was one wrong comment away from ripping someone's head off.

Well, if I was being honest, I was probably one comment about *anything* away from barehanded murder. If I had to watch one more time… I grit my teeth.

"Take the edge off." Mac shoved at my shoulder.

"I'm good."

Drea was face down, ass up on the ottoman, blood dribbled from her mouth where she'd been slapped and cum dripped from her pussy down her thigh.

Every single time I watched her, I got hard. I couldn't help it, I was fucking human, and she was fucking gorgeous. Sure, there was great tits, a perfect ass, and luscious locks, but she was more. She always had been. And as fucked up as it made me, I loved the scrapes and bruises coloring her body. A twisted rainbow on the pure sky of her skin.

"It's been five weeks since she walked in the door, four since I took over the MacCowan family, and, as far as I can count, three since you got laid. What do I have to do to get you to take a dip in my kiddie pool?"

"Say the word, Mac," I answered with a shrug.

"I can't believe I crave her, and you don't even care." He sat on the couch and crossed his legs; he rubbed the toe of his dress shoe against her sex.

She flinched.

Drea only flinched when Mac touched her. Every other man—and woman—she took without hesitation. Half the time she looked like she enjoyed it. That pissed me off to no end, particularly when it was Ardan she was enjoying, but a different and furious rage bubbled up when she flinched. I wanted to let it go, I wanted to give zero fucks, but the memories flooded in. The memories of her spilling her soul that had made *me* flinch.

"I'm losing patience, Niall." Mac pressed his toe into her.

"I don't think she's going to break," I said as I found anywhere to look besides where he was slowly shoe fucking her.

"She will. I'll think of something." He pulled his foot out and planted it on her hip before shoving her off the ottoman and onto the floor. "Take her downstairs, Ardan."

I had to fight against the urge to watch her go.

"Now how to break you?" he mused.

"I'll do whatever you want me to." I tried for complete nonchalance while internally I was screaming *please God don't make me fuck her*. I didn't think I'd survive it.

"I want you to want it," he purred.

"He does," Ailee snapped, materializing from nowhere at the front door. She kept going missing—she'd stopped answering her phone, she wasn't at any of the usual places—only to turn up when I needed her most. "All the time. I have to fend him off with a fucking baseball bat."

"That's foreplay when it comes to you two."

"Hmmm," Ailee mused. "How about I take him home and blow his ever-loving brains out now?" she offered.

"Literally or metaphorically?" Mac asked with a glint in his eye.

Ailee wore an exaggerated frown and shrugged as if she was still deciding.

"Whatever." He waved us off, and we both knew it was a dismissal. Ardan reappeared and strode over to stand by his sister. "We have a meeting with the Murphys tomorrow. Noon."

"We'll be there," Ailee said as she jerked her chin.

I took orders from Mac Ulster and no one else, but I gladly took the opportunity she laid at my feet.

"Jesus fucking Christ." I blew out a deep breath as soon as we got outside.

"Get in the goddamned car, Niall," she snapped.

I shot her a look and nothing more as I slid into the passenger seat of her Rover. Ardan did the same behind me. Ailee wordlessly started the car. Before pulling from the driveway, she scanned the neighborhood street. Then scanned it again.

"What?" I asked, mimicking her and finding nothing.

"I've been followed more than once this week." Her voice was still distant as she pulled out onto the street.

"What? Who? Is that why you keep disappearing?" I couldn't help but crane my neck as we turned down the street.

"It's not disappearing, it's just having a life."

"Mac is your life," Ardan scoffed.

"Mac is *your* life. I have other pursuits." Ailee smirked.

"I don't think Mac would appreciate that sentiment," I warned her.

"Fuck Mac," she spat.

I looked over and studied Ailee. She was tense but it wasn't her usual. I didn't know how to describe it but it looked like she was desperate for something rather than anticipating a fight.

"Do you need to fuck me?" I rubbed my temples as I tried to figure it out.

She blew out a deep breath and leaned her forehead to the steering wheel when we came to a stop sign. "No." She drug out the word.

"Do you want to talk about it?" I asked skeptically and Ardan laughed.

"Fuck no." She rolled her forehead just enough to glare at me. "You want to talk about Deirdre?"

Ardan's laugh choked off in his throat.

"Sure," I sneered. "Let's talk about how I hate her even more now than I did before all this."

"Bullshit man," Ardan said from the backseat. "You don't hate her."

"I would watch her burn in hell and roast fresh popcorn on the flames," I shot back.

"Nah, nah, nah, no way," Ardan countered. "See Ailee and I used to have this treehouse—"

"Oh God, not the treehouse," Ailee interrupted as she decided to whip a u turn.

"Where are we going?" I asked.

"The bar. Any time he brings up that treehouse, I know I need a drink."

"I *loved* that treehouse." Ardan accentuated the word, continuing as if we weren't talking. "It was every little kid's wet dream—"

"Kids don't have wet dreams, Ardan," Ailee tried.

"I mean real boner popping stuff," he continued. "It had walkie talkies and a rope ladder and a mini fridge for snacks. It was camouflaged and far enough away from the house that my mom couldn't hear what we did in there. I was going to live there forever." He sighed wistfully.

"What happened?" I shook my head even as I asked.

"Our parents made us share it, fifty-fifty."

"I know how well you two share." I rolled my eyes.

"She hung curtains. *Pink* curtains. In my treehouse." He made it sound worse than murder. I mean, considering who we'd become that was probably true but...

"What did you do?"

"I blew it up." I looked back into to see him shrug. "Neither of us having it was better than watching her with it."

"So what you're saying is I should shove some C-4 up Drea's ass?" I hated thinking about that perfect ass.

"I'm saying your hate springs from the lack of possession, simple as that." He brushed his hands together a few times as if he was wiping them clean.

We stopped at a light and both Ailee and I turned toward him. His moments of clarity were utterly disarming.

"God, Ailee, remember when I got that possession ticket for my four foot bong?" He started busting up laughing, onto a new story and totally disregarding us.

"You wanted the reason I disappear…" Ailee's voice trailed off as she pointed to her brother in the backseat.

"He's not right," I protested.

Ailee wordlessly parked in the lot behind the bar and we all got out, walking the well-worn path to our table. "Ardan isn't the only one that notices how twisted up you've been since she came back."

"Fuck you," I snapped.

"I don't think that would make you feel better anymore." She arched her eyebrow. I grumbled under my breath as I took a seat.

"What the fuck am I supposed to do?" I crossed my arms on my chest. "I can't be like this. I fucking won't."

"I'm working on it." And since she was one of only two people I could call a friend, one of only two people who'd proved their loyalty, I believed her.

Deirdre

Six weeks. It was easy to count when there was a pattern.

Feed me Go-Gurt, drag me upstairs, beat me for information until I puke, let someone use me and occasionally I'd shower. I retreated far enough into myself that I barely noticed when they finished. I just made a mental tally on the wall I hid behind.

"How's it going?" Saoirse asked just after Go-Gurt.

"Living the dream," I mumbled.

"You have very twisted dreams." She laughed.

"Well all the happily ever after ones are clearly out."

"The bastards have taken everything."

I could picture her throwing her hands up in defeat.

"You two joke, but they take everything from us," one of the other girls added.

"If you think sex is all someone can take, you're a fool." The door whined on its hinges just before the tell-tale light flooded down the stairs. "I'll give them my body over and over and over again if it means I can keep the rest of me hidden…"

Ardan stepped in front of me and I let my words die. I meant it when I said I wouldn't let him have anything else.

"Shall we dance?" he asked as he undid my cage and held out his hand.

"I'd love to waltz today if you don't mind." I smiled despite the ache it put in my cheek.

"Tango taking it out of you?" he asked with his signature chuckle.

"Just bored." I shrugged.

His fingers brushed my spine almost as if he understood. As if he wanted to comfort me. I shot him a sideways look and saw the crazed tilt of his eyes I'd come to know but also… My heart constricted. Sympathy, maybe even pity shadowed his usual mania.

Lust was easy, lust was a game. Vengeance and rage were something I had to absorb but I had years of practice. Hate hurt a little more, but I could meet it head on with mine. But compassion…

We couldn't be humans for what came next. Neither of us.

I wanted to say something. Or punch him in the dick; anything to really piss him off. It was just on the tip of my tongue when I reached the top of the stairs and a knife came to my throat.

"I'm done, Deirdre," Mac hissed in my ear. He pressed the tip in and drug down, the blood fell in a drop down the curve of my breast. "Tell me."

I leaned in. "Just fucking do it."

"She said she was bored." Ardan shrugged.

"I can't tell you what I don't know so just fucking kill me."

I closed my eyes and thought about it. About dying. I probably should have the other day—or last month, maybe even a year ago. Now that I knew where Niall was, *what* he was, the last little bit of something I had to cling to was gone. Fuck it. Fuck all of it.

Maybe my body turning up would get them caught.

I twisted in Ardan's grip and pressed the full blade to my throat and started to lean in.

"You're doing this all wrong," a cool female voice said.

I gave zero fucks.

But the knife fell from my throat.

"Shit," I swore under my breath and opened my eyes just so I could roll them. "You're interrupting."

Ailee had her feet propped up on the table, eating an apple as if nothing out of the ordinary was going on in the kitchen. I prayed that her return didn't mean *his*. As fine as I was meeting death, I probably didn't have the balls to do it with Niall right there.

"Explain, Ailee," Mac commanded.

"See, the process of breaking people taps their fight or flight response. That first hit, the first fuck, they freeze because their body is processing, trying to figure out what to do. Which way they wanna go."

"I like fight," Ardan interjected.

"We know." She arched her eyebrow and it pulled up her smirk.

"She doesn't do either," Mac snarled.

"Because she's been excessively trained on how to respond to force and brutality." Ailee shrugged as an ominous feeling swirled in my stomach. "Marines, firefighters, pilots, etcetera aren't naturally calm and collected people. They train for trauma scenarios. So frequently that the response is engrained in them.

"Doing the same thing with her isn't going to get you new results. Matter of fact, the beating and the screwing and the inhumane treatment are just going to reinforce the coping mechanisms she's developed."

Mac snarled, wild and raw, before grabbing my hair and shoving me into a seat across from Ailee.

"I've been challenged, Ailee. The other families don't think I had the right to take over the MacCowan territory. I now have two weeks. Two *fucking* weeks to prove that she knows what happened. Two *fucking* weeks to prove I have the rightful claim." He slammed his fists down on either side of me; I didn't even jump. "How do I get it out of her?"

Ailee cocked her head and studied me. After a few sweeps she lowered her feet and sat up straighter.

"Find out what makes her uncomfortable. What she doesn't have a trained response to." She shrugged. "Find it. And use it."

I didn't need to look to know that Mac was smiling. "Any ideas?"

"Yup." She picked up her phone and texted someone, the fast clicking the only hint we had.

"Well?" Mac asked.

She smiled wide, evaluating Mac the way she had me. "You're going to hate it."

"This is bullshit!" Mac roared from the other room.

"Then don't do it." Ailee seemed like the epitome of apathetic. "Based on my expertise, this is what I recommend, but Mac, I work for you."

"And what do you have to say, Niall?"

Niall. I had to close my eyes against his name. He'd shown up fifteen minutes ago, and they'd left me in here with Ardan as if it wasn't weird that I was naked and casually seated at the dining room table. I wanted to drum my fingers, but I didn't trust myself. If I moved they would see me shake.

Ailee wasn't wrong.

The unknown—and moreover unexpected kindness—nuked my defenses.

"Answer me, Niall." Mac stomped his foot.

"I fucking hate it, Mac." His voice was ice cold. "But it's always whatever you want."

"I want to be king," he said roughly.

"Well then…" Niall said just before his footsteps echoed through the room.

He wrapped his hand around my forearm and pulled me up. Every fiber of my body reacted to the touch. I wasn't calm and collected. At all. This wasn't fight or flight, this was frozen. I literally had no idea how to react to the situation.

Niall's eyes were furious when they met mine. "Get her some fucking clothes and I'll take her home."

Flight. That was my instinctual answer. Deep in the pit of my stomach. As soon as my body got the memo, I ripped my hand from Niall's, threw an elbow into his crotch and ran.

GOD ALMIGHTY IN HEAVEN AND SAINT CHRISTOPHER TOO. My balls throbbed, pain still radiated through my body and I wasn't completely sure I wasn't going to puke but still I ran after her. With renewed vigor actually, even if I couldn't match it with my speed.

Drea whipped open the back, sliding glass door and took one step out there before I lunged for her ankle. The second I made contact, I yanked. Hard. Her body slammed down with a haggard cry. I'd give her credit though, she scrambled to her hands and knees fast.

Just not fast enough.

I shoved my boot between her shoulders and pinned her down. My eyes lazed down her body for one second before remembering what she'd just done. And why. I shoved my foot harder against her body.

"Just where in the fuck do you think you're going?"

"Anywhere but with you." She still struggled.

"You think I want to be anywhere near you?" I bent down and grabbed her by the arms, yanking her up first to her knees then to find her feet. "Whatever you feel, I guarantee I feel it ten times over," I said as I shoved her back in the house. Ardan shut the door behind me and scanned to make sure the neighbors hadn't seen.

"And here I thought you had no feelings at all," she snapped, and I remembered the fire in her, how it always used to keep me warm.

"Learned from the best." I shot her a look as I pulled her through the kitchen to where Ailee was waiting with a t-shirt by the door.

"Ten days. You three. No excuses. That'll give us time before the challenge," Mac commanded from behind us. "Don't make me regret this, Ailee. Niall, don't fuck this up."

"And me, Boss?" Ardan asked.

"Just like every other day, try not to go off the rails." Mac clapped him on the shoulder. "Unless she warrants it."

Mac's wicked look lit Ardan's unhinged smile. I ignored them both as I shoved Drea toward Ailee. She grabbed her by the arm but didn't move otherwise. I shot her a look that said *put that damn shirt on her so we can go,* and I knew she could read that look. She shot me a smirk that said *she's your responsibility.*

I rolled my eyes and ripped the shirt from her hand. I shoved it over Drea's head only for her to clamp her hands at her sides. The furious grumble came out before I could stop myself, and I saw it. I saw her cheek twitch as she tried to suppress a smile.

"You want to be a bitch, be a bitch, Drea. I expect nothing less." I pinned her with my gaze. "Duct tape," I barked and Ardan left to find it.

We all sat, silent and staring as we waited for him to come back. That sparkle sat on Drea's smile and fuck if I wouldn't give anything to wipe it off.

Or make it grow.

Goddamn, when I sat this close to her for too long, it all slipped a little. And I couldn't let it slip.

"Here." Ardan pressed the tape into my hand.

Drea's cheek ticked again, and I knew it was in challenge.

"Pull her shirt up." I nodded and Ardan did it.

I ripped three consecutive pieces of tape, two squares and one longer piece. With the two smaller pieces stuck to my fingertips, I smoothed a piece across her lips, leaning in as I did.

"I don't need that tape to wipe the smile off your face, sweetheart."

She just batted her eyelashes at me. I smiled then pressed one of my squares onto her breast right over top of her nipple. Then I did the same on the other side. I held my hand up to my mouth and huffed on it, heating the skin of my palm. When it was noticeably warmer, I pressed it to her breast over the tape. I braced her so that I could push hard, making sure the tape was stuck tight. Then I ran my nail over it to really get it stuck. I held her gaze the entire time I did it on the other side.

I didn't even blink when I grabbed the edge and ripped it off, hard and fast.

She screamed against the duct tape holding her mouth. Her whole body jerked, and she stomped her foot.

"Who's smirking now?" I asked as I started pulling out more tape. "You wanted your hands at your side so…" I didn't finish my sentence as I reached between her legs.

It wasn't until I was down there that I really decided to be an ass. I ran my fingers along the slit of her perfect sex just before doing the same with the duct tape and using it to tape her lip to her thigh, wrap around and pin her hand all in one loop. Sure she was going to slip out but it would prove a point. I gave her a few good wraps before doing the same on the other side.

"There," I said as I came back up to standing. Her eyes glimmered but not with the onslaught of tears but rather a pure and fervent fury. It made her painstakingly beautiful. I leaned in and her body bowed against mine, the mirror of my shape. If the duct tape hadn't been there, trapping them, her lips would have been close enough to brush. I cocked my head like I was going to kiss her when I whispered, "Don't fuck with me again," and ripped the remaining square covering her nipple off.

I stepped back and watched her long lean body writhe before throwing Ardan the tape. He dropped her shirt back along her body to catch it.

"One more on her fucking tit in case she acts up then put her in the back of the Rover."

He did what I asked with a slap to her breast, hard and fast, then slung her over his shoulder. Her pussy peeked out where it was still held open. Ailee, Mac and I watched, I wasn't the only one that smiled.

The snap of the Range Rover door perfectly timed with the kick to the back of my knees and me crashing to the ground. Mac had one of my guns pressed against the back of my head before I could even react. I held my hands up in surrender before I even thought about it.

"I need answers. *Need*, Niall." The way he said it left no doubt of the lengths he'd go to get it. How little I mattered if I didn't.

"I'll get them."

"That means you play by Ailee's rules. No questions asked. No fucking games. You get me the answers I need, knowing your pitiful excuse of a life is hanging by this thread." He dug the barrel of the gun into my head. "Got it."

"Got it," I answered, unwavering.

"Get out of here." He slid the gun back into my holster just before his footsteps faded away.

Ailee walked out of the open door toward her brother who stood waiting by the SUV. They both waited expectantly as I got to my feet, straightened my shoulders, and cracked my neck. I was half inclined to stay in the house—I'd take the bullet or a few more kicks to the dick—but with a heavy sigh I walked out.

"Hey," Ailee said softly as she grabbed my arm. "You said you couldn't be like this. That you wouldn't."

"I'm trying. Really. Fucking. Hard." I enunciated every word even though I said them through clenched teeth.

"Get the goddamned revenge you deserve."

I looked over to see the fierce set of her jaw, the steely resolve in her eyes.

"Get revenge by ruining her the way that will *actually* ruin her."

I started to nod.

"No, don't give me a nod, give me a mother fucking yes," she hissed.

"Fine. Fucking yes, Ailee. I'll ruin her." I rolled my eyes. "Just tell me how." I started around the hood of the SUV and she had her hand on the handle. She waited until I caught her gaze from the opposite side.

"Make her feel like you care." There wasn't a hint of jest in her voice. "Make her fall."

F*uck*. *Fuck. Fuckfuckfuckfuckfuck.*

Ailee hadn't said another word as we drove to my house. I knew she wouldn't. Not when my fury was filling up the car. Ardan tried to lighten the mood once or twice but it fell on deaf ears.

"Get out," I said when we pulled up to my house.

"Niall…" Ardan whined.

"Get out and make sure she cannot get out of the house."

Ardan shoved out like a pouting kid. Ailee hesitated just long enough to shoot me a look.

"I'm handling it," I snapped. "Get out."

This time she did. I waited until my front door shut to press the button on my garage door opener. With each foot it rose, I forced myself to take a breath. I backed the car seamlessly into the garage and repeated the breathing as it closed. I sat in darkness for a few moments, steeling myself.

I reminded myself of what she did. How she left me. *Called* me to leave me. How she wouldn't do it to my face. I made myself feel the ridicule I felt as I went back to her over and over and over and begged. How it broke me to learn she was dating Emmett. That she'd chose *that*.

It was enough to fortify me.

I slowed my movements to equal my breathing as I pushed out of the SUV and walked to the rear door. It opened slowly, revealing her body still wrapped in an oversized white shirt and twisted duct tape that betrayed how hard she'd struggled. I swallowed down a knot as I reached for her.

"I'm sorry," I said softly even though the words burned in my throat. "I'm so sorry for all of it, Drea." I reached over and brushed her hair behind her ear. "I never meant to hurt you." I forced myself to smile. "I'm going to take care of you." I reached in and collected her in my arms. Whether it was working or not, I wasn't sure, but she didn't fight me, so I added, "I promise."

Deirdre

HE KNEW I WASN'T STUPID RIGHT? I MEAN, I DIDN'T GRADUATE high school but that wasn't because I was an idiot. That was all Mac, all because of *that* night. Sometimes I wondered if I'd told Niall would it have changed anything?

Would it make the things he'd just said real?

Oh God, there it was. And without my permission. Hope. Blooming in my fucking heart.

I would have elbowed him in the chest and ran if I thought I could get out of duct tape. If I thought he wouldn't rip my nipple off. Again. I fidgeted, hoping I could ease the ache in the one he'd abused back at Mac's house.

He carried me into a townhouse that I guessed was his. Nothing really made it personal, but I knew the places that he'd always wanted to go and saw the photos of them hanging on the walls. I knew that the pillows on the couch were sewn by his mom from a plaid blanket he'd had as a kid. I knew that the pizza menu on the fridge was deep dish. Only *ever* deep dish.

When he set me down in the kitchen, I watched his every move, still on edge. Still suspicious. He reached for the butcher block and came back with a knife. If I hadn't had the tape across my mouth, I would have told the fucker to bring it on. Didn't he know that the dried blood on my neck and chest was from the first knife someone thought they could ply me with today?

But he just cut two small slits next to my wrists, so I was free.

He set the knife on the counter then picked me back up, just as swiftly as he had before and carried me to his bedroom. Just the way I'd known it was his house because of personal artifacts, I knew it was his bedroom. We'd snuggled in that comforter after our first time... My heart shot into my throat. If he threw me down and shoved into me, I wasn't sure I could weather the storm.

Ailee had been right, I was out of my comfort zone.

Fuck.

Niall didn't stop, he just walked through the room to the bathroom. Everything was sleek and modern. Normal but nice. Darker floors and shiny silver fixtures. One towel hung haphazard on the shower bar. Somehow it was reassuring that the room was just so unabashedly *normal guy*. But then I noticed it smelled like cocoa butter, it smelled like me.

My heart thudded.

Niall set me down and reached over and flipped on the shower. Thank God, he left it not too hot—just the way I used to like it. It reminded me that he didn't know me now. He didn't even have feelings for me now. I was just a pawn in a game that I had willingly decided to play.

"I'm not going to take off the tape, I know it will hurt and I'm hoping the water will make it better. Use all the hot water, use anything you find in here. If you need something, let me know. I'll have it for next time."

I tried not to snort at the idea of a next time.

"I'll get you fresh towels and some real clothes to wear by the time you're done."

I would have faked a thank you if I wasn't still taped up. I nodded instead and started to plan my escape. *Treat me like a fool and I'll play you for one, McDonough.*

He stepped toward me, his movements slow and familiar replacing the rough ones of a complete jackass less than an hour ago. His fingers danced at the edge of my shirt, and I hated that my body ached to move closer. Whether he noticed or not, he just pulled it off and smiled before leaving me alone in the room.

And taking the shirt with him.

I snorted and rolled my eyes. That single move said everything that bastard wouldn't. He didn't trust me, and he knew he wasn't fooling anyone.

For a moment I let it go and stepped into the shower. The duct tape pulled at my sex and I made sure to tally that one down in the column of things I'd fuck Niall McDonough up for.

But not right now.

For five minutes—maybe ten—I was going to sit in that hot shower and let it wash the filth of the cage off. Let it ease the ache of my bones and lift the blood from my skin. For just a few minutes I was going to feel human.

I peeled the tape off, using the cascading water to help loosen it as much as possible. Some of the skin was raw and raised where I took it off. My lips were even a little worse, chapped and torn. I took a deep breath as I started oh so slowly on the one covering my breast. If I ever got the chance, I was putting tape on his ball sack. Once I had the tape littering the bathtub, I turned up the temperature of the water and let it scald my skin. This was a trick I learned early on in the MacCowan house. If I couldn't feel my skin for a minute, then I couldn't feel pain or shame or whatever else came with being used.

When I felt one step away from blistered, I took a deep breath and looked around the shower. There was man shampoo and I used it to scrub my hair, carefully detangling the knots I found. A small part of me was crushed there wasn't any conditioner, but I moved on to body wash. It smelled like him. Like him *then*. I could remember the way we smelled together. Even after sex.

Fuck that.

I stepped out of the water, leaving it running, and rung out my hair. I wrapped the towel around me and tried to shove the edge in tight enough that I could run in it. With a sigh I realized there was no hair tie, but a girl would just have to deal.

The water still blasted as I checked my towel again and cracked the door. He'd shut the bedroom door too. I smiled. This was going to be easier than I thought. I tiptoed across the room and had my hands on the window when Niall cleared his throat. My head snapped in his direction just to find him leaning casually against the doorframe into his closet.

"Going somewhere?" he asked.

"Out," I answered with a shrug.

He walked over to me, each step like a predator about to obliterate his prey. A beautiful predator in a button up shirt and sleek black trousers that made my mouth water. My breath caught and I arched back. He simply stuck his fingers into the blinds and pried them open.

"There are things scarier than me out there."

Ardan waved from a lawn chair that was pointed directly at this window.

"Been there, done that," I said with a shrug.

Something flashed behind his eyes, the blinds snapped shut as his hand balled into a fist. He shoved it down to his side, every muscle in his body rigid—even the one that feathered in his neck. I knew I should leave it. Let him be, but I couldn't.

"Does that bother you?" I pressed up against him, somehow his body tensed further. "Do you hate knowing that your crazy ass friend has been inside me?"

I could actually hear his teeth grit.

"And it was vicious fucking." I enunciated each word, daring him to react.

His jaw ground a little longer, every muscle in his neck rolled in time with the bob of his throat. I waited for it. For the shove against my throat, the pin against the wall. He didn't flinch.

"I bet you like it rough these days." I bit my lip and looked up from under my eyelashes at him. Anything to get him to crack. To be the bastard I could hate. "I've known men like you, and I can please you in ways you haven't thought of yet."

My fingers reached for the towel and his eyes flicked to watch, rapt. I thought I finally saw him shake. With a small pull I dropped it and the muffled fabric hit the floor. His eyes flicked up, boring a hole in the wall behind me.

"I'm a whore, Niall, you should use me." I reached up and ran my fingers along the buttons of his shirt. "I'm a filthy, fucking whore that knows who killed the MacCowans." His hand flew from his side and grabbed mine, squeezing so I couldn't touch his shirt anymore.

This was it. The moment that he'd crack. It had to be. We'd return to the brutal back and forth that was infinitely more comfortable than this. I'd beat Mac at his stupid game.

But then Niall's grip softened, and he rubbed his thumb over the tips of my trapped fingers. He pushed my hand back to my side and offered me a stiff and strained smile.

"I'm sorry that I didn't get you clothes before you got out." He turned away and opened first one drawer of his dresser than another before handing me two folded pieces of clothing.

His reaction left me off balance. I took the clothes from him as my eyes darted from the pile to him and back again.

"What did you say?"

He reached up and gently ran his hands through my hair with a sad smile. "I'm sorry that this happened to you, Drea. I'm sorry I wasn't there to stop it."

And with that, he turned and left, leaving me alone in his bedroom, naked, and for the first time in a very long time, feeling like a filthy, dirty fool.

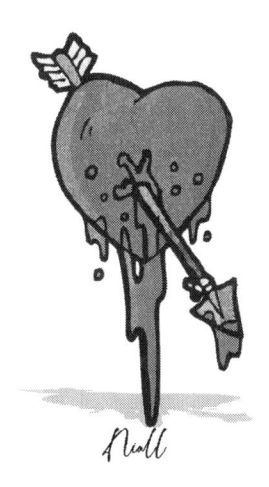

"How'd it go in there?" Ailee asked from where she was sitting on the couch with both a view of my bedroom door and the front windows.

"Get your brother in the house." My voice was so low, so deadly, it barely slipped out from between my teeth.

Her eyes went wide for a split second before she scrambled off the furniture, bolting for the back door. It took everything I had not to punch a hole in a wall. As it was, I kicked the rug in my kitchen as I spun in place, fury as my fuel.

Sorry? I was *sorry*?

Horse shit. She was a whore who deserved everything she got. She deserved to get it from me the way I gave it to Ailee, but rather than letting her play back, leaving her limp on the floor. I grabbed the knife I'd used to cut her tape and rammed it, tip first, into the cutting board on the counter.

I hated this game.

Didn't I?

Each time I saw her she was more beautiful than the last time. Today, getting out of the shower, water droplets twisting down her skin—her skin colored with cuts, scrapes, and scars—she was breathtaking. I had sat there in the closet watching her for more time than I cared to admit.

"Niall?" Ardan pulled me from my thoughts, his worry obvious on his face.

"Watch her. Do not let her leave. Do not let her outside." I pointed at my door. Ailee shot me a look. "Do not upset her. Do not hurt her. Do not *fuck* her. From this point forward, she is your best friend on the whole goddamned planet, and you will up and die of misery if she leaves. Understand?"

"Braid each other's hair, paint each other's nails, watch Bravo, talk about your dick. Check, check, check, check." His fucking maniac smile split his face.

"If you so much as think about my—"

"Boys," Ailee warned, reaching up and pulling on the knife in my hand. I hadn't realized I'd pulled it out of the cutting board. "You'd both do well to remember that we have a job. From Mac. And our lives depend on it."

Wordlessly, I let her take the knife. Her eyes met mine and with a singular sweep toward the garage she knew what I wanted. Or she better. I stomped out and had to keep from slamming the door in her face out of pure rage. My fists balled against the steering wheel before I decided to fuck it and banged them like the Hulk all over the damn thing.

"It's my turn but if you need to win, you can fuck me in the car," Ailee said as she slid in, mid tantrum.

I stopped assaulting the steering wheel and took a deep breath. "I'm fine," I grumbled as I shoved the button to open the garage door.

"You are not fine," Ailee scoffed.

"I will be." I saw her arch her eyebrow out of the corner of my eye. "It's only a few days, Ailee."

"It's only been a few hours and I can see you fraying at the edges." As soon as I pulled onto the street, she checked the side-view mirror then rear. She spun in her seat to stare out the back.

"What? Is someone there?" I asked, ignoring her offer. Ignoring the fact that the mere mention of sex had me thinking about Drea again.

She squinted for a moment before spinning back into her seat. "Nothing," she finally said softly. "What are we doing anyway?"

"Continuing this godforsaken charade," I grumbled.

"What charade?"

"The one where I give a damn about Drea Ulster." I gripped the steering wheel so hard my knuckles turned white.

"No one said you had to give a damn about her." Ailee snorted.

"How else do you suggest I get her to... what did you say? Fall?" I rolled my wrists back and forth.

"Chocolate." She shrugged. "Bitches love chocolate." Her low and hard earned chuckle usually took the edge off the tension in my shoulders.

Today... There was no way that she could know Drea was indifferent to chocolate. The real way to her heart was Hot Tamales or Swedish Fish, dependent on her mood. She also thought flowers were a waste of money and romcoms were for saps. She had always preferred books and spy movies.

I slammed my fist against the steering wheel again. Knowing that stuff about her sucked enough. Sitting here wondering if it was all still true made me worry for my sanity.

"If you're quite finished," Ailee said, crossing her arms with the perfect amount of disapproval. I nodded once. "Good, go to Target." She pointed to the parking lot on the left, and I obeyed.

I noticed her look behind us again. "What is going on?"

"Nothing." She brushed me off. "I'm assuming she needs clothes, bathroom shit, other random, ya know, girl stuff. We can get it all at Target."

"Target?" I'd seen it but never been in.

"Yeah, Target. They have everything. *All* of the things." She looked at me like I'd grown a second head. "Don't you just go to Target to aimlessly wander around?

"No, Ailee, believe it or not, I don't just go to Target to wander around. I tend to be on the busy side." I parked, and we both got out, walking toward the massive store.

"Doing what? Brooding?" She playfully punched my shoulder. "I'm just as busy as you with jobs for Mac yet every Tuesday morning, I make time to come. I get a coffee down the street at Perkies then come and wander."

"Huh." I looked over at Ailee and saw her in a different light. Like she was human. It was fucking weird.

"*Huh* is all I get?" She laughs as she grabs a cart. "I just told you one of my deepest, darkest secrets and I get *huh*?"

"This is your deepest, darkest secret?" I followed her as she pushed the red cart into women's clothes.

"That, despite a degree in behavioral science that I use for reconnaissance and interrogation for the mob, which leads to the occasional murder and a lot of depraved sex, I'm just a normal girl?"

A woman beside us gasped and backed away. She clutched her pearl necklace as she watched us, fear coloring her sagging face.

"Excuse us." Ailee smiled as she navigated around the woman as if we'd simply been talking about the weather.

"Well when you put it that way…" I chuckled just thinking about Ailee as *normal*.

"And speaking of normal…" Ailee redirected. "Is your girl a jeans girl, a leggings girl, a dress girl?"

My girl. I cringed at the words.

"What? You don't know?"

"Don't call her my girl."

Ailee opened her mouth to protest then snapped it shut, taking a deep breath before starting again. "Fine. What do you know about the target?"

"It's been twelve years, I'm not sure how much I know." I prayed to the Son of God and Saint Christopher too that Ailee couldn't see how much that bothered me.

She eyed me for a minute then something caught her attention. She stared across the store, ducking and weaving to get a better view. When she finally answered she didn't really turn to look at me.

"At the end of the day we can probably use that to our advantage. Remembering details from twelve years ago is considered romantic."

"Yeah, that's me. Fucking Romeo." My snark earned me a big, full laugh from Ailee that made a few people turn toward us. "Don't mind her, she's crazy." I smiled an apology then pushed her toward the basic t-shirts.

"That makes two of us you know?" Humor was still thick in her voice.

"Three if you count your brother." I sighed thinking about him home with Drea. The only person that I trusted more than Ardan in this world was Ailee, but I still hated that he was alone with Drea. For a whole myriad of reasons.

"He's at least one and a half times crazy. Maybe even two."

We both started chuckling again as I began to pick things out for Drea. I thought about the closet I'd seen at the MacCowans just as much as I thought about the girl that I'd known. Ailee watched, only helping me with sizes as we went.

I lost myself to it after a little while. Cruising Target for random shit I thought might make Drea smile, casually strolling aisles for things she might want. Not need. I wasn't sure when it had shifted or why but I knew each thing I threw in the cart was a nail in my coffin; I just wasn't sure if Mac or Drea was hammering.

When we were in the checkout line, Ailee picked up one of those terrible gossip magazines and some chocolate. Without thinking, my eyes drifted to the candy rack beside me. I smiled as I grabbed three boxes of Hot Tamales and two bags of Swedish Fish and added them to the basket.

"One trip around Target and I know your deepest darkest secret too." She eyed me from over top of her magazine.

"What?" I looked down at everything in my cart. "That I loved her?"

"That you still do," she corrected.

"Bullshit, Ailee. I hate her." I spat out the word as we started checking out.

She tossed her magazine on the growing pile of supplies and shot me a look. "Yeah and Ardan doesn't give two shits about that stupid treehouse anymore."

Deirdre

"Real Housewives of Jersey? Really?" I asked, unable to suppress the little bit of giggle that came from imagining this tall, cut, gorgeous, and mildly unhinged killer draped across the bed, watching Real Housewives every single week.

"What can I say? I want to be friends with Teresa, I want to throw my drink in someone's face."

"I think I'd flip a table. That's gotta feel fucking great." I leaned back against the headboard as I pictured doing it.

Ardan turned over on his side to face me. "I've only done it during a fire fight for protection."

"Does that really work?" I shifted forward and crossed my legs.

"It's worked so far." He shrugged. "Though I'm pretty sure it's just because it takes away the target unless you've got metal tables."

"True." I started picking at the comforter beneath me. "I've seen enough shot up door frames and walls to know."

"I like that about you." His smile stretched again. "You get it. You get this."

I thought about it for a moment before I started nodding. "I guess you're right. It's the way I grew up."

"You didn't even get to be an actual kid?" His bright and vivid eyes found mine, and I saw it again. Sympathy. "No soccer or summer camp? No fairy wings?"

"I had a roof over my head, I got what I needed," I said sharply as I shoved off the bed. Had he suddenly had an aneurism and forgotten Mac Ulster was my stepfather?

"Whoa, whoa, whoa." He scrambled off the bed too, slamming his body into the frame of Niall's bedroom door to block the exit. "I'm sorry. I didn't mean to hit a nerve."

"I'm not going anywhere, calm down." I walked to the bathroom and snapped the door shut behind me.

"I just feel bad. I didn't think. I'm sorry, Deirdre," he said through the door.

I closed my eyes and turned my back to the door, sagging against it and sliding down. "It's fine. It's all fucking fine. I'm just going to pee," I lied.

"Sure," he said as the door shook. I braced for him to shove in, but the handle didn't move, instead it seemed like he slid down his side to match me.

"I just told you how much I like Housewives." He chuckled and the door vibrated with it. "I know why people hide in the bathroom."

"Ardan, I told you, I have to pee."

"I can feel you talking through the door so please tell me before you go. I'd rather not sit in a puddle of piss."

A smile tugged on my cheek even though I hadn't given it permission.

"My sister is ruthless. She'll call me pee-pants. She still gives me shit about our childhood treehouse."

I couldn't help but chuckle.

"Oh, and she called me puke face for four years when we were little because I ate some candy off the ground on the way to the first day of school that turned out to be *not candy*." He made a heaving noise. "All over my shirt, down the front of my pants. My teacher wouldn't let me change."

"You had to sit in puke all day?" I asked, cringing.

"Yup."

"That's cruel." I honestly felt bad for little Ardan.

"Yeah well, Ailee also beat up two kids that made fun of me

that day. No one else *ever* called me puke face." The warm smile was obvious in his voice.

"The only person that ever looked out for me like that was Niall." As soon as I said it, I wanted to reel the words back in. I wasn't sure why or how they'd tumbled out.

Something jerked against the door, and instead of answering me, it shook and the handle clattered. It opened so quickly I wasn't able to stop it or move. I tumbled out onto my back.

Only to look straight up into Niall's piercing eyes.

"For the record, you're the only person I've ever looked out for like that." That muscle in his jaw feathered again. He didn't say it, but I could tell *And you still went and fucked me over* was on the tip of his tongue.

Wasn't it?

He didn't say it, instead offering a hand up. I eyed it for a moment before reaching for it, still determined to call his bluff. Instead, he used his grasp to spin me in an all too smooth move then pull me to my feet. I wasn't expecting it and my feet wobbled beneath me, making me crash against his chest.

His arm moved around the small of my back and held me close while his hand kept hold of mine. I could feel his heartbeat against mine and that's what unsettled me the most. It was racing, thudding against my chest, in a way that couldn't lie the way his devilish tongue could.

"Are you okay?" He lifted our hands, still entwined, and used his thumb to brush against my cheek.

"Fine. I'm fine." I tried to shove away but he held me tight.

Too tight.

I could feel the muscles of his body, defined enough to make their topography known against my skin despite his shirt and mine. His heady scent tickled my senses as he leaned in, his eyes still boring into mine. When he was close, too close, he wet his lips, letting his tongue leisurely travel the full length of his bottom lip. I couldn't help but watch.

"Was Ardan a prick?" His question was simple and appropriate, but the way he said it, the sin and snarl in his voice, was anything but.

"Nah…" I couldn't really get the word out and had to clear my throat. "No. He's a good guy."

Niall chuckled, and I felt it in every single molecule of my body. "I think that's the first time he's ever been called a good guy."

I shrugged and Niall smiled, finally pulling away from me. But he kept hold of my hand. I tried to shake it off, but he held tight and pulled me back into the bedroom.

"I picked up some things I thought you might need. Or want. Let me know if you want anything else." He gestured to the Target bags piled on his bed.

"What? Why?"

"Did you want to sit in my boxer briefs and t-shirts for ten days?" His eyes raked down me. "I don't mind one bit and Ailee said Target has a great return policy but…"

I yanked my hand from his and dug into the bags to distract myself from every single thing he said. Every single way he'd touched me.

Turns out the bags were worse.

Those bags held every little thing I needed to be… well… me. The real me. Not the pretty toy Emmett and Connor MacCowan had wanted me to be. None of my defensive layers in place. Just me. It wasn't just leggings and t-shirts, but soft slouchy sweaters and slide on slippers, books I wanted to read, make up I would buy, my favorite candy…

My hand fell away, and I stepped back from Niall. "Why would you do this?"

"I wanted you to be comfortable. To have your own things."

"Fuck that. Stop lying to me," I sneered. "A week ago…" I couldn't bring myself to talk about who he'd been this last month or so. That soulless monster that watched Mac finger fuck me, that said I deserved nothing less. "You don't care about me. I *know* you don't." I emphasized the word.

"Nice try, Drea. Look through those bags again then look me in the face and say that."

I shoved my finger toward the bags. "I could find the Saint Christopher in those bags, Niall, and he'd agree." I hadn't meant to end up yelling but I wasn't mad that I had. I clenched my fists and tried to cool the raging fire in my heart. "I know you're playing me. I know this is just a fucking game."

He swallowed as he slowly blinked, almost unseeing.

"Deny it, Niall. Tell me I'm fucking crazy. Tell me that it was all an act in front of Mac. Tell me those exact words and maybe —*maybe*—I'll believe you." I was calling his bluff. I had to. I couldn't believe anything else.

He focused in on me and I could see the emotion spinning out behind his eyes. Couldn't I?

"There was a time that you wouldn't ask those questions, Drea. There was a time you wouldn't need to hear those answers." He had the audacity to look hurt.

I rolled my eyes. "Yeah, well, there was a time that you wouldn't have hesitated to answer."

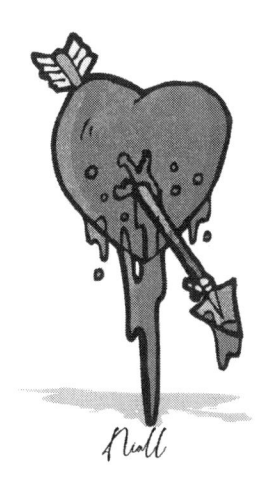

Mac Ulster had me stakeout a building from the opposite roof in the Chicago snow for over twelve hours a few years back. I sat staring through a scope in the dark despite the flakes whipping in the freezing lake wind. The target never showed. I'd almost lost the tip of my trigger finger to frostbite; I still didn't have great feeling in it.

What made it worse was that I'd failed. I was sure I was dead. But when I went back to that house empty-handed, Mac just laughed. The target was a fake. It was all a game. One he thought I'd lose an hour or so in.

I'm not sure how I found enough restraint not to kill him. Ardan and Ailee hadn't been able to pull me off when I beat him so that was all on me. A me that didn't have anything to lose since I'd already lost Drea. I would have killed him—I'd still kill him—but something had stopped me.

I called on that same force now.

Drea was right. Completely right. I was fucking playing her. I was playing her and it was working. The calm, collected, tiger that toyed with men was gone and the girl I'd known had come back.

And that girl was just as dangerous to me as Mac himself.

I held her stare for a moment. This had worked so far because I hadn't lied. I'd been very careful to dodge answers. For some reason I couldn't make my words form the lies.

I hated her even more for that.

"Enjoy your presents, Drea." I turned on my heel and walked out of the room, snapping at Ailee as I passed. She wordlessly took up a post at my bedroom door.

I crooked my finger at Ardan, and he likewise fell into line behind me as I walked to the backyard. He shut the sliding glass door then followed me to the seats still facing my bedroom window. I turned them around and slammed them down into the grass, digging into the soil softened by dew.

"Cigarette," I demanded, "and do not give me shit."

He materialized one immediately and his heavy silver lighter right after.

"You two should talk about Real Housewives," Ardan offered.

I held the smoke in my lungs as I thought about how hard I could beat Ardan before Mac got mad. He must have read it on my face because he offered a wince before lighting a smoke of his own. We sat there silent for a while with nothing but the sizzle of the cigarettes and a few birds chirping.

"I get it." Ardan finally broke the silence when I'd almost pulled it down to the filter.

"Get what?" My voice would have given anyone else chills.

"Why you're so twisted up."

"I swear to God if you remind me that you've fucked her right now, I will slit your goddamned throat." I turned toward him, hoping he'd wither under my stare.

"I was going to say something totally different, you prick." He arched his eyebrow as his smirk pulled into place.

"Fine," I said as I sat back into the chair. "You're on shaky ground, Ardan."

"I know damn well she's a job, a MacCowan, and a whore, but there's something... Something that makes you give a damn all the same." He chuckled.

"What don't you understand about shaky ground?" I snarled.

"Everyone thinks I'm the psychotic one because I like pain and blowing things up and laughing in the face of death, but if you ask me, Ailee is the one with issues. She can detach like a genuine sociopath."

A single laugh huffed out of me.

"Just keep doing what you're doing, Niall. You're under her skin more than Mac ever could be, and that's what we need." He took one more drag on his cigarette before tapping it out on the sole of his boot. "If she gets under yours, who gives a fuck as long as you get the job done."

The sounds of blinds whipping up barely preceded the window directly behind us being shoved open. I knew the little whine of frustration that followed too well.

"Hey there, Deirdre." Ardan turned around and waved at her with his absolutely manic smile.

"You smoke?" she asked and even without looking, I knew the question was directed at me.

"I'm trying to quit."

"Not going too well right now, eh?"

I also didn't need to turn to see that her wicked little smile that paired so perfectly well with her defenses slid into place. "Life a little stressful?"

I stood and strode over, not stopping until we were face to face as I grabbed the window ledge. I let my eyes fall to her lips and swallowed hard before I let my eyes move slowly back to hers.

"Seeing you in my clothes in my bedroom after all these years gets me so damn hard, I don't know how the fuck to handle it." I moved infinitesimally closer. "I think of stripping you down to that simple black thong I just bought and exploring all the freckles I used to know, and my mind just starts mapping them without my permission." I dropped my voice a little lower. "I want that red lipstick on my collar and wrapped around my dick." I bit my lip and closed my eyes. "I am desperate to hear you call my name. Drea…" I whimpered hers.

She gasped.

"So yeah, I needed a cigarette," I growled. "What do you need?" I arched my eyebrow.

Her chest rose and fell a little too fast, her breasts trembled with the quiver of her heart. She started to back away before she even responded.

"Nothing," she finally choked out. "I don't need anything."

Deirdre

Four days and approximately seventeen hours, one on one with Niall McDonough, and I knew one thing—I preferred the damn dog kennels at my stepfather's house. It was far easier to keep track of time here. Oh, and I got to use the bathroom whenever I wanted, clean clothes and good food was readily available, and watching Housewives with Ardan was pretty great.

But then there was Niall.

Mercifully, tonight he was gone, and he'd left me with Ardan. I tried not to wonder whether he was boning Ailee. It didn't really matter. Did it?

We'd moved on to re-watching Real Housewives of Beverly Hills just when pizza arrived—New York style at my request—and I sat waiting for Ardan to come back. I aimlessly grazed at the candy we'd opened and piled on Niall's comforter.

"Ardan come on! We were just getting to the good part," I yelled. No one answered. "Ardan?" I grabbed a handful of Swedish Fish and Hot Tamales before I went to go find him.

Niall hadn't forbidden me from leaving his room but I somehow ended up corralled in there regularly. I didn't fight it. He had a plush king-sized bed, a massive flatscreen, easy access to a bathroom, and a giant window for sunlight and fresh air. Besides, that comforter reminded me of the only home I'd ever had.

"Ardan, where are you?" I asked as I walked toward the

kitchen, my eyes on the candy in my hand. "Who the hell do I have to screw around here to get some pizza."

A plate appeared in front of me and I looked up to find Niall, not Ardan, looking back. I swallowed and heat bloomed across my cheeks, down my neck, and set the tips of my ears on fire.

"Don't worry, I'm not going to take you up on it." His warm smile was rare and something to behold. It sent my insides churning. "I mean, I should because you got fucking *New York* pie but…"

He was wearing a black t-shirt that stretched tight across his chest and showed off intricate full sleeve tattoos. His black joggers were cropped at his ankles and for some reason the small strip of skin between the cuff and his black and white Nikes was sexy. Stupid sexy. His hair had gone a little wild and that curl—my curl—fell into his eye.

I retreated back, first one step, then two.

"I thought you and Ailee…" I started moving again only to run into the doorframe with my elbow, sending my candy flying.

I crouched down and started picking pieces up, Niall set the pizza somewhere and joined me. He twisted and his nose brushed mine. The smell of sweat mixed with his normally delicious scent and the combination struck between my thighs.

"I got it," I managed.

"I'll help," he said softly. "And I'm not sleeping with Ailee." He grabbed my palm and turned it upward before pouring the Hot Tamales into my hand. "I know you're still going to eat them so don't even bother pretending." He took the few Swedish Fish from my hand and rose to throw them away.

He'd remembered; candy with a shell is good as hell, gummies pick up dust bunnies.

Maybe it was that moment down on the floor with me, maybe it was that he wasn't wearing his tailored clothes, but this moment felt real. Real and truly terrifying. Because if it was real, if how he was treating me was real…

No. It was bullshit. It was a game. I looked up at him and internally begged him, pleaded with him, to crack. To remind me.

Instead, he stepped forward and his hand wrapped around me, pulling me up to standing and bringing me flush to his body. His other pushed up into my hair. My heart jackhammered and every fiber in my being wasn't sure whether I wanted to stay right here or run again. I wasn't sure if I even could. My lips parted with the tiniest breath as if my body had already made up its mind.

I knew this was bad. Terrible. Horrible. They wanted me to fall. They wanted me to feel. And if I let myself, there was nothing I would deny Niall. Well, there was *one* thing. One secret. One night. And he could never hate me as much as I hated myself for it. I would lose him if I finally broke, and I knew wouldn't be able to live through that twice.

Niall leaned his forehead to mine, the faint smell of whiskey lingered on his breath, but I didn't care. I wanted that kiss. There was no other way to say it. Despite it all, four days and approximately eighteen hours of him in all his glory, playing all his games, was too much.

All I had to do was lift onto tip toes and press my lips to his—

"Phone call." Ardan's announcement might as well have ripped us apart. He coughed and cleared his throat even though it was way too late and had the decency to look embarrassed when he shot me a look. "It's Mac."

I flinched, and I wasn't sure if it was at the mention of my stepfather or the loss of Niall in front of me.

He took the phone and stilled. Whatever had been there before, whoever I'd thought about kissing, was gone. The cruel man was back. I could tell by the set of his shoulders.

But then his eyes flicked to mine. They didn't match the taut set of his body. He held my gaze as he said, "We'll be right there."

———

"Where the fuck is your sister?" Niall snarled as he hung up his third handsfree call.

"You guys had a drink at the bar and then…" Ardan shrugged in place of an answer.

"Shit. Her and her goddamned *life*," Niall grumbled.

"Or is it that new, weird brand of paranoia," Ardan added.

"You've noticed that too?" Niall asked.

His hands gripped the steering wheel so tight, I thought he might break it as we drove toward my childhood home.

"It's just Mac, man." Ardan clapped Niall on the shoulder, he immediately tried to shake it off. "We've done it a hundred times before."

Niall nodded, but his grip on the wheel didn't lessen. Apparently I wasn't the only one that noticed. "What's got you so on edge."

"I can't believe Ailee disappeared," he grumbled.

"Because you need her or because then someone could have stayed home?" Ardan's eyes flicked to mine in the rearview mirror.

"No one would have been staying home." His voice sent shivers down my spine. "I need her advice."

"Hit me with the question, I have the answer," Ardan offered.

"I don't need to know how to blow this up any worse than it already is, Ardan. I need to start putting it back together."

I expected Niall to hit the steering wheel again, but he didn't. Instead, he just pulled into the driveway and turned off the car.

"I need a minute with her, Ardan," Niall said into the darkness.

Without a single word or protest, Ardan shoved out of his seat and snapped the door shut behind us. I watched him walk toward the house, willing him to come back the whole time, but he stopped at the bottom step, crossed his arms, and waited. When I turned back to Niall, he was watching me. I couldn't read his face, but the set of his shoulders in silhouette, the pinch of his eyes was all I needed to know he wasn't the same man that had watched me earlier.

"Are you hoping he fucks you in there?" Niall jerked his chin toward Ardan standing at the bottom of the stairs.

It was his own brand of a slap and it was jarring after our moment in the house. It shouldn't have been but I'd let down my wall without meaning to and it left my insides spinning. And in pain. I couldn't find words.

"Do you miss Ardan beating you and fucking you with everyone watching? Want me to ask Mac to make it happen?"

My mouth opened once or twice but I couldn't force words out. He hadn't been like this in days. *Days!* Nothing harsh, nothing cruel, and now…

"Or did you want Mac to do it himself?" he bit out, his words had teeth and dripped with venom.

"Fuck you," I said sharply, shoving out of my door and breaking into a sprint.

He was a bastard. I don't know how I'd forgotten. I was in flip-flops and I wasn't really sure how I'd forgotten that either. Niall was on me in a minute, his arms around my body a second before he drew me up against his.

"Did you forget what you were while we were playing house?" he murmured in my ear, his voice low and sultry like a lover. I fought against him. "Did you forget your place in this world?" He shoved one of his hands between my legs, I tried to use the change to elbow him in the chest. "Did you forget how wet this sort of shit makes you." He stroked me just once.

"Arrrggghh!" I screamed as I still tried to break free.

"Ardan, get over here," he called, barely flinching. Niall shoved me into his hands as soon as he found us. "Take the whore into the house."

Ardan held me but not too tight, there was a hesitancy in his grip. I just worked up all the spit in my mouth and launched it at Niall. I wasn't sure whether it hit.

"Back at ya, sweetheart." He laughed low and wicked. "Get her inside."

Ardan pulled me back in front of the Rover and up the few stairs to the front door. He paused for just a second—he probably needed to open the door—and I saw Niall still in the yard, slumped forward, his face in his hands. If I hadn't wanted to carve his lying cheating body into ribbons, it might have made me pause. It might have made me sad.

But after what he'd said to me, I simply wanted to gouge his eyes out.

Niall

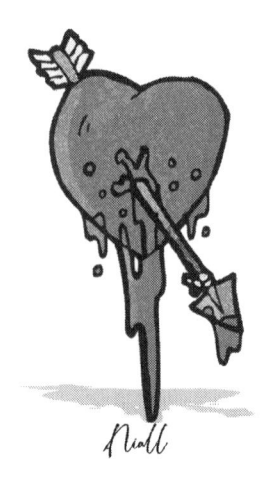

I SHOULDN'T HAVE SAID WHAT I SAID. I SHOULD HAVE LET HER walk in there with that almost kiss on her mind. If I was a good Ulster soldier, I would have fed into it, said some devastating last words, and sent her in there with hearts in her eyes.

But I couldn't do it.

I gave her the only armor I could. Her fury. Particularly aimed at me. Like this we couldn't be each other's weakness in there.

And if I was being honest, she was becoming my weak spot all over again. Her laugh ringing in my house felt *good*. Even if it was just for Ardan. Watching the line of her body as she stretched on tiptoe to reach mugs in my kitchen was addicting. Even her sharp tongue had become something I willingly wanted to cut my flesh on.

Each night I sprawled on my couch with her in my bed, I had to remind myself that she'd left me. For no reason. For someone else. And I'd gotten arrested in the end because of it. I had to remind myself of the shit memories. Of me begging, my heart breaking, over and over and over again. If I didn't, I got lost in the fact that it was Drea, my Drea, laying in my bed.

My head fell into my hands and I left it for only a few heartbeats. That was all I could afford. Then I squared my shoulders and jogged around the car and up the stairs.

"Take your sweet time," Mac said from the sofa in living room as if this was all normal.

Ardan stood in the corner, his arms crossed, waiting for orders. A few other of Mac's asses were doing the same behind him and like usual, two stood at the front door. But it was Drea sitting in the chair closest to me—the one she'd been fingered over—with her back to me that held my attention. I fucking hated not being able to see her face.

"I'm here aren't I?" I tried to sound as flippant as possible. He eyed me, and I couldn't help feeling like he saw straight through me. I had to get it together and fucking quick. "What can I do for you, Mac?" We were all waiting for something, we just didn't know what.

"Do you have answers yet?" His face said he already knew.

"She's not comfortable enough." I held my chin up, challenging him, but I still noticed that Drea tensed.

"Are you not doing your job?"

"I *always* do my job." I tried to hold back the snarl and failed. Didn't he realize how fucking hard this plan was? "If Ailee were here she'd remind you what exactly this job entailed."

Drea's hands dug into the armrests of her seat.

"Speaking of Ailee, where is she?" Mac asked. "I'd had something planned for her tonight."

"I can call her again," I offered, and he nodded.

I opened my phone and flipped over to her number. Almost as soon as I pressed it, she answered, "I'm almost there."

"Almost doesn't fucking count, Ailee."

Mac held up his hand with the number five.

"You have five minutes," I said then hung up.

"And now we wait." He sighed. "While we do, iníon, will you please collect this evening's entertainment?"

Shit.

"What?" Drea asked.

"Go down to The Pit and bring a girl up. Saoirse maybe," he mused, tapping his finger to his chin.

"And if I say no?"

"I can make you say yes." His voice dropped so easy to evil.

I stepped forward and ran my fingers along the neckline of her shirt. "Just do what he says, sweetheart," I said softly. She swatted at me, and I was surprised she didn't throw her elbow. "Please," I coaxed. If only she'd read between the goddamned lines.

Instead she twisted in her seat to look up and me, her face pinched with hatred.

"You're failing miserably, Niall." Mac chuckled. "It seems you are one great disappointment after another where Deirdre is concerned."

That was his brand of slap across my face. It stung just the same.

"We'll be right back," Ardan interrupted. "Saoirse is always so much fun." He rubbed his hands beneath his most devious smile.

Saint Christopher granted us a miracle when Mac didn't protest. Ardan pulled Drea up and over to the stairs that lead to The Pit. I didn't watch to see him whisper in her ear but I knew he would.

"If you fuck this up, Niall, I will kill you. If you fall for her or are just trying to fuck her yourself, I will kill you. If I don't get those answers—"

"You'll kill me. I know." I rolled my eyes.

"I'll kill her, fuck her corpse, and make you watch."

Something roared inside me, but I kept it tamed. "Sounds like a plan."

He eyed me again and mercifully this time I felt like he liked what he saw.

"I'm sorry," Ailee gasped as she wheeled into the house. "What did I miss?"

One look at Ailee and I knew where she'd been. The boy from the bar. Goddamnit. Mac probably saw it too.

As if on cue, Drea returned with Saoirse from the basement. Like a well trained toy, Saoirse didn't put up a fight, Drea would have lost her grip almost immediately if she had. I swore she shook.

"Good. She was your friend, right iníon?"

"What if I say no?" Drea's voice was fraying at the edges.

"Then I'll know you're lying. Just like you did about the MacCowans." He chuckled, amused with himself. "Tie her up." Mac reached back and snapped at one of the idiots standing behind him. They handed her the meanest rope we had, the polypropylene kind that frayed over time and almost barbed. "I want it around one wrist, up through the leg of this chair then down to this wrist." Mac walked Drea through it.

"No." She refused his instructions and the rope.

"Sweetheart, please," I coaxed, and she shot me a look.

It was enough of a distraction that she didn't see Mac coming. He sent a right hook flying into her eye and left uppercut to her stomach before she had a chance to react. She cried out in pain a second before her breath cut off completely and she heaved. She fell to her knees with a sob that combined it all. I would have run to her if Ailee hadn't shoved her arm out to stop me.

"You know this will go faster if she just fucking does it," she muttered under her breath.

I did and it didn't change a goddamned thing.

Drea took her time catching her breath and while she did, Saoirse slid down on the floor in front of her. The gratitude I had for her in that moment shone back in Ardan's eyes.

"Please do it," Saoirse purred. "It's been days." She drug her word out like a cat in heat then met Drea's gaze with one that said infinitely more.

I thanked Christ almighty for her.

Drea started moving, her hands shaking. She knew how to secure Saoirse's wrists, how to tie the knots but every single molecule of her protested. This was Drea's past, and Mac was reminding her it was her future if she didn't talk.

"Good," Mac praised her in a voice that made my stomach churn. "Now run it beneath her, down her spine and tie this ankle." When she didn't move right away, Mac kicked her in the ribs. This time Ardan and I both flinched, only Ailee stayed steady. Tears started running down Drea's cheeks. "It could be you," Mac hissed in her ear. "It could be me fucking you. Never forget that."

That was his endgame. It always had been. She'd been able to keep it to fingers when she was younger; I'd inadvertently kept him to fingers as an adult. I had to swallow down the acid in my throat.

Drea must have figured that out too, because she followed his directions, slow, betraying her ache but she didn't stop until Saoirse was tied exactly how Mac had ordered. Why she hadn't fought him, taken the beating, the punishment I wasn't sure. This sort of treatment was supposed to be what lit her up, made her defenses strong.

Something about this was different.

"Ailee, strip." Mac snapped at her; only I heard the grumble as she pulled off her sleek hoodie. She stepped around Drea and over Saoirse to stand in front of Mac when she was bare.

For the first time in a really long time, I wasn't sure what game Mac was playing.

"Good girl." He patted her on the ass where she stood at attention then snapped again. The same goon that had produced the rope, handed over a strap on. Ailee smirked. "Put it on."

She did, stepping into the leather straps and pulling it up as if it were a pair of her favorite pants. She tightened it easily and started stroking.

"Be savage, my sweet." Mac smiled as he turned Ailee toward Saoirse. She nodded before stepping over Saoirse's tied leg and settling between her knees. "Oh, wait. There's one thing I forgot." He smacked his palm to his face as if it was all a joke. "Deirdre is going to tell you what to do."

"I'm not." She was still fighting for some ferocity. Even if she was losing.

"You are." Mac materialized a gun from behind his back and shoved it up against Saoirse's temple. "You're going to make them recreate that night. Every single touch, kiss, caress you remember."

"No." Drea's word digressed into more sobs.

Fear and worry churned in my stomach. What night? What was he talking about?

"I'll kill her. Don't even think I won't." He shifted to shove his smile in her face. "You know how much I like to paint the roses red."

Her shoulders just shook harder.

"Do it Deirdre." Mac's voice rose. "Tell them. Tell them what to do."

"I don't know." She wept uncontrollably.

"You do. I know you do. You knew what being tied like this meant. I know you remember *everything*!" He screamed into her ear.

"Mac," I started forward, I couldn't help myself.

The gun swiveled at me. "Sit down, shut the fuck up, and watch this, Niall." I held up my hands and chose the seat where I could brush against Drea for support. She flinched away and goddamnit did Mac notice. He started to laugh, his skin crawling, wicked laugh. "Sit there and watch her recreate the night I had her for myself."

With those words my world bottomed out.

Deirdre

I WAS BOTH FLOATING ABOVE MY BODY AND RETREATED SO FAR inside I couldn't see out. Niall had tried to prepare me—I saw that now—but he hadn't succeeded. Nothing could have prepared me for this.

As soon as Mac described the way he'd tied me to my dorm bed frame any semblance of control or defense I had turned to dust. Seeing the gun pointed at Saoirse because of me destroyed any strength I might have had.

Slowly, I found the words. They were etched on my bones, they always would be, so all I had to do was read them. I was numb to what I was saying. What the girls were doing in front of me. To the part of me that watched them. Watched as Ailee ruined Saoirse.

I was Satan incarnate for subjecting the only person that had been nice to me to this. To this… *filth*. Because even if she was fine being used for sex, this was more. This was hate. I hated myself for it.

Ailee played her part well. Saoirse too, crying through it—crying Niall's name—because Mac had made me make her. I shrunk further and further in on myself as his name spun on a loop, echoing in the room, in my ears, and in my soul.

I didn't realize it had ended until a gunshot rung out. The world snapped into sharp view when I saw Saoirse dead and bleeding out on the floor. I started screaming, a sound I wasn't in control of that came from the very depths of hell. Only when Mac shoved the still warm barrel into my mouth, could I stop. Nothing would erase seeing what I'd just seen. What I'd just done.

Or how it had been done to me years before.

"Get her out of here." Mac dismissed me as if nothing had happened.

Niall reached down to picked me up. On instinct alone I shoved against him then let my fists wail against his chest. He froze and let me. He let me flail and fight against his chest over and over and over, kneeling in front of me in silence and strength.

"Get it from her, Niall," Mac snapped inches from my face and my knee-jerk response was to lunge at him to start the assault again.

Niall wobbled but he managed to keep me in his arms and away from Mac. Mac laughed as he stepped out of harms way and started up the stairs. My fists whirled back on Niall until the weight of all of it came crashing down on me.

I curled into his chest and went limp. My tears stopped, my fury fell away, and exhaustion took over. Niall had to adjust me in his arms to keep hold.

Wordlessly, he stood and turned for the front door.

"Where are you going, Niall?" Ailee called after us.

"Home." His word felt like a dagger looking for flesh to cut apart.

She was still pulling on clothes as she ran after us. "After trauma like that—"

"Shut the fuck up, Ailee. Not one word. Not a single fucking word." He jostled me when he reached for the door handle of the Range Rover.

He slid me into the front seat before slamming the door and stomping around the hood of the car. I still couldn't really find a way to react to the world around me. I didn't really want to. Surrender sounded pretty fucking fabulous right now.

Niall slid into the driver's seat a moment before the backdoor opened. I flinched.

"Get the fuck out of my car," Niall commanded. "Don't come anywhere near my fucking house."

"I was following orders," Ailee protested.

"I do not give a single fuck," he roared as he broke. His chest heaved in the seat next to me for a moment. "Your brother can follow later."

She grunted as she slammed the door behind me. I jerked at the harsh sound. Niall didn't speak, he didn't move. If I could think past survival, past breathe in, breathe out, I might have been worried about him. About him learning the truth. If he connected all the dots, he'd know why I left him. He'd know that I hadn't been worthy all along.

I couldn't piece together what would happen then. If he would leave. If I'd be deemed worthless once again. If it was something good… No. I couldn't think of anything good right now. There was no hope in this world. Hell, there wasn't even light.

I wasn't worthy of those things either.

We sat in the driveway for minutes or hours or years or seconds. I didn't know. I didn't know anything anymore. I didn't even want to.

The sound of leather creaking was the first thing that broke the infinite silence between us. Niall reached for me and my instinct was to shove him away again. He held up his hands in surrender and didn't reach again.

"Seatbelt," he said softly.

I tried to reach for it but my body still wasn't working right. I felt drugged. Wrecked. Ruined. Wasn't that what Mac had promised I'd be? When he saw me struggling, Niall leaned toward me again.

"I'm just going to buckle you. Swear to God." He crossed himself, and I nodded.

He was gentle as he reached the strap and pulled, pushing my hair out of the way with his other hand to make sure it wasn't caught. He was good to his word too, and as soon as metal clicked into place he sat back, both hands returning to the steering wheel.

As we pulled out of the driveway, I realized I wasn't sure if he'd started the car when we first got in or after he'd buckled me. Focusing on the absolutely asinine detail helped me keep my mind from going back…

I closed my eyes and leaned against the seat, feeling the tears that wanted to come but wouldn't. All too soon, Niall stopped and shifted into reverse. I didn't have to open my eyes to see we'd returned to his house.

What a difference a few hours made.

He still hadn't spoken to me when the garage door started to lower. He didn't break the silence when it settled. We sat there again. I listened for the moment when he turned the engine off this time, each heartbeat telling myself, now.

Somehow I missed the moment he turned off the car. I'd short circuited. It wasn't until he got out, rounded the car, and opened my door, I realized the engine was silent. *Huh*, I thought, still detached. Still doing every single thing I could to stay that way.

"Do you want…" he started then stopped, his voice falling to pieces. "Whatever you want I'll give it to you."

Pity. Thick in his voice. I couldn't… The tears came back, rolling down my cheeks in twists and turns until they hung on my jaw and quivered. After everything, Niall McDonough couldn't pity me. I couldn't take it. I couldn't…

He reached across me and unbuckled the belt, shoving it out of the way to pull me back into the cradle of his arms. I curled into him completely, unable to do anything but cling to him. Deep down I knew I didn't want to—he'd been callus, cruel, wicked, and right to be all three—but he was here. My Niall was here, and he was holding me so tight.

I knew the moment he carried me into his bedroom. The smell of him was strong, the sense of home was back, even if he knew it was all a lie now.

He started to lay me on the comforter, but I couldn't talk my hand into letting go of that tight black t-shirt.

"Okay," he said softly as he slid onto the bed with me.

He didn't try to shift me or relax my grip, he just found a way to wrap around me. He fidgeted for a second only for that big comforter to wrap around me the next. Something about that comforter cocooning me with Niall underneath started the tears afresh.

Niall just held me tighter.

───

My eyes snapped open and I shot upward, the ghost of Mac's hands on my body fading into memory where I tried to keep him.

"Drea?" Niall asked groggy as he propped himself up on his elbow. "Are you okay?"

No. The answer was no. My heart was slamming against my chest, I couldn't get a full breath in. I was not in any small way okay.

"I want to hold you and tell you that it'll be okay, but I do not want to push you or freak you out." His voice was soft but it wasn't weak.

"Not yet," I managed.

"Okay." I knew the sound in his voice came from his small, sad smile. Even after all these years I had those tones cataloged. The hurt and sad and broken most of all. They were the ones that reminded me I couldn't go back to him. That reminded me I needed a soldier.

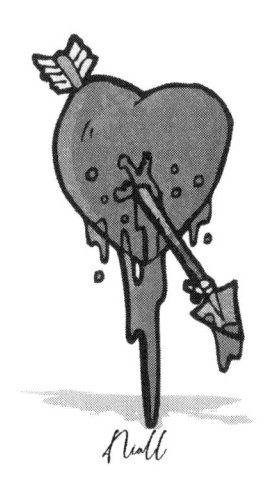

I watched her sleep. Sure it made me creepy but that was better than the other option—fucking murderous. I felt the rage right along with the heartsick. I wanted to tear the world apart piece by piece for her, light it on fire, and piss on the bloody fucking ashes. She deserved nothing less after what Mac had done tonight and… when? That was the real question. What was tonight based off? When had it happened?

The more questions I asked, the more angry I got, quaking where I held Drea. I was going to hurt her if I wasn't careful. Just because she was there and I couldn't control myself. She deserved better than that. Better than me.

This beautiful woman with a broken face, and even worse off heart, needed to be cared for. I let my fingers trace the curve of her body and toy with her dark hair between my fingers where it splayed across the pillows. She pushed the violence back enough that it was contained. But barely.

If Mac were here there would be no restraint.

And speaking of Mac, had he made her what she was today? Was he to blame for it all? Even us ending?

Drea broke out of my arms with a wild gasp that turned into a sob. She drew her legs up to her chest and wrapped her arms around them.

"Drea? Are you okay?" I moved to run my hand down her spine only to stop short.

She didn't want my touch, not after that. How could she? All the questions quieted and only one remained—how could I take care of her? It was the overwhelming urge in the pit of my stomach, the tingle in my fingertips. She looked so small and so alone where she sat up in my bed, and I wanted nothing more than to hold her— hatred all but forgotten.

"That's why I left." She barely breathed the words. "I couldn't look at you after he…" She shuddered. "I couldn't face you. You deserved someone who hadn't done… that. Been *that*."

I had to bite back fury and bile. "I loved you."

She flinched as if that was a slap. "I know. And you were so perfect and the life we were going to build was so… I had to save you from that." She wouldn't look at me. "Then I chose Emmett because I knew he could save me from Mac. In my mind it made so much sense. He was wicked and awful, but he could be a *soldier*." She spat out the word. "I was so stupid. So naive." Tears choked her words.

The desire to touch her was almost painful. No, not almost. It was fucking excruciating. Now that I knew the truth, I wanted to rip away the years and get my girl back.

It just wasn't that simple anymore.

"I want to hold you and tell you that it'll be okay, but I do not want to push you or freak you out." I wasn't sure if it was the right thing to say but… fuck, I said it anyway. I wanted nothing more than to respect her right now. All my hurt and anger had died.

Like Saoirse.

"Not yet," she said.

"Okay." I hadn't expected anything different. I hadn't wanted her to want to bury herself in me and forget the world around us. Had I? "I have cold pizza, hot tamales, and real Housewives when you're ready," I offered up instead.

"You'd watch that with me?" She turned back to look at me, her cheek resting on her knee.

"If it'll make you smile," I said it and meant it. I really fucking did.

She nodded, her cheek still firmly notched against her kneecap. I picked up the remote in response and flipped around until I found the show on demand. She watched me the entire time. The joke was just on the tip of my tongue when I forced myself to swallow it.

The show started playing and I recognized the intro from when Ardan watched it. I added that little realization into the column below *reasons that I hate myself*. What I didn't recognize was the feeling of relief and contentment when Drea laid back down next to me.

I filed that under the same fucking column.

About an episode in, I noticed she'd fallen back to sleep. I thought about closing my eyes and cuddling into her, but I knew I couldn't. Not quite yet. Instead, I slid out from her grip and moved quietly to the door.

Ardan jumped off the countertop and stood at attention.

"Don't *ever* step up and try to protect her again." I stepped to him, knowing that we were pretty evenly matched if he decided to swing back.

"She's my friend." He held up his hands.

"Yeah, well, she's just fucking mine," I snarled.

He arched back, and his eyes went wide, but he didn't question me. Thank Christ. I wasn't ready explain. I wasn't ready to say it out loud.

"Whatever you say, Niall." He nodded. "I have her back though. If either of you need it."

I didn't say anything, I didn't even ask for the cigarette I so desperately wanted, choosing a beer from the fridge instead. Drea hated smokers.

"Did you know?" Ardan asked tentatively.

I snarled as I popped open the beer and chugged. I wanted to roar and rip his head off for that question but also…

"I had no idea." I slugged back more.

"Sorry, man." He clapped me on the shoulder. "Not like it was your problem, I guess."

The way he said it made everything snap into place. That hunch before was right. I'd known her so well, the way her mind worked, the way she reacted to things. *This* was our problem. Our only insurmountable one. Mac was the reason she'd left me.

And now the reason we were back together.

"I'm going to kill him, Ardan," I said as I drained more of the beer. "I hope it's slow and fucking awful."

"Pin his balls to the floor and shoot him in the stomach. Let him bleed out." He shrugged.

I nodded my agreement as I finished the last of my beer.

"When you gonna do it?"

"I haven't decided yet." I slid the can across the counter to the recycling. "She might want to watch."

"True." Ardan chuckled. "But in the meantime, we need answers," he said it so seriously for him. "I won't touch her, I won't step forward, but I can't watch that ever again."

"That makes two of us."

"Are you really going to do it?" Drea asked from the hallway.

"Hey." I crossed the kitchen to stand close to her, I had to ball my fists at my sides not to grab her. "Why are you up? Can I get you something?"

"I hate myself a little for this but… I can't sleep without you there. My mind just starts going over…" She swallowed audibly. "You know what, forget it."

I knew how vulnerable that sentence made her. I felt it fishing for the chinks in my own armor.

"I meant it, Drea. I mean it with all of my black and dead heart." It was the only reassurance I could offer. "I will kill Mac. I'll kill him for what he's done to you."

She stopped her slow retreat and slouched against the wall, her eyes searching the opposite side of the hallway rather than coming back to mine.

"How can I trust you?" Her gaze fell to her toes. "You've been jerking me around for almost a week, Niall, and I know it's the game you're supposed to be playing. I can't tell which version of you is real. I don't know which words are either."

"I could say the same about you," I said as I leaned against the wall opposite her. "One minute you're a venomous viper, the next we're here. Just you and me."

"There can't be a you and me. Ever."

I had to hide how badly that stung. I wouldn't let that be the truth.

"Well there's a you and me right here, right now, and we're in it together whether we like it or not." I sighed. "And I am being one hundred percent serious and utterly honest when I say I hate him." My fists balled automatically. "I hate what he did then, I hate what he did tonight, and I will kill him for both." I softened, wanting to reach out for her so badly. "I'll protect you until I do it too."

She scoffed.

"I mean it." This time I reached out before I remembered myself, and I grabbed her hand, my fingers lacing in. She let me keep my hold.

"I've carried that cross for long enough by myself, I'll be okay." She offered me a small smile. "If you gave a shit, you'd protect people like Saoirse from becoming collateral damage."

I looked at her, really looked at her. I saw the girl she'd always been grown into the woman in front of me. I saw that woman and knew what she was thinking.

"That's what this all is, isn't it?"

"What?" She crossed her free arm across her chest, shrinking away from me.

"Who are you protecting when it comes to the MacCowans?"

She shook her head and said nothing. My temper percolated under my skin. She thought she was doing the right thing by keeping her mouth shut when it really just made her an island with an army of one. Again. Did she see I could fight for her?

"Are they worth dying for?" I wouldn't look away, I wouldn't let her hide from this question.

"Who?"

"Whoever you're protecting," I snapped.

"You're being an asshole again." She turned for my bedroom, but I used my hand, still holding hers, to pull her back.

"Am I just supposed to lose you all over again and like it?"

"Lose me? You don't have me," she answered softly.

"You are in my house, in my bed. I fucking have you, Drea." I reached up to push a small piece of her hair behind her ear.

"You're not going to lose me like that Niall." She leaned into my hand. "I'm already gone."

Deirdre

Two days and ten hours. Now I counted to keep myself from monitoring Niall's every move. I knew the way he'd been the other night after Mac was real. What he'd seen had terrified him. I'd felt it in my bones.

And that terrified me.

We were so much better off as frigid cold and uncaring. We made sense that way. I could push him, and my feelings about him, away. He could keep that thick and mile high wall intact to deflect anything I let slip through.

But now we were wide open and raw.

Like this, was his allegiance with me or my stepfather? When it came down to choosing, who would it be? And why the hell did I want that answer to be me?

I took a deep breath and shifted from cobra pose to downward dog, hoping to find my center. The ghost of that night haunted me. No matter how many times I showered, I felt it on my skin. If someone wasn't with me, Mac was. Mac from then, Mac screaming at me now. I would see Saoirse. It made me desperate for some inner peace. I pushed deeper into the stretch and instead of calm, my shoulders popped, and the yoga shorts Niall had bought me slid up a little too high. I closed my eyes and tried to push past it and breathe.

"Bagels?" Niall asked, and my eyes popped open.

There he was, between my legs, upside down, sinfully sexy

where he leaned against the doorframe. Clearly he'd been watching me, his easy pose and hooded eyes said plenty, so I felt no shame eyeing him.

He'd been running lately. Or running to the CrossFit gym. Where he had to lift, and drink sludge smoothies, then lift some more to be as bulky as he was. Hell, if I knew anything besides that he looked amazing and came back soaked in sweat. His dark t-shirt clung to his skin and showed the tattoo sleeves blanketing his arms, the tattoos I was trying not to inspect too close. His joggers hinted at the thick musculature of his legs, rode just high enough to show his ankle bones, and gathered at the waist in a way that made his dick print my constant companion.

"Goddamnit," I cursed when my eyes darted to his crotch. Again.

"What?" he asked with his smirk pulling into place. "Hungry for something else?"

It may have been my imagination, but I swore he suggestively pressed his hips forward. I gracelessly crumbled out of downward dog to sit cross-legged on his floor.

"What kind of bagels?" I ignored him and his body as I reached for the bag.

He held them out but just out of reach. I threw my legs out to a V and reached past my ankles for them.

"Yoga's paying off, Drea." He pulled them back just an inch to make me lunge. This time I caught the bag and ripped.

"There better be…" I was going to threaten him, demand the correct bagels, but when I opened the bag, I knew. I should have known.

"Cinnamon raisin with honey granola or garlic with plain."

My smile that spread was genuine. I couldn't help it, I was too grateful to hide it.

"If only there was coffee."

He held up one finger before turning to leave, returning a minute later with two cups. "An americano or a vanilla latte with whipped cream and cinnamon." He smiled as he folded his legs beneath him to sit on the floor across from me, the cups barely shifting. "Pick whatever combo you want, I'm fine with the other."

This was the Target bags all over again. The small little things about me that really didn't matter. That he really could have forgotten. I wouldn't have been upset if those sorts of things had gone. But he'd remembered. All of it.

"I know where those pillows on the couch came from," I blurted out.

"And you knew to order New York style pizza to piss me off," he said with a chuckle.

"You're an ass," I muttered as I grabbed the savory bagel and extra sweet coffee.

"You're the one that purposefully fucked with pizza."

I stuck out my tongue and made a face as I mocked him before taking a bite of my bagel.

"You still have that big freckle high up on your inner thigh?"

I choked on the bagel, sucking it into my throat and shutting off my ability to breathe. I coughed so hard I know I was turning a throbbing beet red.

"You okay?" He set down his coffee and bagel and started toward me.

I held two thumbs up even though I was still coughing wildly.

"Verbally, Drea, or I'm going to have to come over there, wrap my body around you," he paused for effect, lifting his eyebrow, "and give you the Heimlich."

I couldn't help the sharp intake of breath or that it started the coughing all over again.

"Drea," he asked again, this time concern coloring his voice.

I tried to cover my mouth and held up and arm to keep him from coming over, but I couldn't stop. I couldn't tell him to keep his ass to his side of the room. My eyes watered, my face and ribs hurt with the force of it all. I wasn't choking but I really wasn't breathing either.

Niall scrambled over and did exactly what he'd said but it lacked the sex and sin his words had a moment ago. His big arms wrapped around me just when I managed to squeak out a *stop*.

"Wait," I gasped, finally clearing my windpipe. "Water," I begged.

As quickly as he'd gotten behind me, he disappeared again.

"Here." He jogged back in with a water bottle in hand.

I snatched it and sucked down the water, finally clearing my throat. I took a deep breath before taking another long drink. When I pulled the bottle away, Niall was crouched close, watching me intently.

"Thank you," I said softly, my eyes falling from his.

"You're welcome." He reached out for my chin and pulled my eyes back to his. "Are you okay?"

I swallowed the lump in my throat. Christ, he seemed like he could see into my soul and I didn't know what he would find there. Not anymore. This week, these two weeks, had changed so much. Or had they really changed anything at all?

"Drea, answer me. Please?"

I didn't know. I wasn't going to die, but him, here with me, like that…

"You smell." My mind glitched and it was the only thing I could think to say.

"Sorry about that." His hand fell away but he stayed crouched right in front of me as he whipped his shirt off.

Holy Mary Mother of God.

I'd seen him about to split out of just about every shirt he owned, I'd seen hints of the tattoos, but not once did I indulge this fantasy. The one where he was a made of muscles stitched together with ink and nothing else. Over the years I'd see enough men nude to know many shapes and forms, not a single one of them did it for me like the one in front of me.

The bastard knew it too.

"Better?" he purred, his eyebrow in a wicked arch.

"I… uh… God. Christ, what is your workout routine?" I couldn't stop myself. Again.

"You don't really want to know about my workouts." He dropped his knees to the floor, bringing the whole mass of muscles closer. "You want to know what it feels like to touch."

Fuck yes I did.

But if I did… If he was still playing me… How would I ever recover from Niall McDonough? I didn't really the first time.

"Do it, Drea." He inched closer.

I couldn't swallow this time. My throat was so dry it was the damn Sahara. I shook my head.

"One finger, down the center of my stomach." He leaned in and I balled my hands. "You can lick cream cheese off me if you want."

I would have choked on my bagel all over again.

"What the fuck is wrong with you?" I barely managed.

He started laughing, loud and brash and free, a sound I hadn't heard in twelve years. If butterflies hadn't been going apeshit in my stomach already, they would have at that sound.

"It's what you get for having your ass out and in my face." He kept laughing as he rocked back from the balls of his feet and swiftly stood.

His fingers brushed my shoulders as he walked past me to the bathroom, toeing off his shoes as he went. My skin sung, somehow more alive than it had been when he'd been topless in front of me, just because of the simple touch. And his bare feet.

I bit my lip as I looked after him, his backward glance over his shoulder complete with a wicked smirk told me he was waiting for it.

"Don't you dare." I saw where his hands were resting at the edges of his waistband. "Shut the door you savage."

"My house." He shrugged as he shoved his pants down.

My hands snapped over my eyes. Nudity was fine but *his* nudity would kill me. I had to be a prude when it came to Niall, it was self-survival.

Then again so was one, tiny, little, insignificant, basically nothing peek.

I let my fingers split—just for a glimpse of what was likely an insanely tight, horseshoe shaped ass that I could bounce quarters off—only to find his semi-hard cock pointed in my direction and the bastard laughing his insanely tight, horseshoe-shaped ass off.

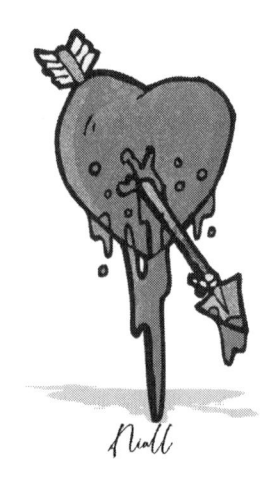

I looked down at my phone as the call from Mac faded. Something was wrong. Well not wrong, but *off.*

"Where's your sister?" I asked, my eyes still on the screen as I walked toward my room where Ardan and Drea were watching something stupid.

"I don't know," he called as I walked in.

They both started laughing.

I looked up from my phone to find Ardan laying on my side of the bed with Drea sprawled across the bed with her head on his stomach. Jealousy flared in my chest.

"Why don't you find the fuck out," I snarled.

He glanced down to Drea before his eyes went wide and he scrambled out from beneath her.

"Sorry," he muttered.

"Just find her."

He slunk past me, and I heard him pressing buttons on this phone a moment later.

"He's not his sister's keeper, ya know." Drea had rolled on her side to watch me.

"But you're his?" I snapped.

"What's that supposed to mean?" She propped her head on her elbow.

"If you want to fuck him, do it on the counter or some shit I can bleach later." I walked past her to my closet, swapping my sweats for my slacks and started in on the buttons of a shirt.

"So you're back to being a fucking jerk?" Her voice was right behind me.

"Never stopped." I fiddled with the buttons at my wrists.

"Bullshit," she snapped.

"I lost my head for a second."

"Fine. The other night after Mac…?" Her voice cracked as it trailed off, my shoulders tensed.

"Despite all evidence to the opposite, I'm fucking human." I turned toward her and knew just how human I'd become this week. Like this—yoga shorts, a sheer, soft hugging t-shirt, and hair piled high—she could bring me to my knees. Somewhere I increasingly wanted to be in front of her. "He's fucking scum. Worse than that. He doesn't deserve to live." I let my eyes rove down her body before I sighed and closed them. "But then again, so am I."

"If you're such a goddamned terrifying monster, why don't you rip my shirt off, shove my shorts down, and fuck me?" She uncrossed her arms and stepped toward me. "Use me. Make yourself feel better."

I said *nothing*. There was nothing that I could say. I couldn't admit how fucking great that sounded. I couldn't admit how gutted that left me either. She wasn't something to use and throw away. My teeth gritted, and my heartbeat thrummed in my throat.

"Or is this still the game? The back and forth fuck with my head until I cave?" Her voice said she was challenging me, but her eyes scanned my face. "I'd rather you just fuck me," she said softly, turning for the bed and crawling on.

I wanted to touch her. I wanted to feel her thighs brush along mine—but more—I wanted to feel her warm breath on my skin as she said my fucking name.

"I'm not going to fuck you."

"If you're toying with me, you already are," she grumbled as she pulled her knees into her chest and wrapped her arms around.

"Ailee for you," Ardan interrupted from the doorway.

"Great," I snarled as I strode over to him. "Watch her while I'm out." I pointed at Drea even though I didn't need to; it gave me a reason to look at her one more time before I grabbed Ardan's phone. "Answer me when I fucking call you, Ailee." I clicked the phone off and shoved it in Ardan's hand and didn't give either of them a chance to say anything.

As soon as I got in my car, I realized that I should have said something to Drea. I should have told her that we'd talk about this when I got back. That she didn't know what she was talking about. I could have even said this stopped being a game for me that night. She'd snapped back to being Drea, my Drea, and I couldn't shake it.

Sure there was still hurt but hadn't we both lived with it long enough?

I was about to put my fist through the window when my phone rang. I answered right away.

"I'm not the kind of girl who sits by her phone, waiting for a man to call," Ailee snapped.

I started the car, started driving, and put her on speaker before answering.

"I need you," I said as I started navigating across town toward where Mac had asked to meet.

"You don't need me," she scoffed. "You *want* me to babysit and that's just bullshit."

"*Mac* wants you to babysit," I corrected her as I rushed from the neighborhood to the highway.

"No, Mac wants *you* to get an answer." She put me on speakerphone, and I could hear the rustle of fabric across the line. "It's not my fault that you fell back in love with her along the way."

"I don't fucking love her," I roared when she hit my bruise. I didn't want to. I didn't want to feel anything anymore. I'd been fine doing just that for twelve years.

"Fine, you'd love to be fucking her. Whatever."

"I don't—"

"Oh come on. You want me there and Ardan gone because

you're jealous they've boned," she groaned. "Get over it. She's a job and a whore."

I slammed on my breaks, swerving to the shoulder. "I don't know who the fuck has gotten into you Ailee and why the fuck he's made you such a complete cunt but it's not a good look," I sneered. "He better have a magical dick, a penchant for manslaughter, and the willingness to put up with your mountain of shit if you're going to pick him over me."

"You know where my loyalty lies," she said, her voice as deadly as a blade.

"I thought I did."

"You're going to let *her* ruin our friendship?" She picked the phone up and took me off speaker.

"You're doing it all on your own."

"We will talk about this after the house—"

I hung up before she finished. My fingers hurt from the grip I kept on the steering wheel. I had to cling to it to keep from beating the ever-loving shit out of my car. Or some bystander. Fuck, Mac would be lucky if he didn't get the shit beat out of him when we met in the parking garage he'd indicated.

Warning bells went off in my head.

Ailee had said *the house*. She'd been getting dressed. Whether it was at the prick's house or hers, she was leaving. And soon. But Mac had asked me to meet him across town. The feeling that I'd had before came back tenfold.

I tried to call Ailee back only to be sent to voicemail after one ring. I called back again, and she let it ring three times before doing the same thing.

"Damnit, Ailee."

I flipped over to Ardan's number.

"I am on the way. Do *not* give me shit, I was doing what you told me. I didn't know we had to fucking be there," he kept rambling.

"Ardan," I tried to stop him.

"I thought you were going across town, how was I supposed to know we needed to be at the house?" he barreled on.

"Ardan!"

"Five fucking minutes, Niall," he shouted then hung up.

"No, no, no." This time I did slam my hand against the steering wheel.

I called him back only for it to ring and ring and ring.

Drea.

She could be with Ardan, he hadn't said anything and if he was following orders… *Shit*. If he was following my orders, he wouldn't have moved his ginger fucking ass from my bed unless the Apple TV got out of sync and he needed to unplug it and plug it back in. But if Mac had made him think otherwise…

That feeling grew in my stomach until it choked me and made my throat go bone dry all at once.

I slammed on the gas, veering back into traffic despite the chorus of horns that followed. The concrete barriers kept me straight and narrow as I reached for Saint Christopher where he hung around my neck, pulled him up, and kissed him in prayer. I just needed to get to the next exit.

Each turn of my tires seemed to stretch on for hours when it was usually instantaneous. I'd never known real fear until now. I swerved off the next exit and ran two lights to get back on the highway going the other way.

Sending us in different directions, getting Drea alone—please God and Saint Christopher let me be wrong—couldn't mean anything good. Couldn't mean anything less than awful. I prayed my mind was fucked up because of the way things were left between us. I would take the punishment Mac handed out if I was *just fucking wrong*.

I blared on my horn as I wove in and out of traffic back the way I came. My tires squealed on the pavement as I exited the highway. My heart thudded in my ears urging me forward. My fingers tingled making each movement seem disconnected and surreal.

This couldn't be happening.

But when I turned onto my street, it was. Oh fucking hell it was. Mac's Range Rover was parked in front of my house and the front door hung wide open, shattered on its hinges.

Deirdre

I RAN MY FINGERS OVER THE HANDLE OF THE GUN ARDAN HAD left. This was... *different.* They'd left me alone. And with protection. I could kill Ardan or even Niall if I wanted out.

And I definitely wanted out.

Didn't I?

I'd tried to run naked from Niall in my desperation when I left the cage. And a few times after that. But now... Now I wanted him to own up to his feelings. No more jerking around, no more games. I wanted to know where we stood and if we could ever take a step forward.

There was a small chance I'd hold the gun to his head to get *that* answer but... I smiled. I'd do it. Niall would probably find it funny. Or see it as a challenge. Which seemed to shut him down or turn him on. If it was the later...

A knock at the front door stopped my thoughts cold.

People like Niall didn't have friends. No one randomly knocked on these front doors. I knew it because it was the same type of front door that the MacCowans had. It was the one I lived behind for twelve years. It was equal parts prison and protection.

The knock sounded again.

I grabbed the gun and slid beneath Niall's bed, willing my breathing to slow. When I couldn't, I said the silent prayer I used to say so very many times asking God or whoever deigned to still listen to bring Niall back to me. I prayed that this time it would work.

The door splintered a moment later, wood protesting and screeching before plinking on the ground. My hand shook against the gun Ardan had left me, and I tried to remember what Emmett had told me about using one. I hadn't wanted to learn, I hadn't wanted to retain a single word out of his shit eating mouth, but now I desperately tried to dredge it up.

Why hadn't Ardan gone over it?

Maybe he assumed—

"Iníon, where are you?" Mac's voice slithered through the house, and I balled in on myself as best I could. "Come out, come out and play."

I tried to hold my breath as his footsteps moved into the kitchen.

"I know you're alone," he taunted. "I *wanted* you alone."

He stopped in the kitchen, and I knew he'd be finding the still-warm take-out on the counter. We hadn't even opened it when Ardan started spinning around in a frenzy. It said plenty even when my mouth stayed shut.

"Do you know what I liked most about that night? That night when you were in boarding school?"

My teeth chattered once as I shook before I was able to control it. He chuckled.

"Are you thinking about it again, iníon? About that night?"

I squeezed my eyes shut hoping to block it out or forget it or put up some defense against him here and now. Or all of it. Any of it. Please God.

"I loved that, knowing I was taking what wasn't mine." His foot falls went from clacks against tile to shuffles against carpet. My heart was in my throat, threatening to split it open. "I've become rather fond of things that aren't mine." He sat on the mattress, barely more than a shift and whisper but I knew.

I opened my eyes to find his feet inches from my face.

"When you were just a whore, it wasn't fun. Not even to get the information that I want." He must have rounded forward because his fingertips came into view. "But then I realized something."

He paused, waiting for me to say something. I couldn't have managed even if I wanted to.

"You really won't play with me?" he asked in a high and wicked voice. "Fine." His voice flattened out. "I'll tell you." He shifted and my breath caught.

He spun and dropped to the floor in a single fluid movement. His hands shot out and tangled into my hair and pulled. I screamed and thrashed against his pull. I beat at one of his hands as I tried to grab the bed frame with the other.

I didn't remember the gun near my fingertips until it was too late.

Mac had me out from under the bed when he dropped down on top of me, his full weight on my chest. I didn't stop jerking, writhing. Anything in my ability to fight him off.

"See, iníon, I realized you were his again. You were his, which means I can take you as mine."

His hands were at my breasts, his fingers digging into my shirt to rip it.

I couldn't do it again. After everything, this would be what broke me. Years of sexual favors, years of being used, and this, the circle back to that first night, the one where everything was upended…

A sob tore at my throat as he ripped at my clothes. I knew I kept screaming, crying, wrenching my body beneath him even as I sunk deeper, trying to find that spot inside me. The one that used to offer me safe haven when it all went sideways.

The place where I kept Niall.

"Drea," Niall said, his voice smooth and supple. *"Close your eyes, sweetheart. Close your mouth, too."* His voice wasn't cruel or urgent, just steady and true.

Tears slid from the corners of my eyes as I did what I was told, desperate to cling to his presence. His voice.

A heartbeat later a bang echoed in the room, deafening almost. Mac pinned me and… and stilled.

I started screaming only for Mac to roll off me a second later and Niall's hand to cover my mouth.

"Shhhhh," he started, again soft and strong. "Shhhhh, it's going to be okay." He brushed the hair out of my face and tucked it behind my ear. "Did he hurt you?"

I shook my head as a sudden cascade of tears poured down my cheeks.

"Shhhhh, Drea." He gathered me up into his lap. "I'm so sorry I left. I'm sorry I wasn't here," he murmured against my temple. "Forgive me."

My hands curled into his shirt, clawing at any hold I could find. His arms around me didn't waver, they just held me tight to his chest as his lip ring brushed against my skin.

"Forgive me for all of it," he whispered so quietly I wasn't sure I'd even heard it.

My tears started fresh.

"I'm not going to let anyone hurt you again, okay?"

I couldn't help but nod.

He let me sit for a while without saying a word. His hands didn't wander or stroke my skin, he just held me. As if he'd never let me go.

"Do you want to take a shower?" he asked after a million heartbeats.

"I want to get rid of the body." My words and how wicked they sounded just came out. "I want to watch it burn or sink in cement or get eaten by lye, I don't fucking care. I just want to watch the true end of him."

"I can do that, I just need Ardan or Ailee or both." He rested his chin on my forehead.

"What are we waiting for?" I shoved against him to stand.

"Breathe, Drea." He let me go only for my body and brain to fall apart when I actually saw my stepfather lifeless on the floor. "I told you to breathe," he said a little more firm when my knees wobbled.

He unfolded from where he'd crumpled on the floor, keeping a hand on the small of my back. "When you're ready, I need you to change. We have to go over there. I'm going to keep the peace, we're going to get rid of the body."

"Simple as that?"

"Simple as that." He gave me a look that made me believe. "He's just a dead body. It's just a family without an heir."

I nodded. I could deal with that. Corpses and coups were normal. They were nothing.

My shirt hung loose at my body where it had been stretched. I fiddled with the fabric as one question surfaced. Things like this could be bloody, borderline insane…

"Niall, what's going to happen to my mom?"

He stepped into the closet with me, his arms around me just as they had been before. Holding me up. He leaned his forehead against mine.

"What? What are you going to do?"

"Drea." He kissed my forehead, his lips hesitant, shaking even. "He killed your mom years ago."

My jaw hurt, a little unhinged from where she'd decked me. Drea could punch. I didn't deserve the hit, but I took it all the same.

And I let her kick and beat on Mac's body, unleashing the pent up fury of a lifetime on his already rotting flesh. After one full-bodied kick to his kidneys a new wave tears took over, and I knew she was going to crumble a second before she did.

I rushed over and caught her as she melted. She sank into me, only to punch me again. I took that too. I let her cry as I started to pull her out of the room and perched her on the arm of the couch.

"We have to get moving okay?" I said softly as I pushed her hair behind her ears again. "Someone might have heard the shot, the screams. The front door is split wide open."

She looked toward where I'd propped up the door for some semblance of privacy with a glazed over gaze then nodded.

I turned and got her a shirt and some leggings from the drawer I'd given her. The same vacant look greeted me when I came back.

"You wanna get changed?" I asked as I set the clothes next to her. She nodded again but didn't move. "I can help you if you want." All I got was a matching weak nod.

I made sure to move slowly and deliberately as I reached for the hem of her shirt. "Do you want a bra?" I asked softly.

"No."

"Okay."

I pulled her shirt up slowly and tried really fucking hard not to look. She was so fucking beautiful I didn't think I could control myself. The thought of someone taking that from her, taking that for themselves, infuriated me. I wouldn't do it now.

I wouldn't do it ever.

She helped me slide her arms into her shirt and I pulled it over her dangerous curves until she was fully covered again. Her body was just as sexy in the soft, sheer fabric as it was out of it.

"Leggings?" I turned it into a question so she would know I'd only touch her if she gave me permission.

Drea found some semblance of motor skills and stood. She pressed her shorts down as if it was nothing and I made a vow that would never happen to her again. The next time she took those pants off in front of a man—in front of me—every inch would count. It would be torturously slow, I'd kiss every single inch. She'd feel worshipped.

I held them down so she could step out of the fabric then tossed the shorts to the side. I slid one slipper off, cupping her heel as I pushed her pant leg on. I repeated it on the other foot before pulling them up, coming nose to nose with her. My eyes met hers and I couldn't help but wet my lips, flicking my lip ring as I went.

"I hate you right now." Her arms wrapped around her stomach. "I hate that she's dead."

"Okay." I held in my heavy sigh as I crouched down and helped her slide back into her slippers.

"You should have told me." Her voice broke.

I stayed at her feet, unable to rise with the weight of those words. After everything tonight, that's what had overshadowed it all. There was just so much between us. Too much maybe.

"It was years ago, I thought you knew." I leaned my forehead against her thigh. "I didn't think I needed to."

Her body shifted beneath me and I looked up to see her nodding. Sorrow hung on every inch of her. Her throat wobbled and her mouth opened before she snapped it shut again. Tears pooled in the corner of her eyes again.

"She wasn't up for mother of the year back then, and I wasn't allowed to contact her when I lived with the MacCowans, but she tried to protect me. She tried."

I had some really choice retorts to that. One of which was bullshit. She'd brought Mac into their lives, into all of ours if I was being honest. And what sort of protection was Drea talking about? Boarding school? That was nothing more than a wall for Mac to climb.

It took every ounce of restraint I had not to yell all of that in her face. How easy it was for her to forget... My teeth ground together despite my words. Drea narrowed her gaze at me, fury evident on her face as if she read my thoughts.

"Thank you for tonight," she managed.

"I wish I'd made him suffer." I would have ripped his fingernails off one by one and cut his tongue out just to start.

"Me too." She slid out from under me and stepped away.

I wanted to hold her. I wanted to make her lose herself. Her mind, her heart, her body. Fuck, maybe I wanted that for myself too. It wouldn't be tonight though, judging by that face, we might have been back to never. Her anger was the only thing keeping her from falling to pieces, I could see it in the way she barely held herself together. For that reason alone, I let her keep it.

With a heavy sigh I got up, walked into the bedroom, and grabbed one of my sweatshirts. I unzipped it and slung it over her shoulders when I returned. I had to stop myself from running my hands down the length of her arms or the curve of her hips.

"Let's go."

She nodded again as she shoved her arms into the big baggy sleeves then turned to follow me. I had to pick up the pieces of the broken door and move them to let her out. I kept one eye on her as she shuffled across the grass to where I'd left the car. Each step, each movement seemed like an effort as she hauled herself into the SUV.

As we drove the familiar roads to her stepfather's house, my eyes kept flashing to her. To the sadness and pain that enveloped her features. To the hurt she tried to hide behind the hood of my sweatshirt she'd flipped up. I liked her swimming in my sweatshirt. I liked her sitting in the front seat of my car.

I hated that the whole situation was so fucked up.

How had we gotten here?

I knew the actual events that had happened but how had I forgotten this? All of this? How good she was, how gorgeous. How the vulnerable part of her was more beautiful than the strong. Hurt and hate had clouded my vision of her for far too long.

Red and blue flashed and I realized everything had clouded over with my thoughts of her. I hadn't been paying attention to the road, not really anyhow. Everything in me tensed at the sight of the police cars lining the street. Particularly because the street was Mac's.

"What's going on?" Drea sat up a little in her seat.

"Nothing good," I replied. "Get down."

"Why?" she challenged me.

"You look like hell, if they stop us—"

"It'll look suspicious that I'm hiding on the floor," she interrupted me.

"Point taken. Pretend you're asleep then, hidden in that fucking hood." I pointed at her, using a voice she shouldn't question.

She *humphed* but did as she was told. We moved forward in a creeping line of traffic toward the barricades. I tried to survey the area, to get a feel for what was going on. One cop was shining a light into cars and directing traffic, two stood behind him and the orange and white striped barricade, chatting idly. Beyond them the street was littered with regular cop cars and a few unmarked ones. I couldn't see Mac's house but they all seemed pointed in its direction.

"Shouldn't you turn around?" Drea murmured as we rolled forward.

"That looks too suspicious."

"And if they decide we look suspicious anyway?" she snapped.

"I'll deal with it."

I didn't have to look to know she was rolling her eyes. She'd never given me enough credit. The reminder had me tightening my hands on the steering wheel.

We pulled forward and the metal of the cop's flashlight tapped on my window. I put a small smile in place as I rolled the window down.

"What's going on officer?" I asked, pushing all my irritation and edge aside.

"Federal matter." He brushed my question aside. "Where were you two headed?"

"Home. I had business in St. Louis today and my wife came with." I always had a lie ready. It was one of the first things I'd learned from Mac.

"Do you live on this street?" He gestured past the barricade with the butt of his flashlight.

"Just trying to avoid the highway." I shrugged. Many more questions and I'd have to figure out a way to off this guy.

"You'll have to take an alternate route," he said sternly.

"No problem."

He waved us on, and with a nod, I pulled the Rover forward.

"Do you think he knows?" Drea asked as soon as the window was shut.

"If Ardan and Ailee were there, they'd know Range Rovers are the vehicle of choice, but he didn't even ask for identification." I followed the flares until we were a few streets over then turned into an alley and parked. "Stay here."

"What?" Her voice shot up a few octaves.

"Don't get out of the car. Don't turn on the headlights. If you need out, it's a left, a right, a left, and you're back on Mac's street, likely past the cops. It won't look like this car fits through the second alley but it does."

"Are you fucking serious right now?" She scrambled over and grabbed my shirt.

"As a heart attack, Drea."

"You're going to leave me?"

"If there is even a chance that Ardan or Ailee got out, I'm

going to get them. And it's not because there is a dead body at my house or a federal matter involving your family and my employer. It's because they're my friends. They're the only two that have ever been loyal to me." I realized what I'd said, what it implied about her betrayal all those years ago, a moment too late.

"Feel free to sit up there on your high horse, Niall. I hope you enjoy the view."

I shook my head as I shoved out of my seat.

"It'd do you good to remember, some of us haven't had the luxury of loyalty, we've been too busy trying to survive."

I slammed the door and stalked away, turning her words over in my head. Survive. That word chipped away at my anger. She'd weathered so much, more than anyone I knew and that said a lot. I didn't mean to make it harder on her but somehow I managed. Almost every time I opened my mouth.

Shit.

Fucking shit. I swore again when I crept down the alley just over from the one we'd been diverted down. A lone officer stood at the mouth, aimlessly kicking rocks in an excuse of a patrol. I studied the buildings beside me, trying to recall what they looked like from the front, trying to remember if they had cover. A general picture formed but the details were lacking. Ailee was always the one to know the details.

Fuckingshitpiss.

That meant I couldn't sneak past the officer with guaranteed shelter on the other side, and standing in the open wasn't something I was willing to risk. I slunk back into a small alcove, picking up both a brick and a handful of gravel as I went. When I was tucked in the doorway, I tossed the gravel into the alley. The sound of each small rock echoed like rain in the alley.

The cop tensed and turned, drawing his gun and his flashlight, pointing both in an X down the alley. He swept the space, and I shoved back further into the shadows, watching. Waiting. If he kept going maybe I could let him live.

His radio pierced the quiet. *They've almost got 'em all. We might be out of here in twenty. We'll take the girls, feds will handle the perps.* Each word crackled like a live wire.

And the officer turned around, almost pointing the light right at me. Poor, unfortunate fool.

The second he stepped past me, I bludgeoned his temple with the brick in my hand. He dropped soundlessly into my arms. I'd planned to snap his neck or choke him, but he was out from one perfectly placed blow. I gathered him up and dumped his body in a nearby trash can. It wasn't that I minded killing him, I was just short on time.

I crept to the opening of the alley, keeping to the darkness. When the alley met the street, and the world opened back up in front of me, only two words came to mind.

Holy fuck.

Deirdre

Where was he? Where in the ever-loving world was that gorgeous, disgusting, ruthless, beautiful bastard? Every second that he wasn't back in this car with me my world spun a little further out of orbit.

Today was too much.

I leaned forward and let my head rest against the dashboard. My mom was dead. I was livid no one had told me. No Ulster, no MacCowan, not even Niall. It was like they hadn't given a shit. Which was probably true. Each and every one of them was heartless. Each and every one of them viewed death as a toy to play with. Had he killed her quickly or was it something slow and torturous? Had she known she was going to die? Did she feel pain each of those last minutes or seconds?

Had she died alone?

The questions stirred up a sorrow so complete that tears started streaming down my cheeks without my consent. I wanted to kill Mac all over again.

I tried not to look too closely at those events tonight either. He'd had his hands on me again. I could feel him all over me. Heat. Pressure. Pain. Shame. Loss unending.

Twelve years ago, Niall had been strong and steady. He'd loved me simply but entirely. He was sweet and kind and good. And after Mac took from me, I was damaged goods. And Niall had deserved so much more than damaged goods.

God, I was worse now.

Then again, so was he.

He was cold and ruthless but there seemed to be a soft spot too. One that laid beneath all those layers of muscle and ink. One that seemed to exist only for me. Niall was something else entirely, and I had no idea what he deserved these days.

And speaking of Niall, *where was he?*

I scanned the alley and saw nothing. No one. The brick of the buildings seemed to inch in closer and grow taller. I'd never been claustrophobic but now, with the world around me whirring out of control, there was a pressure on my chest I wasn't used to. An unease that sent the hairs on the back of my neck on end.

A massive thump on the hood of the car stopped my heart and made me scream. The whole car swayed with the force of it and I braced myself against the leather of the seat and the door. A figure moved on the hood and I cursed myself for not getting into the driver's seat. Tears renewed on my cheeks, these ones born of true fear, as I tried to get my seatbelt unbuckled with shaky hands.

I screamed again when the man jumped down from the hood of the car and whipped open the door.

"It's me," Niall hissed.

"What in the fuck are you doing falling from the sky?" I screeched.

"Christ above, Drea, keep it down. There's an entire precinct down the street and an FBI task force." He buckled up before driving forward, the alley every bit as dark now as it had been a minute ago.

"What happened back there?" I couldn't see his face, I had no way of knowing.

He didn't answer me, instead he drove the route he'd told me earlier—a left, right, left—and we were back on my childhood street, down a little ways by the Irish pub Mac had frequented. I wanted to spit just at the thought of his name.

Niall flipped on the lights and drove on as if nothing had happened. Not just now but all night. He acted like this was all so fucking normal.

"What the hell is wrong with you, Niall?"

"Excuse me?" He shot me a sideways glance.

"This is all just so normal to you," I accused.

"Well this may come as a surprise to you, sweetheart, but being one of Mac's men isn't exactly take out and Real Housewives all the time."

"Very funny." I rolled my eyes.

"Those days, the ones with you that were quiet and calm were the exception. Killing people and stuffing bodies into trashcans are a bit more par for the course." His voice was somehow cruel and seductive all at once.

"You stuffed a body in a trashcan? Fucking Christ, Niall."

"Yes, it was that or snap his neck and leave him in the alley." He flashed me a fake smile in the haunting blue of the dashboard. "Twelve years with the MacCowans, with *Emmett*," he sneered, "and this shit makes you squeamish?"

"*Emmett*," I emphasized his name in a similar huff, "treated me like a set of fucking holes. I was a possession. A toy let out at playtime. I wasn't involved in this sort of shit unless I was sucking someone off while they did it."

He roared in response and slammed his hand against the steering wheel. "Don't say shit like that."

"Don't tell you the truth?" I huffed. "Fine. It was bliss. I enjoyed every single fucking moment of it. Just like this go round, Niall."

"Shut the fuck up, Drea," he snarled.

"The best part was when he fucking branded me. The pain was indescribable, but it was nothing compared to learning it was all a lie. Every word he'd said, every reason that I'd left you, complete and utter bullshit," I shouted at him, my myriad of emotions unleashing in a torrent as he pulled the vehicle over. "The only thing that wasn't a lie was what the fortune teller had said, because that day, the blood on my hands was my own as it poured from the inside of my lip!"

His hand flew from the steering wheel to my neck and shoved me back against the passenger side window.

"Stop talking." Niall's voice made my skin grow cold.

"Just because you don't like what I have to say?" I sneered, lifting my chin to give him better access. "Do it," I taunted him. His hand tightened on my flesh. "Throw me in a trash can when you're done."

"We'll never be done." He bit out as he used his grasp to yank my face to his.

The moment our lips touched it was like fireworks, searing and explosive, stealing my breath. My hands flew to his shoulders, equally wanting to shove him away and draw him closer. His hand tightened on my throat, but the reason I couldn't breathe was him. His lips, his tongue. This kiss.

Each of his movements was aggressive and I met them, one for one. Our lips tumbled over one another, his teeth caught my lip and pulled. Each time I gasped, the heady smell of him filled what little of my senses were left. His taste danced on my tongue. The thump of my head against the glass was second only to the wild crash of my heart.

As quickly as he started, he stopped, flopping back into the seat and breathing wildly.

"Don't ever say those things to me again," he murmured.

"They're the truth." I leaned my head back against my headrest and looked up at the ceiling. "They're my truth."

"Well my truth is that I'm a goddamned monster. I cling to Saint Christopher because it's my way of clinging to humanity. I lost that the day I lost you."

I closed my eyes against his words.

"So yes, I kill people without batting an eye and I stuff them in fucking trashcans. It doesn't bother me much anymore, I don't know that it ever really did." He blew out a deep breath. "I can tell you that it won't even make me flinch if it helps protect you."

"Stop saying things like that to me."

His finger appeared at my chin, and he turned my face toward his then waited for me to open my eyes. When I did, the pad of his thumb rolled over the plump of my lip.

"The thing is, Drea," he said softly, "that's my fucking truth too."

Niall

THE ROAD STRETCHED IN FRONT OF US, EVERY BIT AS LONG AS THE silence between us. There hadn't been much to say after we spoke our truths.

Or much I wanted to say anyway. I could take a lot of carnage but ripping myself open didn't feel great.

Neither did the realization that Ardan and Ailee were in custody and that left us with only one option. One really shitty gamble of an option. I hadn't managed to tell Drea about any of that, what with all the yelling. And that kiss. That fucking amazing kiss.

She didn't know that I'd seen the twins' fire red hair easily in the night as they were loaded into unmarked Suburbans rather than the cop cars. Suburbans meant FBI; I knew because the bright yellow letters emblazoned on their jackets had been just as easy to recognize as the twins. The twins, my friends. Sure, it wasn't all fucking kitten memes between us, but they were the only people that had kept me sane over the years. I owed them more than this.

Not to mention, if the FBI had them, they would have my name, cell, and home address by now too. There were too many damning text messages on those phones not to look into. I'd destroyed my phone back in the alley but there hadn't been time to torch my house. They would find a body. If they already had…

Fuck.

She also didn't know that without Ardan and Ailee, I couldn't do this all alone. The only choice left was to follow the escape plan laid out for the entire Ulster family. We all had the details, we all knew when to run. The only safe haven we'd find was in Montana with Mac's dad, Cochlain Ulster, on the ranch where he'd retired when he left the business to Mac.

He was a monster. He'd want things from Drea. He'd kill me if he found out about Mac, but I had to take the risk. Everyone we knew was incarcerated. No one knew Mac was dead. No one *could* know. Just like no one was there to help us. It was us against the feds now, and I wasn't going back to jail.

I had to protect her.

"We need new plates or a clean car." I wasn't sure why I'd said it out loud, maybe just because I craved to hear Drea's voice again.

She just nodded.

"Do you need food or water or something?"

She shrugged.

"Damnit, Drea, say something," I snarled.

"Something," she said with a snap.

"That's real mature." I laughed one singular and utterly sarcastic laugh.

"It's been a day, Niall. It's not personal." With a heavy sigh she drew her feet up onto the seat and shifted to lean against the window.

"Not talking to me sure feels personal," I challenged her.

"What do you want me to say?"

"Anything." I glanced over. "Whatever you're thinking about."

"I shouldn't have kissed you," she said softly.

"I kissed *you*." I couldn't help but smile.

"I shouldn't have kissed you back," she amended.

"Why not?"

"Because, well, because…" She stumbled over her words

"We've been heading for that kiss since you walked back into Mac's house."

"Yeah those first few weeks when you watched Mac abuse me and Ardan fuck me really screamed romance."

I couldn't think of a counter argument. My anger had been blinding when she first came back. It took me too long to realize that it was because I was hurt and hurt could be healed with truth. I never stopped to think that my hurt lingered so fully because I never stopped loving her.

"I'd change it if I could," I offered, not expecting it to mean much.

"There's a lot of things I'd change too."

I didn't know what those things were, or how far back they reached—honestly, I was afraid to ask. Yes, *afraid*. After all the things I'd said and done, after all the demons that I'd faced, this was maybe the worst. That after all of this, she might still walk away.

I refocused on the pavement in the small swath of my headlights and settled into the rhythm of the road. My mind wandered over the details of this trip. The next step, the best way to scrub the car, Cochlain Ulster himself, but I always came back to that kiss.

The lights of Fargo, North Dakota came in to view when I'd been driving long enough that my eyes watered. There was a truck stop on the edge of town that was busy enough it would serve its purpose. I pulled in and parked toward the back, near enough cars but far enough away from where any cameras would be pointed.

"Go inside, get snacks, maybe some sandwiches."

"With what money?" She shot me a look.

"There's a bag under the carpet in the back where the spare tire is, take the small bills."

She shot me a look, complete with a wickedly arched eyebrow. "You just happen to have a bag of cash in your car?"

"Yeah, why wouldn't I?" I smirked.

"Don't look at me like it was a stupid question."

"It was a cute question." I chuckled.

"Fuck you."

I looked her dead in the face. "Love to."

She turned a brilliant shade of pink that I was lucky enough to catch in the gas station lights before she shoved out of the car without a second look. She rooted around in the back for a second before slamming the hatch. I was going to end up with hard boiled eggs or some shit like that, but I just couldn't help myself.

I watched her walk across the parking lot before slipping out of the SUV and over to the adjacent diner parking lot. There was a Uhaul and I figured it was the easiest mark. Its size provided a ton of cover and had Kentucky plates. A state that mercifully only required a rear license plate. I smiled as I pulled out my knife from my pocket. With a silent prayer to Saint Christopher, I snuck over and used the knife to start unscrewing. The screws unthreaded fast enough that I was back at the car, changing them out when Drea came back.

"Is that going to work?" she asked.

"It'll buy us enough time." I looked up to find a trace of fear behind her eyes. "I need to get the front one off then we'll go."

She hesitated by my shoulder. "Want me to drive?"

"No, we're going to find somewhere to sleep."

"I call backseat." She pointed for emphasis. "And the Hot Tamales."

"Sweetheart, I'm going to do you one better—"

"You're not going to do me."

"I'm going to get you a bed."

Deirdre

One room, that was all they had left. One room, with one bed. I shouldn't have expected much from a place that was fine with us checking in at five a.m. and paying by the hour. It was a small place called the Wagon Wheel Inn that was an odd mix of adobe motel rooms, teepees people could sleep in, and actual covered wagons as decor. The one room was one of the adobe ones, built in a long thin line with the others, which meant mercifully it wasn't a teepee. It had odd shag carpet and puke colored flowers on the scratchy comforters. There were pioneer pictures bolted to the wall, and a baby blue lamp sat next to the bed. I would never dare to turn a black light on in the room.

God almighty, someone up there had a sense of humor. It was probably my mom, and that simple thought made my heart hurt.

"Why here?" I asked when I flipped on the lamp and the filament actually hummed. "There was a Hilton back by the highway."

"They'll look there first if they're on to us," Niall said as he set my haul from the gas station on the enamel dresser next to the TV. "And I doubt seriously this place has cameras."

"Ahhh." I nodded as I looked around again. "Perfect place to dispose of a body."

"No, hotel rooms are a fucking bitch," he said casually.

"Don't." My word barely made it out. "My mom?"

His brow darkened then he turned to lock the deadbolt and hook the chain on the door. "Do you really want to know?"

I swallowed and shook my head. I didn't. Nothing he could say would make it better. Even if she had some giant, ornate gravestone at a church and the few friends she'd made had stood there mourning the loss of her, I couldn't. Specially not now.

"Yes." I didn't want to know but I needed to.

"I didn't kill her. Mac just called and said he had a body and it needed to go into a foundation being poured in Elmhurst. I couldn't do it," Niall said softly. "I was supposed to do the usual but I couldn't."

"What did you do?" My voice shook but it was nothing compared to my hand and my heart.

"I called in a favor and had her cremated then went at sunrise and spread her ashes at Montrose beach and out on the point."

How I had more tears to cry, I wasn't sure, but they spilled out and I hid my face in my hands.

"I'm so sorry, Drea. I figured someone would contact you." He gathered me up in his arms and this time I didn't fight him, I just wrapped my arms around him and let the puddle of water spread beneath my cheek. "I would have swallowed my ego for that," he murmured, his face buried in my hair. "For you."

I just nodded. Split between love and hate and hurt, I didn't know what else to do.

He pulled back the comforter on the bed then drew me down with him. We were sideways on the mattress with the pillows at my back, but I still felt exposed. Part of me wondered if that feeling would ever go away.

"You don't have to forgive me," he said after my tears had run their course.

I still clutched his shirt. "I already did," I whispered. His hand clasped over mine as he pressed up to his elbow. Those deep and piercing eyes scanned my face. "That's exactly what she would have wanted, and I'm... I can't... there aren't words." I couldn't find the right ones anyhow, the right sentiment. "It just hurts." A sob shook my shoulders. "It all hurts."

"I hate that any of it came at my hands." His lips brushed my forehead.

"It didn't. Not really." For some reason it seemed incredibly important that he know. The words started spilling out. "Back then Mac hurt. What he did to me hurt—"

"I'd kill him for it all over again," he interrupted, fierce but quiet.

"I'm the one that died that night."

"No." He cupped my cheek and leaned in to kiss me again, this time soft and gentle.

The weight of his body on mine was too much. I couldn't breathe. I felt Mac's body on me then, his body where it had crumpled on me tonight.

"Stop." I shoved my arm to his shoulder.

"What? Sure. Fine. What did I do?" Niall sat up, his hands poised in surrender.

"I can feel him…" My voice choked off.

He snapped up and stood by my knees, still hanging over the edge of the mattress. "I'm sorry."

"It's… Well it's not… but… I mean…"

"It's okay." He couldn't quite hold back the snarl as he flipped off the lights.

He grabbed the mangy blanket and started to pile it on the floor.

"No, Niall. Don't." I patted the bed beside me. "Please."

"I don't know if I trust myself." He eyed it in the small bit of streetlight shining through the curtains.

"I do," I said softly as I turned to make room, lying on my side of the bed.

His eyes met mine, barely more than a glimmer in the dark.

"I want to fuck you, Drea," he said, his voice low and sultry. "I want to dominate every inch of your body. I want it to hurt. But I want you to be so completely lost to me that you welcome it. That you crave it and couldn't stop it even if you wanted to. That kiss I gave you earlier?" He paused for effect. "That was a spark when what I really want is to burn you to the ground."

I swallowed. *Holy shit.* I wanted that too.

But as soon as I imagined him pressed up against me, I wanted to heave. That was what I remembered most, how heavy Mac was. How I couldn't fight against him.

"I couldn't get out from under him. That's what I remember most." My throat went bone dry at the memory. "I tried, I fought like hell, but I couldn't get anywhere.

"I knew what was coming and that fear was very real but in the back of my mind I just kept thinking, *if I can just get out*, then none of that other stuff would happen."

Silence fell on the room.

"But you didn't get out," Niall finished softly. I shook my head.

"No," I said softly. "And I will feel what he did to me forever."

Niall toed off his shoes then slid into bed beside me. "I still wish you'd told me."

"I couldn't come to you with my stepfather still staining my thighs. I couldn't ask you to take me to the drugstore for Plan B. I couldn't look you in the face like that." The edge in my voice hurt even me.

"I don't know what to say."

"I don't either. All I know is you wouldn't have killed him then." I looked over. "And I'm glad he's dead."

"I told you I'd kill him."

"Yeah but I expected it to be one of those, life-long quest kinda things." I turned onto my side to face him. He had his arms crossed behind his head as he played with his lip ring. "One of those, *my name is Inigo Montoya* kinda things."

He laughed and his body shook. "Sorry to disappoint."

"You didn't." I reached for his hand and laced my fingers with his. "And you won't."

"How do you know that?" he asked, casually moving our hands to the washboard of his stomach.

I closed my eyes and breathed in deep. Exhaustion hung on my limbs every bit as bad as my eyelids. The words on the tip of my tongue were stupid but then again, the ones he'd said earlier showed the cards he was holding in his hand too. I took a deep breath and moved closer to him.

"I think you may have turned into a soldier after all."

I knew what those words meant to her and they kept me awake long after her breathing had gone soft and steady.

Sure, I'd been saying I wanted her, body and soul. I'd been pursuing her the last few days even, but to hear her have faith in me made it real. So real. All my old insecurities washed back over me. Was I good enough for a girl like Drea? Was I making the right choices? Could I protect her?

She was the kind of girl that could catch the stars. The only thing that could be said about me was that I could catch her.

We were so different now. I was a monster and I liked it. She was jaded and broken. I wasn't lying when I said I wanted to debase her, but would she want that version of me? Would it wreck her further?

And Cochlain... I'd only met him a few times but it was enough to know he was an asshole just like the rest of us. Was I insane to even consider that as an escape plan? To take her there? And if we didn't go there, what the hell would I do?

Christ, the questions kept spinning up with the fantasies making it hard to breathe. My clothes felt tight, too constricting. I unbuttoned a few of the buttons of my shirt, wishing that I'd stayed in my sweats. I wouldn't be able to sleep like this—confined, cocooned, and next to her.

I stripped my shirt off first, the crisp cotton was almost itchy. Or maybe that was just my skin crawling with want. For her. For a future with her. I could take it…

God I was spiraling. I needed to sleep but my brain wouldn't shut off.

Flashes of her skin. Of her body bending to mine. Doubt in my eyes not hers. A future falling to pieces. My cock splitting her as it slid in. How she'd moan. How she might scream if someone hurt her…

Fuck.

I needed to stop. The only thing that was going to come true if I worked myself up like this was that I'd ruin it. All of it.

My belt felt like it was digging into my skin, so I undid the buckle and turned on my side. Drea was curled there in a ball, swimming in my sweatshirt and tucked beneath the sheets. The soft repose of her face, the soft sigh of her breathing…

Shit. This was going to make me hard.

I pushed up to pull the belt out from my waistband and Drea groaned beside me. "Good Christ," I snarled as I flopped back to the bed. As if responding to the movement, Drea reached out, her hand coming to rest on my chest. She purred again at the feel of my flesh.

My dick twitched, pushing against my fly. Her fingers slid in the groove between my pecs. What I wouldn't have given for her hand to move lower. My dick pushed harder against the fabric of my pants.

"Fine, I'll ditch them too," I mumbled.

I was left in nothing but my boxer briefs, but I felt like I could breathe again. Like Drea knew, she moved closer to me, her body wrapping thoroughly around mine.

"I'm being punished aren't I?" I said to no one in particular.

But her so close, her breathing so even and steady actually soothed me. I matched my breaths to hers, using her as my own brand of hypnotist. When I rolled into her and truly let myself hold her, I felt satiated. My limbs sunk into the bed, my eyebrows sagged, and the last thing any of my senses knew before sleep overtook me was Drea.

———

"Do you want to explain to me why in the fuck you're naked?" Drea's voice cut into the dream that I'm pretty sure was about her too.

"Boxers?" I nuzzled back into the bed wishing I was actually naked. And so was she.

"Niall, why did you strip?" She shoved me and I finally managed to crack one eye open.

Bright sunlight filtered in from the crack in the curtains, giving her a halo of gold and gorgeous but it was wrong. It should have been coming from the east. How long had I slept? I shook my head and focused on her. She'd ditched my sweatshirt at some point, leaving her curves on display beneath the t-shirt that she'd been wearing because of the lighting. Her face was pinched, her lips thinned, but there was a playfulness to it.

She'd never been more beautiful.

"You try sleeping in a suit with a boner," I said as I buried my face back into the pillow.

"Try sleeping in leggings with a boner pressed against your thigh."

"I'd be happy to put it elsewhere if you'd like." I couldn't help the smile that spread across my face.

"You were so sweet last night." She feigned disappointment.

"You know what goes good with something sweet? Something salty." I pressed my morning wood hard against her.

"You're disgusting."

"You know monstrous is a synonym of disgusting?" I rocked my hips against her.

"I've had bigger."

That was a bucket of ice water thrown on me. Not only was it a reminder of the past but fuck… My feelings of inadequacy came back all over again. One sentence and I was spiraling down the same black hole I'd been in last night.

I wasn't going to get the girl. This wasn't going to be the fairy tale. Whether it was her or me or the combination, that moment that I'd seen the future crumbling last night was the one that was going to come true.

"I'll get dressed." I pulled away from her and rolled to my side of the bed, grabbing clothes from where I'd tossed them.

"Niall…" she protested after me.

"Do you want to stop somewhere for clothes or are you good?" I said simply as I pulled up my pants.

"Niall." Her voice was almost a scold this time.

"I'm concerned about the weather in Montana—"

She grabbed me from behind and turned me, cutting off my words. I arched my eyebrows at her but didn't say anything else.

"I thought we were joking," she said softly.

"So my dick's a joke to you?" I tried to hide the sting from my voice. None of this was a good thing coming from the woman that I wanted. That I fucking *needed* now that I knew the truth.

"No, Niall—"

"It's okay, Drea. I can take a hint. I'll lay off." It was really my only choice. My pride couldn't take another hit when it came to her.

"That's not… I'm just… you're, ya know…" Her words always went a little haywire when she got flustered.

"I don't know, but it's fine. It's cool." I shrugged into my shirt and started buttoning it. "Let's get going."

"Niall—"

"Stop." I was harsher than I meant to be, so I took a deep breath. "I'm a big boy—maybe not the biggest you've met—but I can handle rejection, Drea."

"See the funny thing is that your dick is actually pretty great. I said something stupid." She bit her lip and reached up to smooth down the fabric of my shirt.

"I've done that once or twice. No harm, no foul." I forced a smile onto my face. "I'm going to go make sure the coast is clear. Give me a minute or two, okay?"

She nodded but her shoulders hunched, and her eyes were downcast. I wanted to cup her face or gather her up in my arms, but I'd said I'd leave her be and I needed to mean it.

"If you look out that window and there are any cops, any hint of any trouble, you shove yourself out of that bathroom window in back and run like hell, understand? You get to Massacre Junction, Montana."

Her eyes flicked up to meet mine, panic clearly lining the corners.

"I don't think anything is going to happen but just in case." I didn't wait for her answer before walking out of the room and into the unknown.

Deirdre

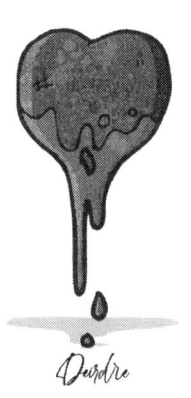

My heart had stopped when Niall walked out of that motel room. I couldn't breathe, my hands went clammy and there was a definite possibility that I was going to pass out. Fear, true and real, gripped me. And I wasn't afraid that the FBI were waiting.

How would I manage without him again? I was shit at it before. Worse than shit honestly. And I never wanted to do it again.

Luckily I didn't have to wonder about it all too long. He came back five minutes later, but they were the five scariest minutes I'd weathered in a very long time.

There was a different kind of fear holding me back from saying anything about us now. From giving myself over to my feelings. He couldn't really want me. For more than my body anyway. I'd left him, I was the reason he'd been in jail, the reason he was in this shit now. I was used and abused. That wasn't the kind of girl guys fought for.

I sighed.

"What's wrong?" Niall asked cutting into the weird 90s radio station we'd found after shopping in Fargo.

"Nothing. Just thinking." I turned from the miles of grassland whipping past my window to look at him. "Want me to drive."

"I've got it, Drea," he said simply.

"I know… but if you wanted… I mean… I can." God, I was such an idiot.

Why on God's green earth had I made a joke about his dick?

WHY? Particularly because I wanted his dick and every little thing that was attached to it. Not that anything about Niall was little but… Waking up next to him this morning had given me a complete lady boner. I think my nipples had even stood up on end. The fact that he'd pumped the breaks last night when I asked had done something pretty damn similar to my heart.

I was an idiot.

"I know you can drive, Drea. I taught you." A smile tugged at his lips but it was small and sad. "I honestly just like having the control. I don't feel like I have much right now."

"Oh." It was all I could think to say before turning to look back out the window again.

This was a disaster. An actual certifiable disaster. I leaned more forehead against the window.

"Talk to me Drea," he said softly.

That alone told me how bad this was. Niall—the new Niall anyway—didn't do soft. Fuck.

"You can yell at me, I get it." I twisted on the glass so I could see him.

"For what?" He chuckled.

"For anything." I shrugged.

"I mean, you ate the Hot Tamales for breakfast and that's really not healthy…" He tried to sound upset and failed.

"Niall…" I whined.

"Drea, I don't know what will happen once we get to Montana so let's just sit, enjoy each other for the next ten or so hours, okay?"

"What's in Montana?" I arched an eyebrow.

He blew out a deep breath, and his hands tightened on the steering wheel. "Cochlain Ulster."

―――――

I'D MET Mac's father once. It hadn't been good. That was the first time I'd seen a dead body. A girl had been splayed out on the living room floor, blood spattered everywhere, and he'd been thrusting into her sex with the shotgun that killed her.

I was thirteen.

"Why are we doing this?" I shoved my hands under my ass when we turned on the long county road. "Why are we going here?"

"This is what Ulsters do when shit hits the fan, and we don't have anywhere else to go." The hard lines of Niall's face were falling back into place.

"You've got that money…" I couldn't hide the fear in my voice nor the inherent question.

"Money runs out, specially if we try and get out of the country. Getting you documentation will empty that bag at least." He started playing with his lip ring. "And if the feds know Mac is dead…"

"What if *he* knows Mac is dead." I pointed down the long driveway.

"That's the gamble." He took one hand from the wheel and shoved that one curl out of his face. "But I'm willing to take it. No one else knew. Everyone was arrested."

"The FBI?" I drug out the word as if it was obvious.

"They're not going to pick up the phone and call Cochlain. If they're onto us, they know about him. He ran that family for a long time."

His name sent shivers down my spine. "I don't like this."

"I don't either, but I have to protect you, Drea."

"You don't walk into the lion's den, wearing a meat dress, hoping that it'll bite whoever follows you in." She gestured wildly to accentuate her sentence.

He slowed the car on the dirt road, sending whorls of dust up around us. He put the car in park and turned, waiting until I gave him my full attention to speak.

"Do you trust me?"

"It's Cochlain I don't trust." I glanced back down the road.

Niall reached over and with a single finger notched beneath my chin, turned me back to him. "That's not an answer." He took a deep breath and held it as his eyes searched mine. "Do you trust me?" He finished with an urgent exhale.

"Yes." The word was a reflex from deep inside me.

"Funny," a new voice with a thick Irish accent said, barely muffled by the car window. "I don't."

We both turned to find a double-barreled shotgun pointed at us through the glass and Cochlain on the other end. He'd appeared from nowhere but now that he'd shown himself, a slew of other men came out from hiding and what had seemed like an empty country road before now looked like a war zone.

"I didn't know who to expect first, you or the feds," Cochlain said, his accent was thick enough that I had to listen closely. "What are you doing here, Niall, and who'd you bring with you?"

"Lea's girl," Niall said as he held his hands up in surrender.

"A MacCowan?" He pumped the shotgun once

"She's Mac's. She was in The Pit up until very recently."

Cochlain's eyes swept over me and I knew the hunger behind them. I knew what The Pit meant to him, what it said about me. I couldn't help but heave.

"Why's she out?"

"I'll tell you everything at the house, I swear."

"Who said I'm letting you in my house?" he asked rough and ready.

"This is what we're supposed to do when shit goes sideways. Mac always said—"

"And speaking of Mac, where is my son?"

"I don't know." Niall enunciated each world clearly. Maybe a little too clearly. My stomach flipped.

"What do you know then?"

"All the MacCowans are dead or missing. Mac took over their territory, and I don't know if it was that or something else completely, but it tipped off the feds." Niall was speaking in a calm, cool, collected voice. Too calm and collected. Like he'd practiced.

Cochlain eyed him, seeming to formulate a theory on his own. I couldn't swallow past the bone dry of my throat.

"And is she here because she's responsible, a loose end, or just a place to put your cock?" The gun moved back toward me.

"She was Mac's," he said a little more vehemently. "We take care of what's ours."

I wanted to reach over, brush his arm or squeeze his thigh as a thank you but I didn't dare move. We both knew it was an out and out lie but he was willing to face down the barrel of a gun and say it.

"Roll down your window," Cochlain commanded. Niall's hand moved slowly to the buttons on the door and rolled it down. The second it was out of the way, Cochlain shoved the barrel of the shotgun against my temple. I tried to swallow the knot in my throat and failed. "We don't give a shit about possessions like this. They're for fucking and fucking up. Simple as that. You should have left her in her kennel."

I sat stock still.

"Maybe she belongs in mine."

He moved the barrel of the gun down to the hem of my sweater and started to lift it. The cool air from outside kissed the slowly exposed skin of my stomach but the goose bumps came from something else entirely. I sucked in a breath when the bottom curve of my breast was exposed. Tears pricked the corners of my eyes. I couldn't do this again. Could I?

Niall still held his arms up in surrender, but he shifted his elbow just enough to stop Cochlain from lifting any further. Everyone sat frozen for a moment before the world lurched into fast forward. My shirt dropped and Niall listed forward just before Cochlain swung the barrel of the gun and slammed it into Niall's face. Niall bellowed as blood started to spill down his white shirt. I shrieked and covered my mouth in true shock.

"How dare you. If I want her, she's mine." Cochlain aimed at me again.

"No." My screech was barely covered by my hands.

He swung the butt of the gun and slammed it down on Niall's thigh.

"Stop!" I screamed.

"Tell me the truth." He shoved the barrel beneath my chin.

"That is the truth." The knot welled in my throat.

This time he lunged into the car and pinned Niall's throat with his gun. Niall didn't fight back. He knew he couldn't if he wanted to. Not if we wanted to live through this.

"I could pull the trigger so he can watch you die while he chokes to death." Cochlain laughed.

"Please. I'll do anything." My voice trembled just as bad as my hands; I knew what I was offering up.

"If I tell you to strip?" he asked.

"I'll do it." My shaking hands went to my hem.

"If I tell you to put your cunt on display and let all my men fuck you on the hood of this car while Niall watches?"

I was going to throw up. It wasn't far off from what happened in the beginning between us but everything was different now. "I… If that's…" My words tripped over the acid in my throat.

"No," Niall's choked growl had a fierceness that renewed my goose bumps.

"How about you just tell me why my son won't answer my call?" He pulled his rifle back until it disappeared.

My heart jackknifed as I looked over at Niall, bleeding and beet red. He barely shook his head, but I knew what he was saying. I tried to keep my mouth shut but my teeth started to chatter both from the cold and the terror.

Cochlain moved so fast I didn't see it coming, I just felt the boom echo in my ears as it unhinged my bones. Blood oozed from the hole torn in Niall's pants as feral cries did the same from his lips. Cochlain held a small handgun that he'd pulled from somewhere to shoot Niall. Actually fucking shoot him.

"He's dead," I screamed as I lunged to put pressure on Niall's thigh, just above his knee. "Mac's dead."

Niall winced.

"I know." Cochlain smiled.

"What else do you know then?" Niall gritted through his teeth as he woozed.

"See I still have boys on my payroll in Chicago. I know things

Mac never did. I know that you love this traitorous girl. I know your loyalty has wavered. And guess what else?" Cochlain smiled, shouldering his shotgun, still holding his handgun. "I know that you did it."

Once again the world seemed to stop spinning for one singular breath before it jumped back on track, moving far faster than before. Our tires started spinning a second before two shots rang out. Dust kicked up wildly around us, spilling into the SUV before I could really survey whether those shots had landed anyway. I screamed without meaning to.

"Get down," Niall yelled just before the world around us seemed to explode. I ducked down as low as I could and tried to shield my ears. But the cracks, booms, and thumps of bullets hitting the vehicle, smashing into glass echoed until my ears hurt. "Shit," Niall swore as the SUV wavered on the road, but we kept speeding in reverse, zig-zagging as we went.

A massive bang barely preceded the sound of broken glass. I looked up, expecting to see the windshield cracked into a web, but it must have been a headlight. We swerved again, but Niall hadn't let off the gas once.

"Fuck," Niall swore again but this time his voice had changed; it was scared. It was fading.

I looked over at him to see him wooze again.

"Niall!" I shot up and reached for him.

I held him upright and took one look around to try and get my bearings. We were almost down the lane and back to the main road. I couldn't see the men anymore and despite whatever damage we'd taken, the SUV was still speeding backward.

Before I could digest it all, we shifted, the nose of the Rover rising up. The new angle was disorienting. I couldn't figure out why the hood kept lifting.

But then came the crash.

Niall

THE PAIN WAS ALL CONSUMING. I REALLY TRIED TO FOCUS ON Drea, on getting her out, but the tear and burn were excruciating. Time was speeding up and slowing down all at once. My heartbeat slowed but the steady thump in my leg seemed to speed up.

"Niall?" Drea asked. "Niall, are you okay?"

We'd crashed into the ditch, and I knew I needed to answer her, but I couldn't quite say anything. Pain, pure and simple, ran through me.

"God, give me your belt." Drea fumbled at my waist and pulled. "I hope this works."

She pulled it and I watched detached as she wrapped it around my leg and pulled tight. She shoved out of the SUV and circled the hood, her feet crunching on the gravel. I wanted to yell after her. I needed to. She couldn't leave me.

"You gotta move over." She reappeared at my door, albeit far lower than she should have been, and held the belt as she shoved against me.

"I can't." My words ran together.

"You *have* to." The urgency in her voice gave me a little bit of umph.

She helped me as I tried to scoot up and across the console and navigate the awkward angle of the vehicle. New pain ripped through my body and I knew by the heat that blood had streaked across the leather.

"Get in the seat, Niall," she said roughly as she pushed me. I bellowed in pain as the SUV likewise protested its injuries. From here they didn't look as bad as they should, and agonized as I was, I still thanked Saint Christopher for choosing bulletproof glass as I settled into the passenger seat.

Drea slammed the SUV into drive and the dirt kicked up again. We lurched a little but didn't move much. She switched into reverse and did much the same. The vehicle rocked wildly as the world wobbled, black edging back into my vision. From what I could see we were moving, but not far or fast enough. They could catch us if they tried. If I died here, now, at least I was with Drea. My head lolled to the side and I looked her over. She was still beautiful even in her panic.

"Drea." I smiled. "You're so pretty."

Her eyes went wide. "No," she said sternly. "You stay with me, Niall. Stay with me." Her eyes kept darting into her mirrors.

"Where else would I go?" I asked just before I blacked out.

———

"It's actually a pretty good place to get shot," an unfamiliar female voice said. "Not that getting shot is great."

"Is he going to be okay?"

Drea. That was her voice. She was here.

"Drea, sweetheart," I mumbled.

"Niall?"

"He'll be okay as long as you keep the dressing clean and look out for infection. Keep the dressing on for as long as possible then wash the wound with regular soap and water and diluted hydrogen peroxide. Do not let it soak. He'll need to see someone about the stitches."

"Okay." Drea blew out a deep breath.

"And it'll hurt like hell. He can't be very active or his blood pressure will plummet." The unfamiliar voice was edgy and rushed.

"Thank you," Drea, beautiful Drea replied, and I basked in the sound of her voice saying anything.

"You have ten minutes to get him up and get him out."

"We'll be gone." Drea's hand found mine and I squeezed.

"There's a motel down the way. They don't ask many questions."

I opened my eyes enough to see Drea up against a stark white ceiling. She looked like an angel hovering over me, one I didn't deserve to have.

"Thank you," Drea said as her eyes found mine. Her whole face twisted with hurt.

A door shut behind her and a new silence took over. Only the hum of fluorescent lights filled the room.

"What's wrong?" I asked, reaching for her face even though my arms weighed a thousand pounds.

"You got shot."

"I remember." I smiled. "Not the first time."

"Well it was the first time in front of me. That bullet ripped straight through you. It was a hole." She bit her lip and shoved her hand through my hair. When she leaned in closer, I noticed that her eyes were red, puffy, and still shimmering with unshed tears. "I thought I'd lost you."

"He shot me there on purpose." I managed a small smile. "No arteries, no chance of nicking an organ. Stay away from the bones and someone can even walk after. I've done it plenty."

"You passed out." Her hand trembled in mine.

"Getting shot still hurts. Blood loss still sends you into shock." I tried to make light of it if only to smooth the lines of her face. "I'll be okay."

"We barely made it out." She sounded so small like that.

"I'm so sorry I took you there. I thought—"

"It's okay. We don't have to do this now. We only have eight minutes."

"Eight minutes?" I tried to sit up only to sag back against whatever I was laying on. I was too weak. Weakness didn't sit well on my shoulders. "What the fuck happens in eight minutes, Drea? Where are we?" I was starting to get my bearings back.

She reached for my shoulders and helped pull me up to sitting.

"We're at a vet's office about thirty miles from Cochlain's place."

I sat sharper at attention surveying the place, willing myself to focus. The room was small, and kennels lined one side of it while a blinding light and magnifying glass hung on mechanical arms above me. The table I laid on was stainless steel and built for surgery. A variety of cabinets covered the other wall where there weren't windows. A swinging door at one end seemed to lead into the building, another, closer to us, lead to outside. My car was parked close.

"And she just volunteered to fix me up?" I scanned outside, noticing a barn and a few outbuildings. One seemed to be a house with a living room light on and a small face pressed against the window. *Shit.* There were witnesses.

"About that..." She pulled a wad of cash from her pocket. "This is all that's left."

I studied the roll. Two rubber bands. That meant two packs of twenty bills. Four thousand dollars.

"I pulled up at dusk in a wrecked car with someone covered in blood. I didn't really have a choice."

"She's the fucking thief," I snarled.

"Good to see you have your delightful sense of humor back." She rolled her eyes. "Can we get going now? We have, like, five minutes."

"What happens in five minutes?" My temper was building again.

"I wasn't planning on finding out."

"I could just kill her." I slowly tested my legs, pain shot from the wound, but I grit my teeth and made myself stand.

"We could just leave," Drea snapped.

"Don't be naive, Drea. This is the moment that our future hangs on," I snapped right back as I snatched a nearby scalpel.

"I know." She lifted a single finger to my cheek and turned me to look at her. "What if it could be the moment we decide to have a good one?"

"We're not those people, Drea. Monsters don't get happy endings. Those are reserved for the heroes and we're left with kill or be killed."

"What if I know a way?" Her eyes were wary as they ran over me. "Could you be happy? With me?"

I still held the scalpel and for a moment I wanted nothing more than to cut the bit of my heart that had leapt at the idea out of my chest. I didn't deserve her.

"Look I know. I know how fucked up everything is between us. How it's one step forward and two back." She sighed, glancing at a clock as she did. "But when I thought you were dying…" Her eyes came to mine. "I can't lose you, Niall. Not again. I won't."

"I don't think you get to choose, Drea." I softened.

"But I get to fight." She smiled that same small, sorrowful smile. "And I want to fight for you."

She pushed her hand into my hair and lifted onto her toes to press her lips to mine. Her teeth sunk into my lip just before her tongue smoothed that spot back over. Her lips pulled on mine, kissing me fervent and hard, and I was simply at her mercy until she pulled back.

I sat frozen after that kiss. It wasn't a simple chaste, romantic kiss but it was softer than the crash landing we'd had before. It was passion incarnate. I craved it completely.

I craved *her* completely.

Deirdre

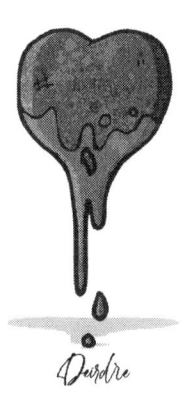

THE TENSION VIBRATED IN THE FRONT SEAT AS WE DROVE TO Missoula. I wanted him to be safe, but I also just wanted him. Feeling like I was losing him had put everything in perspective. We'd been dancing around this too long now.

With a heavy sigh I realized we'd probably be dancing around it a little longer too. Gunshot wounds were a buzzkill.

"Only a few miles left," Niall said, though I wasn't sure if it was meant for me.

"Any idea where we're going to stay?"

"Somewhere with a bed because I'll be damned if I wait another minute to fuck you," he said roughly.

I almost choked on my tongue. Both my protest and my yes please caught in my throat. I bit my lip to keep from moaning at the mere thought of him following through.

"Tell me, Drea," he urged, his voice spun of sin. "Tell me that you want that. That you want me."

"I do." I grit out the words past the sandpaper of my throat. "Of course I do.

"That's not enough." His voice found that edge from before, the one that drove me insane. "Tell me that you want my hands on your body, my face between your fucking thighs."

He reached over and every inch of my flesh was acutely aware of him, of his touch. I shoved my head back against the headrest when his whisper touch started moving higher and higher. His fingers found their mark between my thighs, and I couldn't keep it in any longer. I whimpered and my eyes fluttered shut.

Shit. I forced them open and stared at the road.

"I'm driving. You can't…" My voice was shredding to ribbons.

"I can't do what?"

"Touch me like that."

"Why?" he purred. "Because you want it, want me, so bad that you might fall to pieces?"

"I'll wreck the car. Again." My breathing had hitched up too.

"Finger fucking you? What a way to go."

I moaned again as he pressed against my slit over top of my leggings.

"Stop. Please stop," I begged as I had to swerve back into our lane.

With one final, devilish stroke against me, he leaned over and let his lips brush against my ear. "You won't be able to ask that once we get to our room."

Turned out, I didn't have to. Pain shot across Niall's face when he stood, so much so that I had to run to help him. I got under his arm and the two of us barely managed getting his bulky body to bed in the motel I'd checked into.

"Are you okay?" I asked as I helped him lay back.

"No," he said sharply.

"What can I do?" I leaned down and moved that singular curl away from his eye.

"Wrap your lips around my dick and suck," he said causally, closing his eyes where he was sprawled out.

"What?"

"You asked if you could help, and I have the most painful fucking hard-on I've ever in my life." He shifted his hips to highlight the steely column of his erection. "I'd fuck you until you forgot your name, but I couldn't get on my knees to worship Saint

Christopher right now, let alone worship you the way you deserve."

How was each thing out of his mouth sexier than the last? He had me wanting the worship he promised but more than that, I wanted him. Any way I could have him.

"Niall," I said softly, waiting for him to open his eyes and look at me.

When he did, his usually piercing eyes had changed just the slightest. They weren't sharp to cut right through me, they just saw *everything*. I'd been right to trust him. I'd been right to save him. Even after everything, there was nothing else I'd ever wanted more than to have him look at me exactly like that.

I held his gaze as I lifted up the hem of my shirt, putting my chest on display for him. He sat up, propping himself on his elbows with a wince. I almost stopped but then a smile tugged at the corner of his lips. My fingers were at the waistband of leggings when he stopped me.

"What's the rush, Drea?" His eyes stayed fixed on my naked breasts. "Play with yourself. Prolong the magic as if I were the one bringing you to your knees."

I went on autopilot, I couldn't help it. Years of being told to do this sort of thing gave me a choreography. When it was just moves, it wasn't me giving my body. It was a defense I didn't even realize I'd fallen into until Niall sat up and wrapped his hands around my wrists, stopping me.

"Don't give me a show, give me you. Your body, what you like, what you want."

"I want you."

He shoved his hand into my hair while the other threaded behind my back and pulled me close enough that his lips closed easily around my nipple as he began to suck. My hands moved up his shoulders and across the broad line of his shoulders to thread into his hair.

"Gentle," he reminded me with a few good laps of his tongue before he scraped his teeth along the length.

"Fuck." I had to consciously make an effort not to grab him.

"You like that?" he asked, his voice hot puffs against my skin.

"I like that you're the one doing it." I pressed my legs together at the pleasure.

He started his work on my other breast, starting gentle with a suck that hollowed his cheeks below his defined cheekbones and was punctuated by the lazy lap of his tongue. Where he'd scraped before he bit down. Hard.

I cried out and shoved against him. He dropped me and sat back, pain clear on his face. Where I'd thought that the images of Cochlain smashing the butt of the gun into his face and choking him with the barrel would stay with me forever, they up and disappeared the moment pleasure overrode my own pain.

"I'm sorry. I'm so sorry."

"It won't happen again," he said sharply.

"No, I swear."

"That's not what I meant, Drea. I won't let it." His hands moved for his belt. "Take your pants off and drape that perfect ass, right here."

He gestured to the bed beside him. I did as he said then laid my torso down on the bed and bent my knees on the carpet to be positioned exactly as he wanted. Not once did I have to remind myself I trusted him or that I wanted this. Not once did I have to remind myself that this was my place in the world. Every bit of me knew.

I was waiting for the snap of the belt across my skin. How many men had punished me for slights like this. No matter how hard I tried to push them away, they were still the ghosts watching these moments, these movements. I couldn't deny that my body responded to the snap or slap either.

But he just folded my arms behind my back so my forearms rested against one another then wound the belt around them to keep them in place.

"You don't need your hands when you've got a mouth like this," he said as he leaned back and brushed his thumb over my bottom lip.

His hand slid down the line of my arm and traced along the

edges of his belt before finding the space between my thighs. His hand splayed out across my cheeks and one finger dipped into me.

"That's my sweet little pussy. I missed you and the way you dripped for me, Drea."

I groaned. There really had never been another man who owned my body like him. No matter how he'd touched me, I wanted it. No matter what'd he'd said, it turned me on. Then it had been more innocent but then again, I'd been more innocent too. Now he was wicked to match my sinful soul.

He added a two more fingers and used the leverage of his hand to thrust fast and teasing into me. My body shook with the force of it and my breathing went ragged right along with it.

As quickly as he started, he stopped. "Your turn."

He pushed me up from the mattress before undoing his fly. With that same damned irresistible smile on his face, he shoved at the fabric, freeing his dick. I'd been a moron to make fun of him for two reasons. One, I wanted this. More than I'd ever wanted intimacy in my entire life. And two, I was going to choke without my hands for help.

"Don't keep me waiting, Drea. I get creative when my mind wanders." He flexed his hips.

I shuffled against the rough carpet of the motel to slide between his legs and with my eyes locked on his, I wrapped my lips around Niall McDonough's dick.

If there was a way to build the perfect woman, I would have built Drea. Just the way she was now. This mix of confidence and vulnerability, hard and soft. The body and moves of a porn star but knowing that the moments she was honest and here during sex were few and far between. And they were mine.

She was mine.

Today proved it. She'd protected me in every way she knew how. She'd made decisions that being with a man like me required while staying the girl that the boy inside me still held a candle for.

"Holy shit," I half said, half chuckled as she swallowed me.

All of this was too good to be true.

Well, as long as I forgot that we were wanted for murder, and by the FBI, and had only $3,876 to our names with nowhere to go.

Fuck.

Drea slid her tongue out along my dick and moved me even deeper in her throat. Then she fucking swallowed. I moaned. I couldn't hold back. Until her shoulder hit my thigh. My cry turned pained and she froze, swallowing again. God, the combination…

"Don't stop," I managed.

Pain made me alive, made me feel like this moment was real. Pleasure was going to kill me all the same and in the best way possible. It felt right to have both consume me.

She was careful as she went back to moving up and down the length of me. The noises were so animalistic that they churned a new hunger inside me, one that I didn't think would ever be satiated.

Her mouth moved expertly up and down my cock, a slickness of her own making made it even easier for her to move. She knew when to tilt, when to add her tongue and when to stop completely and just let me relish the feel of her wrapped around me. The scars on her bottom lip were a new and heady feeling.

Maybe I'd died and gone to heaven. I sure as shit wouldn't imagine it to be much different than this.

She let me fall out of her mouth, and I landed with a thwack against my stomach. She inched forward and licked my length from balls to tip with the broad side of her tongue. I twitched and she caught me again, using that magic mouth to massage the sensitive tip of my cock. Each flick and squeeze made me jerk. Each jerk had that bite of pain on the end.

This was torture of the best kind and fuck if I wasn't going to come from it.

I reached for her and pushed her down. I wanted that tongue out, wagging, and her nose against my skin when I shot into her. She scrambled against my hold and it took everything in me not to lose it. I'd spent too much time being rough and ruthless with women.

"I want you inside me," she gasped when her mouth was empty again.

"Put your lips back around my dick and I'll show you just how far I can get inside you." I used my grip to urge her back toward me.

"No, Niall..." she whined.

I'd known exactly what she wanted but that wasn't going to happen here, tonight.

"Drea, I told you to put your mouth on me and I fucking meant it," I said as seductively as I could manage. "When you have my dick inside that pretty little pussy, it's going to be on my terms." I flexed my hips back toward her face. "My terms will be absolute and utter annihilation. Destruction. You will surrender to me, body and fucking soul." I let one hand leave her hair and pump twice on my cock before I fed it to her. "Tonight is not the night I can follow through on that, so you will finish me in your fucking mouth. You will think about how no man has ever been in you this deep and you're going to devour me whole. Hear me?"

"Holy shit." She barely got the words out before I pushed back in. Deep. Just like I'd said I'd do.

Her tongue splayed out along me as she worked herself further. I felt her gag a few times on me and the warm, wet, vise grip was almost too much. It wasn't going to take long but I'd made her a promise I intended on keeping.

I used my hand still tangled into her hair to push her down the last little bit. She choked again but she didn't resist me. Not really anyway. The moment she relaxed, I flexed my hips and shoved up into her. Pain shot through my leg again and I couldn't help but cry out. She tensed but she didn't fight me, she didn't waver. Drea just took it as I thrust into her throat. As I walked the line between pleasure and pain. As I made good on my promise.

Everything beneath my belly button tensed, my forearms went taut and that familiar build up in my body sent a single shockwave before it broke. I held her in place, feeling the heat of her breath against the base of my shaft and low stomach as I shot into the depths of her throat.

My hands wavered mid-orgasm, sliding away from her but she stayed put until I finished. Every bone in my body felt as though it had turned to mush when I melted to the mattress. I barely noticed when she collapsed back onto the floor.

Only heavy breathing filled the room.

"I never stopped loving you." Eventually I broke the silence. "I was hurt but it was because you were my world."

She shifted just enough to lean her forehead against my uninjured leg.

"But I think we needed the time apart," I continued even as she tensed against my body. "Because the world will eventually end in brimstone and fire, but I'll still love you, Drea. You're heaven and the religion I'll worship to get there."

"I love you, Niall," she said from her spot at my feet. "Whether you're my salvation or damnation, I don't care as long as you're mine."

I sat up, slowly, my body aching worse than it had before but unhinged in the best way too. I reached down for her against my body's protest and helped her to standing. As tenderly as I could, I unwrapped the belt from her arms. I leaned in and kissed the red marks her skin still wore, trying to communicate the true reverence I had for her in each touch of my lips.

"Come here." I turned her as I pulled her over my good knee and down to the bed with me. "Thank you," I murmured against her lips where they landed so close to mine.

"Better now?" she asked, almost shy, and fuck me if it wasn't the sexiest thing she'd done.

"Yes and no." I brushed some of her hair behind her ear. "Yes, because the immediate problem of being so hard up for you it hurt has been solved." I smiled. "No, because now all I want is you. I think I'm an addict."

She hid her face again.

"None of that."

"I know how fucked up this makes me, but the feel of this…" I pulled her bottom lip out and ran my thumb over the brand that infuriated me if I thought too long about it, "…is incredible."

"Don't say things you don't mean." Her voice shook.

"I promise." I used my nose to turn her face back to mine only to remember how bad it hurt.

She sat up with a wince. "Do you want some ice?"

"Would it ruin my savage masculinity if I said yes?"

Drea laughed. "Probably. But I'd still do you." She winked and it didn't just bring a lightness to the room but to my chest that only she'd ever been able to manage. "I'll get the clothes and food from the car then some ice. Give me a few minutes."

"Fine." I huffed so she knew exactly how I felt about losing her from my grip. "Don't go naked, I'm not in the mood to kill anyone tonight."

"From this day forward, only for you." She held out her pinky, knowing that I knew what to do. I wrapped mine around hers, staring into those big beautiful eyes of hers and finding home despite everything. I shook our entwined pinkies once just before she leaned in and kissed them. "From this day forward, everything is only for you."

I tried to find the words to tell her the same, but I couldn't. My throat was too tight, my heart beating a little too fast. So I held on to those words, to that hope, like it was the lifeline I should have taken twelve years ago.

Deirdre

One question kept repeating over and over. Was saving him also betraying him? I sat staring at the pay phone, asking myself over and over again.

The answer was so complicated I would never find a yes or no.

I just knew we didn't have many other options. Okay, we didn't have any other options. Niall's desperate attempt at seeking refuge with Cochlain had spoken volumes about just how out of choices we were. Whatever I felt about making this phone call I knew it wouldn't result in a gunshot to the knee.

Probably.

I had one number. Ten digits that were to be used in case of emergency. I'd memorized them then swore to myself I wouldn't use them. Ever. That promise had last about two months. I rolled my eyes. Then started staring at the pay phone again.

Niall was going to be furious. Men like him were conditioned to explode at a certain set of words. What I was about to do would light the fuse to no less than three different ones.

But there was no other way to save him. Us.

I grabbed the phone this time and picked it up. I shoved the quarters in and started dialing before I could talk myself out of it again. It rang and rang, each one making my heart fall toward my toes. *Please.* I sent my silent prayer to anyone who would listen, I begged God, his Son, the mother Mary and Saint Christopher too. *Answer the damn phone.*

Just when hope was about to drain out of me and puddle on the floor, a deep male voice answered.

"What?"

"Brye, is that you?" The question rushed out of my mouth and bled into one mushed up word.

"Deirdre?" His voice softened fractionally. "I was wondering when you'd be calling." He sighed.

"How did you know I'd need your help?" Emotion churned inside my stomach worse than it had before.

"Filly made me promise I'd answer the phone when we saw."

"*You're damn right I did, I owe her for giving me my entire world*," Filly yelled in the background and I couldn't help but smile. There were all the reasons I'd gone to her, all the reasons I'd played my part in bringing down the MacCowans, and all the reasons I'd kept my mouth shut wrapped up in a nice little bow.

"That's still not an answer," I chided gently.

"Drea," Brye said, back to utterly serious, "turn on the news."

"Here." I shoved the ice at Niall, barely giving him a glance as I dropped the bags of clothes and food we'd bought before leaving Fargo on the bed and turning for the TV. I hit the remote harder than was really necessary as I searched for a nightly newscast.

"What are you doing?" he asked, his voice still blissed out.

I didn't need to answer as the evening news started right in on it.

"The national manhunt continues for two persons wanted in connection to the murder of mob boss Machlenan Ulster and for their possible connections to the Ulster family crime syndicate that was publicly apprehended two days ago."

Niall and I flashed on the screen. The photos both looked recent, I wore the bruises from after Mac had hit me.

"Where did they get those pictures?" I turned to find him watching intently.

"Shhhh." He waved me off.

"The couple was last seen just outside of Fargo, North Dakota in a black Range Rover. They are assumed armed and dangerous.

"The Federal Bureau of Investigation has set up a tip line for any information regarding their whereabouts. Any tips that lead directly to their detainment may be eligible for a reward."

They moved on the next story brusquely as if they hadn't just leveled a sentence against us. I'd known it was coming but that didn't make seeing it, seeing us any easier.

"How did you know?" Niall asked.

"What?" I pressed mute and tried to dart out of his way.

I wasn't fast enough. He grabbed my wrist me and stopped me from fidgeting with the bags.

"How did you know to turn on the news?"

I eyed him and swallowed.

"Did the woman at the front desk have it on? Could she have recognized you?" His words were rushed, his temper pushing each one forward.

"I didn't go into the lobby."

"God, Missoula is like the only city on this highway." He tried to jump up only to remember his wound.

"Calm down." I rushed over to grab him.

"Calm down? They just broadcast us on national TV, and we have nowhere to go." He hobbled over to peer out the blinds. "Why shouldn't I be freaking the fuck out? Why aren't you?"

This was going to hurt.

"See... the thing is... I... well..."

"What, Drea?" His voice dropped, infinitely colder.

"I have somewhere we can go." My teeth dug into my lip.

"Where?" The temperature of the room followed his voice.

"Pyramid Peak, Colorado." It was the truth after all.

"What the fuck is in Pyramid Peak, Colorado?" He shoved his hands on his hips.

"Umm... well..." I inched backward. "See about that whole thing at the MacCowans house..."

He went preternaturally still. My throat constricted.

"Who helped you that night?" His ruthlessness sent shivers down my spine.

"No one helped me." I took a deep breath and let it sit in my lungs. "I helped Brye MacCowan and the girl he loved, Filly Ryan."

He didn't have to say anything. The way his body went rigid, and the vein on his neck jumped, I knew just how furious he was. My words went rushing out in the hopes of smoothing this all over.

"He loved her more than anything. He tried to sacrifice his life to make sure she was safe." I remembered back to the desperate man he'd been and the feeling in the pit of my stomach that I'd never have that. That was why I'd done the only thing I could to protect them. Because someone needed hope. "So I sacrificed the only thing I had to get them back together."

"And what, pray tell, was that?"

"My security." That's what the house, Emmett, and the MacCowans had been. They were what I traded. "I had been hiding what Emmett was from Brye for years. Brye had no idea he framed you. He had no idea we started off *together*. That I chose to be there at first." God that word was awful to get out. "I spilled everything, and Brye decided that he had to take a stand to stay with her. He killed his father."

"All those other men?" His voice was deadly.

"Filly's dad and uncle." That sounded better than Horse and Cole Ryan didn't it?

"And Emmett?"

I flinched at that name. "Filly," I answered simply.

He started nodding, his lips pursed into a thin line. Slowly he returned to the bed, his head still nodding even though his eyes narrowed further. He barely moved until he shoved his hands through his hair.

"And you think because you all swam in this cesspool of deceit and betrayal together you can trust them?"

"No. I can trust them because they put love above this life." I stepped closer to him, aching for that closeness from before. "They put love above everything but each other."

"And what makes you think they're going to help us?" Each of his words cut.

"Because they believe in that sort of thing, and I think they might believe in us."

He shot me a look that had hope bottoming out in my stomach. I backed away from him and returned to the bags I brought in. I grabbed the pair of pajamas, a toothbrush, toothpaste, and some shower stuff. When I reached the bathroom, he hadn't moved. He barely breathed.

I cleared my throat and leaned out of the doorframe. "If my word isn't good enough for you, Niall, how about because they owe me, and they said they would. They swore."

My world was officially dust in the cosmic wind. It had already fallen to shit when Drea blew me and blew my mind. All the reasons that I wanted her tangled up with all the reasons that I wanted her body and became this whole new universe to dwell in.

But then she'd thrown in the Ryans.

The mother fucking Ryans.

Stories about them were whispered myths and legends amongst the Irish crime families. They didn't follow the rules or live by a code, at least not one that the rest of the families understood. They were brutal and ruthless.

We couldn't trust them.

Or rather *I* couldn't trust them. Drea was out of her mind if she thought she could.

And Brye MacCowan? That fuckhead and I had met in a dark alley one too many times. There was absolutely no love lost between us and not just because his family had Drea and I didn't. The last time I'd seen him, about two years ago, I'd held him still while Ailee had sliced his stomach open over a cocaine dispute. How could I tell Drea that? How could I tell her that she was naive or delusional if she thought they'd extend any courtesy to me. Maybe she was both.

But she'd thrown the T word out. And of course I trusted her.

About everything but this.

The shower water shut off and the subtle sounds of her drying off and moving around the bathroom replaced them. I hefted myself off the bed to meet her. I had to impress the gravity of what she'd done upon her. About what it meant for us.

I leaned against the door frame just in time for her to whip the door open. She tried to duck out of the way, but I filled the space, leaving her shit out of luck.

"Years ago, there was this guy called The Butcher. He was unhinged in a way you see more in serial killers than typical enforcers. No one talked back, no one disobeyed him."

She eyed me.

"Except the Ryans. Rumor has they gutted him with a butcher hook and left him to rot in his own entrails."

Drea crossed her arms. "Sounds like he deserved it."

"You don't get it. *No one* fucked with the Butcher," I tried to plead with her.

"No. You don't get it." She pushed me out of the way. "I've been around these kinds of people, around this life, longer than you. Just because I was a *thing* doesn't mean I was a nothing. I know what happens when people cross each other or get crossed. I know how bloody and brutal and violent everything is. I'm the one who saw *all* the scars. Every scrape and bruise and wicked, jagged cut."

She closed her eyes against the memories but kept speaking.

"I was there when Connor MacCowan wanted to make the Ryans hurt the way he hurt. I helped. I'm the one that saw the hatred in Brye's eyes fade and fizzle out. I knew what I was doing when I went to Brye. It was for them, for their future, but don't think for one second I didn't know what that would mean for me. I knew the rivers of blood would change this landscape. I was fucking *destined* for that."

"The fortune teller?" I asked skeptically reaching back to stop her.

"Sure." She shrugged. "But also just fortune. As if my life as a lonely, abused little Ulster was going to end up any differently."

"It still can. It so can." I pulled her in.

"How?"

"I'll figure it out." I leaned in only for her to arch back. "Let me fucking figure it out."

"I already did."

"They Ryans aren't the solution, they're just another problem." I tried to keep the venom out of my voice.

"I'm going." She pulled her arm from my grasp and looked me full in the face. Something seemed to crumble as she did, and I'd never wanted to pick up the pieces so badly. I just didn't know what pieces I needed to. "I'll go without you if needed."

"No," I roared before reeling my temper back in. "You aren't leaving me ever again. You promised. Everything only for me, right?"

"This is for you, you fucking idiot." She shoved past me and grabbed a box of Hot Tamales from before shoving herself back against the headboard. "For us."

"And if it goes wrong?" I crossed my arms on my chest.

She emptied a handful of the candies into her mouth, wrestling with the gummies for a minute before speaking.

"What exactly about us has gone right?"

Her question kept popping back into my head. Strictly speaking, nothing had gone right. It was just that *we* were right.

That was the reason I was driving the highway that snaked along one of Colorado's many rivers as it carved its way through the thick mountains and changing scenery. With each bend in the road, I expected to find a family of ruthless killers ready for an ambush.

The story that Drea had painted was beautiful but naive. That wasn't the way things worked. It wasn't the way men like me worked. Was it?

"It's beautiful here," Drea hadn't said much to me but her presence still spoke volumes to my soul.

"I haven't been able to look around much." My hands gripped tighter on the steering wheel.

"I've offered to drive a hundred times."

She leaned forward to inspect the canyon walls closing in on us. Part of me wanted to point out that she hadn't said a hundred words to me since leaving Missoula, let alone offering to drive a hundred times, but mercifully I managed to hold back. I didn't want to pick a fight.

I just wanted to pick anywhere else on the globe to go.

"We're getting close." Drea pointed to the mileage posted on the roadside sign.

"I want to go over how this is going to go at some point." I twisted my hands on the steering wheel, hoping it would ease some of the tension.

"What do you mean?"

"There are two guns in this car and a knife. I need to know which you're more comfortable with. I can lead with both handguns and you can follow with the knife or if you've had practice shooting, I can go one and one, and you can back me up." I kept running through scenarios, ways that I could use the car or the cover of pine trees if the property had them.

"Or we can walk up like civilized humans and say hello." She rolled her eyes and went back to looking out the windows.

"They aren't civilized. They're fucking murders," I countered.

"So are we." She snorted.

"We're not the same." The tips of my ears were getting warm.

"You're right." She crossed her arms. "We're lucky they're not as stubborn and pig headed as you."

"Being cautious has kept me alive this long."

"Being difficult now is going to get you killed." Her voice was growing claws and digging in.

"Fine! As long as it doesn't get you killed who fucking cares?" My temper bubbled up and over. "For a while now it's just been about you, Drea. About keeping you safe and making you mine. Don't you get that?"

"Don't you get that I feel the same fucking way?" she asked, her voice soft and soothing rather than rising to meet mine.

"But you're…" I started.

"Say it," she challenged right back.

"A girl. You're my girl." I knew what an ass I sounded like. Ailee would have pummeled me, and I knew I deserved it.

"I am a girl. I am your girl but don't mistake that for being weak. Look at what I've lived through, what storms I've weathered." She reached over and found my hand, lacing our fingers together. "I'm not fragile like a flower, but fragile like a bomb, or however that quote goes."

"The funny thing about that quote is that either way, you die. It's just whether it's with a whisper or a bang."

Her grip tightened on me and her smile spread.

"Yeah but if things go bad, as a bomb, I'm taking some fuckers with me."

Deirdre

Thank God we were walking into this as a team. I hadn't quite known how to get back there for a minute. The lingering doubt as to whether Niall trusted me and the prick to my pride at his assumption I was weak were hard pains to ease. With deep, centering breaths I was trying.

Sure, Brye MacCowan owed me for reuniting him and Filly Ryan. Sure, Filly owed me for crawling back bruised and bloodied to help her save his life. But each and every single thing Niall had said was true too.

Pyramid Peak was a hole in wall, a couple thousand people in the middle of mountains and hay meadows. Nothing was within thirty minutes of the town and even then what was was tiny too. The only thing that put it on the map was the mountain it was named after and the ski area that afforded the massive log homes dotting the landscape. I'd never known this type of isolation, and I wasn't sure if it boded well for us.

We'd come to a compromise leaving the historic town center and climbing up a dirt road deeper into the wilderness. Niall would carry both guns, and I'd be unarmed but I would go first. We turned off the county road where the map said to, dipping down into a grassy valley before climbing up a tree lined ridge on the other side. When shade from the pine trees covered the road again, we came to the gate.

Niall punched in the code Brye had given me and we waited

for it to rise. I took a deep breath as we drove under it and couldn't help but turn to watch it settle back into place with a finality that set unease churning in my stomach.

"That fence will fuck you up," Niall said as he surveyed the grounds. "There's barbed wire and razor wire hidden in with the rocks and wood."

I studied the bits I could see closely as we slowly climbed the dirt road. What had at first looked like a decorative country ranch fence was far more menacing on second glance.

"If you have to run, you don't go over or through, understand? You find another way." He was sharp, direct, but I could detect the fraying edges beneath.

"I understand," I answered, picking up our entwined hands in my other to hold tight.

We broke out of the trees again onto a small grassy plateau. A singular, massive log home stood in the middle with a barn tucked back closer to the tree line. Mountains arced up toward the sky behind the home and the plateau fell into a deep ravine via a steep plunge close to where the road had spit us out.

"Jesus Christ." Niall breathed.

"It's a fortress." I knew enough to know that it was built strategically.

"That's what worries me." Niall couldn't stop scanning the landscape.

"Why?"

"One way in, one way out doesn't bode well for enemies or escape." He audibly gulped.

"Here's hoping we don't need to do either."

Niall nodded but said nothing more as he started driving toward the house again. When we pulled close, three figures stepped out onto the stairs leading down to the drive. They were all imposing men. Tall and built for brutality. The cut of their muscles said just as much as the squint of their eyes or pinch of their faces. They all took up similar positions, wide legged stance, arms crossed over barrel chests. Well, crossed as best as possible considering the weapons they held.

Brye MacCowan stood front and center, the wounds and wariness he'd worn the last time I'd seen him were gone, replaced by utter certainty and severity. Cole Ryan stood over his left shoulder. He might have been old enough to be my father but he didn't look it. He was blanketed in tattoos that were menacing in and of themselves and still had the unnerving glint I'd noticed last time in his eyes. He hadn't used age as a reason to stop working out. Or maybe it was just that they were all trying to keep up with Horse standing over Brye's right shoulder. Horse had the kindest face of the three, but it was likely because he could feed someone their own asshole with sheer strength alone. Between them four handguns, one shotgun and an AR-15 were visible. I shuddered to think what wasn't. If the geography of the house had been imposing, the welcoming committee was terrifying.

"Maybe walking out armed isn't the best idea." I tried to keep the confidence in my voice.

"Fuck that," Niall said with a snarl. I didn't argue. The idea that he'd have my back gave me the smallest reassurance.

We parked a few feet from the stairs, facing them head on.

"You leave that door open, okay? Walk around the back of the car to me, then we'll go up there together."

I squeezed his hand in answer. "Niall, I—"

"Not until we're out of this, Drea." He jerked his chin toward my door, and we pushed out in unison.

I had to stop myself from shutting it as I rounded the car, taking deep breaths as I walked toward Niall. Each step I waited for something to happen, but the only sound was my feet crunching against gravel and wind blowing leisurely through the trees. I reached up and brushed my fingers down Niall's spine when I reached him. He flicked the handgun in his left hand to urge me on.

With a deep breath I stepped out from behind the shield of the Rover.

"Hi Brye," I said, sure it was stupid but unsure what else to say.

The answer was Brye drawing both the handguns he wore at

his shoulder holsters while Cole leveled the AR-15 at me, the mirror to Horse doing the same with the shotgun. I raised my hands in surrender only for two more handguns to appear in my peripheral as Niall stepped up behind me.

"Hi Deirdre," Brye replied without flinching. "Why don't you start with the introductions?"

I went to take a step forward when Niall hissed at me and I froze. "They'll know I'm hurt," he whispered in my ear.

"They're going to find out." I turned just enough to be able to mutter the same thing back.

"Stay put. Play his game," Niall commanded.

I turned back toward the steps, shielding my eyes from the sun to hold Brye's gaze. "So remember the guy I told you about, Brye? The one I'd loved but that Emmett had destroyed."

He gave me one curt nod in reply.

"This is him." I thumbed toward Niall at my back.

"Niall McDonough," Brye said, making Niall's name sound like cruel joke as he did.

"So you know him then?" My chest tightened.

"Met in a dark alley once or twice." Brye cocked his head, making him seem even more cold and calculating than he usually was. "That bitch Ailee get what was coming to her?"

Niall growled and pressed his body up against mine.

"Ardan blew your house to pieces," Niall said with the hint of a cruel smirk.

Brye tensed but only the slightest bit. "Good."

The wind replaced our words again, the slight sway of the spindly pines was the only movement. I wracked my brain for something to say to diffuse the tension and came up utterly short. I didn't think *so about that favor* was going to go over real well. The tension kept ramping up with each heartbeat. I wanted to move but didn't dare, even the scratch of gravel seemed like it could be the pin pulled out of the grenade.

Just when I couldn't take it anymore, when I was sure someone was going to shoot someone else just to make something happen, the front door flew open. Filly Ryan in all her five foot two glory came charging out the door.

"What in the hell is going on out here?" She skipped down the steps in her high-top Chuck Taylors and spun to face her dad, her uncle, and her... Brye, with her hands on her hips. The wild bun on her head swiveled as an echo of each of her movements.

"Go inside, Filly," Cole said, his voice even and heartless.

"Fine." She spun again, this time heading straight for me. "Sorry Deirdre, none of them are crate trained." She rolled her eyes. "Come on." She grabbed one of my hands out of midair and started pulling me toward the stairs. "You can come too if you promise not to whip your dick out and be part of this pissing contest." She shot a smile over my shoulder at Niall.

She was able to drag me a couple of feet before I glanced back to Niall. He was keeping up but barely. Pain had creased his face and pulled a fraction of his attention from defense.

"Wait, Filly. Please?" I asked gently.

She followed my gaze back to Niall and smiled softly. I dropped her hand and reached back for his. He let me take the gun, and I clicked the safety before shoving it into my pants at the small of my back and reaching back for his hand. I pulled it over my shoulder, taking some of his weight.

"Been a rough few days?" Filly asked, no accusation or pity in her voice.

"Oh, you know, just the usual." I shrugged even though he was draped across my shoulders.

Filly opened the door. "Mom, they're here," she called.

"Are they hungry?" A voice floated from somewhere past the fireplace.

"Oh hunty, I have been utterly starved for beefcake like this." A tall man with head to toe tattoos and a short pink silk bathrobe walked down the stairs.

"This is my Uncle Conrad, he's married to Horse. I don't think you met him in Chicago, Deirdre."

"Hello." I held out my free hand, but he was still focused on Niall.

"What on earth do they feed those boys in Chicago and please let the answer be wieners." He fanned himself.

"Sorry, *she's* going through menopause or something." Filly rolled her eyes. "I've had to physically pry him off this local kid named Swany with a crowbar."

"Move it or lose it, Conrad. They've been through enough." Elle came up from behind and hip checked Conrad even though she was just as petite as Filly. "I'm Elle, darling." She leaned in and hugged Niall's big ole body. "I was planning on steak, sorry it's not fancy but it's usually good to keep at least one of those hotheads occupied with fire and burning flesh if we want a peaceful meal." She rolled her eyes and I almost smiled at how similar they were. The memory of my mom weighed the corners of my lips down though. "Filly, do I need to go out there?"

"Couldn't hurt."

"Okay, Conrad go back to trying those fake eyelashes that came via UPS, they're mink and they're expensive. If they don't sit on right, I want my money back." She pointed toward the staircase. "Girls, this man's been shot, get him comfortable."

She shook her head at us the way only mothers really could.

"How'd she know—" Niall started.

"Don't ask." Filly went to duck under Niall's arm only to realize how he truly dwarfed her size. She stepped out with a giggle. "Come on."

"When you're done, Filly, go grab a bottle of bourbon and a case of beer from the cellar. I have a feeling we'll need it," Elle called as she walked out onto the porch.

"Yes, Mom," she answered, and it was so childish that I almost choked.

I'd done really debasing and perverted things to Filly high on ecstasy but here we were being treated to steak and bourbon at her parents' house. After being greeted at gunpoint. It would have been the weirdest day I'd ever had if I was anything close to normal.

"I'm glad you called, Deirdre. I want nothing more than to return the favor," Filly said as she moved a stray sweatshirt and a blanket off the recliner.

"I think I'll be owing you a few extra this time around." I sighed as I helped Niall into the chair then took up a perch on the armrest.

"It's a recliner. My dad seems like such an old man sometimes." She laughed. "He's becoming obsessed with recliners. He shipped two to our Paris house. Ruthless killer my ass…"

Niall snorted.

"See?" I smiled, knowing he saw what I saw now.

"Thank you for helping us, Filly," he said.

"He speaks." Her eyebrows rose as she shot a look over to me.

"With the voice of a sexual god." Conrad reappeared, complete with long, lush, and fully mink eyelashes batting at Niall.

"He's mine to worship, thanks." I hadn't meant the edge in my voice but I didn't mind that it had appeared. Niall's fingers found the valley of my spine.

"And he's an old married lady." Horse stepped through the front door, shotgun still in hand, and gave Conrad a knowing look. Niall's fingers tensed at my back. "Niall, I'm Horse." He nodded. "If you're good with Deirdre, you're good in my book."

"Thank you," I said before Niall could.

"Don't thank me yet…" He sighed just before the door kicked in, slamming against the coat rack behind it.

"You and me." Cole pointed at Niall, his voice rumbling through the room. "Outside." I stood up and put myself in Cole's line of fire. He just gestured me to move. "Now, Niall McDonough."

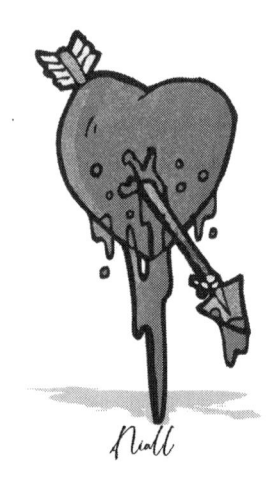

"It's okay, Drea," I said, as I hefted myself out of my seat. She still stood guard like she could do something if Cole Ryan decided to turn his fury on me. "Drea, sweetheart, have that beer okay? I'll be right back."

I didn't trust Cole or Brye as far as I could throw them and the jury was out on Horse and Conrad, but Elle and Filly were something unexpected. Something I could trust. At least when it came to death, dismemberment, or detainment.

"I'll come with you." She bit her lip.

I looked to Cole and one look said it all. "No, we're good."

"I have news for you, you're the farthest thing from good," she muttered under her breath.

"If they wanted me dead, they could have killed me a few times over." I lifted my hand and ran the pad of my thumb over her lip. "We're just going to talk."

She pressed her lips into a thin line, her brow furrowing, but she didn't try to stop me again.

I tried to even out my steps as I crossed the room. Cole and I stood nose to nose for a moment. I was bigger than him in stature and musculature, but I still shrunk in front of him. He vibrated with every ruthless story I'd heard about him. I wasn't afraid, but I knew when to sit down and shut up. I'd learned the hard way.

"He's not gonna bite," Elle said as she clapped me on the shoulder in passing. "And if he does, he's not going to get laid until Paris."

"What?" Cole snapped.

"You heard me," she called, walking into the kitchen. "You heard me, Cole Ryan. You're getting old but you're not going deaf."

"Like you could go that long," he shouted after her.

Both Horse and Conrad winced behind me.

Elle wrapped back around the corner. "Is that challenge?" Even I knew her face said *don't fuck with me*.

"Ladyface," Cole softened.

"Think back over *everything* we've been through and tell me which of us has survived worse." She shoved her hands on her hips. "A few months without dick, even one as fantastic as yours will be easy."

"Mom," Filly whined. "You have *got* to stop. Dad, get out there, wrap this up, and give me back Brye."

Cole looked back at me. "It's a lot easier when you just get to kill the people who fucking talk back."

"I'm learning that," I said.

He pointed out the door and I wordlessly went. Brye was leaning casually against the railing that lined the wrap around porch. The door shut behind me, and Cole stepped past me to do the same on the other side of the small stairway. Neither of them seemed armed.

"Who would have ever thought a Ryan, a MacCowan, and an Ulster man would stand within five feet of each other to *talk*," Cole said as he crossed his arms on his chest.

"Is that what we're doing?" I asked.

"We both owe her a debt, and we have every intention of paying," Brye said with a huff. "Filly will fillet me if I don't help."

"And Filly is my baby girl so what she wants, if it's within my power to give, she gets," Cole grumbled. "That's why he's here."

"Same to you," Brye shot back.

"I can go back inside," I snapped. "My knee fucking hurts."

"We'll have Elle look at that after dinner," Cole said as he jerked his chin down the porch. We wrapped around the corner and found a few Adirondack chairs. "But for now, we need to know what happened."

"And what's coming," Brye added.

"How far back do you want me to go?" I sighed as I settled into a chair.

"How far back do you need to?" Cole asked.

I started with the MacCowan house. It seemed like the right place. That's when it started for Drea anyway. I detailed her life in The Pit, what Mac did; neither of them flinched.

"That's when we changed tactics." I sighed, remembering how furious I'd been. Now I thanked my lucky stars. "She moved in with me."

"Give her some comfort, some humanity..." Cole mused.

"Really fuck with her head," Brye finished.

"Only I started to remember the reasons that I loved her. All the reasons that I wanted to spend my life with her back when we were young." I sighed and leaned forward to let my head fall into my hands. "Mac sent us all in different directions so he could fuck her. I figured it out in the nick of time, came back, and killed him."

"Deserved it," Brye interjected.

"And then some." Cole shook his head.

"We went to the house to get Arden and Ailee to get rid of the body, and I was pretty sure I was going to take the head but..."

"That's where the FBI come in." Cole sighed and leaned forward, his elbows on his knees.

"They have Ailee and Ardan, so I just kept fucking driving." Just saying their names hurt. "I changed the plates. The only place I could think of was Cochlain Ulster's."

Brye snorted.

"He *shot* me." And I shot Brye a look.

"You fucking deserved it for thinking you could go to Cochlain Ulster's." Brye laughed again. "The families made him move out of Chicago because he was fucking unhinged."

"As if anyone who raises shit bags like us is sane." Cole sighed.

We let those words hang between us for a little while. I listened to the wind sounding in the trees, sure that I could hear the crunching of gravel under tires. I tensed a few times against it.

"So you need to cover your tracks then get out of the country. Non-extradition?" Brye asked.

I thought about it. About that life, away from here and with Drea. I could imagine it—sort of. When it was good, it was great, but we were still figuring this out. Figuring each other out. The sex had always and would always be phenomenal but the rest of it… I was scared of screwing it up almost every time I opened my mouth. I wasn't sure I was ready for her and me against the world.

Besides, every single moment of every day that I was lying on a beach somewhere, I would know I'd left people who deserved to be by my side to rot. I'd been there once, and it took a lot not to be bitter as hell about it.

Getting Ailee and Ardan out felt right. Drea and I could do it together, learning more about how to work together, live together, and love through this all. Then the four of us could disappear. We'd be our own fucked up family unit like the Ryans here.

"I need to get them out before I can go anywhere." When I said it out loud it felt right.

"Excuse me?" Cole asked at the same moment Brye called *bullshit*.

"All I need is a clean car, some documents if that can happen, and an introduction to the kind of people that make this happen."

"Fucking shit," Cole swore as he scrubbed his face. "Why would you start that when you have a chance to finish everything else?"

"They're my friends." I glanced back to the house, wondering what Drea would say. Cole followed my line of sight to the house and I knew I had him. "Tell me you wouldn't do the same for your friends?"

He blew out a deep breath. "I can't. I get it."

"I fucking don't." Brye looked at both of us like we were crazy.

"Filly is fucking everything and if it was anyone, even Elle, or Filly, I'd pick Filly. Every. Single. Fucking. Time."

"That's the only reason you're allowed to touch her," Cole grumbled.

"Like I really need your fucking permission," Brye snapped.

Cole shot up, fists clenched and even more wicked and intense than he'd been with me. "Remember you're alive because of me and my friends that I'd rescue from the pits of hell, you ungrateful little…"

"Little what?" Brye taunted.

"Hey." I winced as I pushed up from my seat and in between them.

"Hey yourself." Brye pushed up into my space.

"Even shot, I will fuck you up—again—Brye." I pushed my chest up against his.

"One shot to that broken nose or a finger above and to the right of your kneecap and I'll level you. Spare me the fucking theatrics." His wicked little smirk pulled into place. "Besides, fucked up or not, Deirdre and I have a history. Twelve years of one. And it's weird and convoluted but it's a hell of a lot stronger than the one you and I have. I'm on her side."

"I'm on her side. I'm her whole fucking side. I'm her whole fucking team." I ground my teeth.

"Bullshit." Brye popped his knee so it crashed into mine. I howled, almost crumpling to the ground. Cole of all people caught me. Brye bent to get right in my face. "If you were what you claim you are, you'd put her fucking first."

Deirdre

THE SECOND NIALL BELLOWED I SHOT UP AND BARRELED FOR THE door. I was about to whip it open when Brye beat me too it.

"What's going on out there?" Filly asked, suddenly right behind me.

"Nothing," he snapped before softening. "Promise." He grabbed her behind the neck and pulled her in roughly for a hot and heavy kiss. I tried to look away but heat radiated from them. From the way he held her and took and took from her, sucking on her bottom lip. The way she'd fisted her hands in his shirt. But as quickly as he'd grabbed her, he let her go. She sighed, longing heavy on each note. "You and me." His eyes met mine as he jerked his chin back the way he came.

"Hurry back." Filly took her time letting go of his shirt.

"Anything for you." He knocked her chin before turning to lead me out onto the porch.

I followed him down the steps and we each pushed a Rover door shut before walking beyond it toward the sharp edge of the plateau. He kicked a few rocks as we walked out there, his hands shoved deep into his pockets.

The view was incredible. The creek we'd driven across in the dip of the drive, tripped and fell over rocks below the plateau, far enough away that we couldn't sit on the banks but close enough that the slight sound reached me. A small dirt road hugged the rolling hills and mountain sides below, winding into the distance to where Pyramid Peak sat nestled at the valley floor. The peak for which it was named rose high above the town and though it was miles away, I felt like I could reach out and touch it.

It made me smile.

That smile lasted exactly two and a half heartbeats, or in other words, until I looked at Brye.

"What's that face for?" I asked.

"Why did you ask for my help, Deirdre?" His face twisted up and he wouldn't meet my eyes.

"What do you mean? Because you offered it." I tried not to sound like I wondered when he'd been dropped on his head. "And we were out of options."

"No, not that." He sighed. "And Filly's happy to help—"

"But not you?"

"We slept together. A lot. And even if it was forced or misguided, it feels weird now, knowing that I found her. That I found the one." He smiled toward the house. "I wish it was only ever me and her."

"I get it." I followed his gaze back to the house.

"You love him." He didn't ask the question.

"I think so."

"What does that mean?" He rocked on his heels, his hands still in his pockets.

"It means this is new and fresh even though we have history. I think I know but I want to know more." I couldn't help but smile. "He was my everything back then. We were perfect. Our life was going to be perfect. But we've been apart a long time. And while we were, we both became really raw and fucked up creatures. Sometimes I think that makes us impossible, sometimes I think it made us even better for each other. Is that wrong?"

"No it's not wrong." Brye smiled, somehow both knowing and sorrowful.

"Good, because I plan on finding out when we get out of the country."

Brye froze and looked at me. Really looked. "That's why you called me," he said simply.

"I know the Ryans travel the world, I remember Filly talking about it in Chicago. I knew they'd be able to help with documents or transportation or something."

"But that's what you want?" he clarified.

"To get out and start over?" I blew out a deep breath. "It's terrifying but yes." I started nodding as I looked out on to the valley. "I haven't had control of my own life since… well, maybe ever. Now I get to do it with him."

"I have two things to say, Deirdre, then I won't bring this up again." He sighed. "One, I'll get you the papers and get you out. Two…" He reached up and ran his hand on the back of his neck. "You two need to talk."

I'D FOUND a perch on the edge of the plateau, a rock where my feet could dangle. Brye had been nicer than I anticipated. Sure they owed me, but he'd acted like he cared. Like what happened between us and between Niall and him mattered. Brye hadn't said as much but his face…

Something was wrong.

I kept scanning the road where I could see it, sure that the cops or a convoy of black Suburbans would be pulling up any moment. The voice in the back of my head that reminded me Brye was trustworthy, that we were safe, but the way he'd looked…

"What are you doing out here?" Niall asked, his feet crunching on the gravel as he came to meet me.

"Thinking," I said, turning to look up at the beautiful man limping up to me. He was gorgeous even now, battered and bruised. Strong and steady despite it all. A soldier that would fight for me and a future.

Wasn't he?

"Brye said that you might be." His brow furrowed. "He insisted we talk. That it was integral to how we all move forward. Like it was life or death. Fucking insufferable," he added as he sank down to the ground with me.

"He's not so bad," I said as I leaned against Niall's shoulder. "Dramatic sometimes but not bad."

"At least it's only for a day or two."

"I don't think even they can get passports in a day or two." I chuckled.

"We don't need passports," Niall said as if it was obvious.

"What?" I sat up and looked at him but the feeling was already there. The one that had materialized when Brye said we needed to talk.

What did Brye known that I didn't?

"We're staying stateside." He turned and cupped my cheek. I backed out of his hold. "I think our next move is to get Ardan and Ailee out. Then we have a team, we can tackle the rest of it with a team."

"*Our* next move?" I asked. "As in you and me?"

"Yeah. Bonnie and Clyde for a little longer." He smiled at the thought. "But then think of it, building a place like this, the four of us."

"The four of us?" My heart felt like it was going to burst.

"It's not right to leave them. You know that," he said softly.

"I *don't* know that." My chest was tightening, it was hard to breathe. "I don't need a team. I don't need a family like this. I need freedom."

"So you just want to up and leave like this life never existed?"

"Yeah," I said, this time it was my turn to sound like that was the obvious answer. "You're the only thing I want to take with me."

"I want you with me too but running away isn't the solution." His eyes pierced through me like they had in the beginning.

"We're federal fugitives, I think running away is the only solution."

"The Ryans know a guy who can help us. He specializes in

illegal extractions but works under cover of a K&R company." Niall added some gestures to his arguments.

"And how do you propose paying someone like that?"

"We'll figure it out. We'll give him whatever we have," he answered earnestly.

"We have service and sexual favors, Niall." I knew because that was all I'd ever had. I closed my eyes to find my strength. It took me a minute to wash that pleading face from behind my eyelids. "I won't give either of those away again. I can't." *Not even for you.* I said the words with all the conviction I could muster even if I couldn't bring myself to say that last bit.

"I…" he started then fell quiet.

"Want them free," I finished, feeling tears well in my throat.

"It's my fault they're in there. If they'd stayed home that night. If Mac hadn't wanted…"

He looked over at me, his eyes frantic and sorrowful in a way I'd only seen once. Twelve years ago when he'd tried to get me to talk to him after Mac raped me. Those were the frantic eyes of a man about to lose me.

"Stop," I said softly. "I can respect your reasons."

"I can't lose you again." His words almost got lost on the wind.

"I can't…" I started only for the words to fall short. I couldn't pledge my life to someone dirty all over again. I wouldn't. "That life was nightmare and I just got out…"

"Was it really so bad?" His words barely squeaked out.

I looked over at him and waited for his eyes to meet mine. I brushed that single beautiful curl out of his face then traced the bruises beneath his eye from Cochlain. The way he softened said he knew. He remembered what my life had been like if he was forced to dredge it up.

"Would a life with me really be so bad?"

"No," he said, his voice soft and tender. "But I would always regret not fighting. I regret the hell out of not fighting for—"

"We have a day or two. That's what you said, right?" I interrupted, knowing that I couldn't hear him finish that sentence.

"Yeah."

I traced my thumb lower, copying his move when I swept it across the swell of his bottom lip, thumbing the lip ring that I'd already miss when it wasn't pressed to mine. I focus on him, on that lip ring, as I begged him.

"Then kiss me like that's all we need."

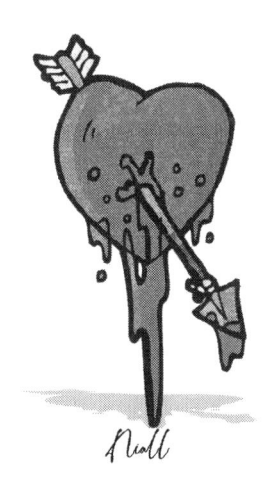

"You're quiet," Horse said as he sat down next to me where I had my leg propped up. Elle had cleaned it and bandaged it after dinner. "That's a rarity in this house." He offered me a rocks glass with something brown and neat.

"I'm not a man of many words," I said as I took it.

"I don't think any of us are." He gave me one single laugh, but it wasn't mocking or cruel. We sat in silence in the living room, a fire roaring in the hearth to stave off the early fall chill. Horse had an easy presence and I was grateful for it. Without him I kept thinking of Drea.

I'd kissed her out on that plateau with every bit of feeling that I had for her. If I thought long enough about it, I could feel her lips glide against mine, the way she tugged on my lip ring, or the way her tongue begged entry to my mouth. The soft sounds of her pleasure resonated in my ears. The salt of her tears where they tumbled into our kiss left a haunting taste on my lips. One that not even scotch could burn away.

"How do you know you're making the right decisions in a world where every fucking thing is wrong?" I asked, not really thinking that Horse would answer.

"Follow your heart and hope like hell it hasn't turned black before you do."

I thought about his words. Each of them. And how they applied to me, or rather whether they still could. My heart said it was Drea, just Drea. My fear and an overwhelming sense of guilt said Ardan and Ailee too.

"You really think it's that simple?"

Horse laughed again, still low and husky, so I knew it wasn't a malicious thing.

"I know it's that simple," he said. "Figuring out what it's saying is the hard part."

I nodded and took a deep pull of the scotch, letting it burn down my throat.

"Am I interrupting?" Drea said, pulling my attention from the fire and my thoughts to where she stood between the kitchen and living room.

She was wearing those short pajama shorts with a scandalous split up the sides and another one of the basic tees we'd bought that were soft, almost sheer cotton. I would remember her like that *if* this ended in a few days. I refused to say *when*.

"Nope." Horse stood from his seat next to me, raised his glass in a small toast and walked toward the stairs. "I think everyone's… uh… retired for the evening." He smirked as he took the stairs two at a time.

"Hi." Drea waited until Horse reached the top of the stairs and started walking down the hall to break the silence.

"Grab some scotch." I pointed my glass to where Horse had poured mine.

She grabbed a glass and the decanter and walked over. She filled my glass before filling hers and settling onto the floor to face me. Her long legs were stretched out in a V, framing the scotch glass, and making her shorts more scandalous than they'd been before. I wanted to run my fingers along the long lines of her.

As if she could read my thoughts, she undid her hair and let it fall in dark brown waves around her face. My fingers itched to comb through it.

And fucking yank it hard.

"Why are you all the way down there?" I couldn't help the heated growl in my voice. I didn't want to.

"Easier to commit every inch of you to memory," she said with a sip.

It was a slug to my chest, there was no other way to describe the small acknowledgement that we'd be a memory at some point. Like so many wounds before it, I smiled through the pain. I'd given up twelve years ago, I wasn't going to give up now.

"There's a few inches you definitely can't see from down there."

She smiled. The shape of her lips tempted me to crawl down there and kiss her. She shifted her hips, pulling my attention lower. To deny the peek that gave me of her perfect pink pussy lips would be torture.

I pushed up from the seat and slowly folded down onto the floor with her.

"What are you doing?" she asked softly. I crawled the few feet to her as best I could, keeping my weight on my hands and good knee. "Don't hurt yourself."

"Denying me what I want is the only thing that would hurt." I took a deep drink of her scotch, my eyes never left hers.

"And what do you want?" she asked, drawing her feet up so they were flat on the floor and her knees fell open a little further.

My eyes fell from hers and fixated on the apex of her thighs. "To eat you like you're my last fucking meal."

She started to lay back.

"Oh no." I stopped her. "You're going to sit on my face."

"Here?" Her eyebrows almost shot off her forehead.

"Right here." I pointed to the ground with my hand still wrapped around her glass and settled onto my side.

"What if they see?" Drea glanced toward the stairs.

"Let them watch, knowing that no one has ever eaten your pussy like I'm about to."

"Jesus, Niall," she scolded me, but I knew by the way she shifted she wanted it. Badly.

"It's Jesus Christ and you can pray to him later. For now,

you're going to be saying my name." I smirked. "Take it off and mount up." I laid back.

"That's it?" Drea took a sip of her scotch. "No foreplay?"

"I know what my mouth does to you even when it's not on you." I leaned up just enough to arch my eyebrow. "When I tell you I want to taste you, that I want to tease you until you drip down my face, and torment you with an orgasm that makes you see stars, I turn you on just the same as if I kissed you."

She sucked in a deep breath that told me every button I'd just hit.

"Stop stalling." I wanted to hit the rest.

Drea stood and unceremoniously shoved her shorts to the floor and stepped over me. The view was fucking fantastic. Her long legs were the supple lines that led straight to her sex. Her slick sex. I smiled something wicked as I watched her shift.

"Do you like me staring at you, Drea? Watching each little twitch and clench."

She did it as if on command.

"Shit, sweetheart." I couldn't help my low, husky chuckle. "You're perfect. I'll never get over how perfect."

I let my hands wrap around her calves and run up that long, lean line of her legs. She shuddered in my grip.

"Get down here," I growled.

She whimpered before she even folded. "I don't want to hurt you."

"Take off your shirt and I'll be fucking fine. Promise." I reached up and palmed her breast then tweaked her nipple to prove my point.

She kept most of her weight in her thighs as she pulled her shirt over her head and notched herself against my lips. The curve of her breasts from below was one of the most arousing, pornographic shapes I'd ever seen. I reached up and brushed my thumb along the curve just like I usually did to her lips. Goose bumps spread in my wake.

"Niall," she moaned.

"Quiet," I said against her skin before I stuck my tongue out and went to work.

I rimmed around her a few times first, slow and leisurely. My hands found a spot on her thighs and urged her to rock ever so gently, her hands dug into mine. I flattened out my tongue and pulled her back and forth across it. She murmured something unintelligible as I folded my tongue to slide inside her.

She moved up and down on what little of me was inside her until I coaxed her hips to rock back and forth instead. Her thighs trembled beneath my hands—our hands—as she moved to my rhythm, slow and steady. Arousal spread across my face just like I'd wanted. She tasted like her and skin and sex.

I changed my tactic, finally wrapping my lips around her clit and sucking it into my mouth. She moaned as my lip ring notched against her, and her body rounded forward. Her hair fell like a curtain in front of her face and my view changed, her full breasts on display. It changed the angle of her hips, so I nipped her sensitive bud to keep her still.

"Ah." Her voice was ragged and pained.

I lifted her up enough to chastise her. "You give it to me, don't you fucking dare take it from me."

She nodded and straightened out, pressing her clit back into my mouth. God, I wanted to tell her *good girl,* but I wasn't about to let her move away again. I wasn't about to let her go anywhere.

As soon as I thought it, something thudded in my chest. I had to stop myself. Distract myself. I couldn't face that thought. So I used the tip of my tongue to trace the inner knot of nerves of her clit.

Without warning, she exploded. Her body quaked with that telltale shake, and I slid my tongue into her to feel her body clench on me.

God, she was good. Perfect even. For me, anyway. The way she reacted made me feel like a god. The way she was with me made me feel whole. She made me feel whole and yet she was about to leave…

She slid off my face and collapsed on the floor beside me. I propped myself up on my elbow, then bent down, pressing my lips to her hip then over to her bellybutton. She pushed her hand into my hair but didn't pull me, she just held me as I kissed leisurely up her body.

I wiped my face in the crook of my elbow and reached for a glass of scotch, whether it was hers or mine. Mercifully the burn left the taste of her in my mouth even as I bent down to kiss her, taste her, again.

"I'm going to take you to bed." I pushed up to standing and scooped her up.

"My clothes." She tried to reach for them.

I bent down and leaned my forehead to hers and smirked. "Drea, you don't need them."

Deirdre

"Were those your pajamas on the floor?" Filly asked as she settled into the chair beside me. I almost spit out my coffee.

"I... um... we... Niall said..." I'd burnt my throat and the flames of embarrassment lapped at my cheeks.

"Relax." Filly chuckled as she sipped her coffee. "It'll take a whole lot more than discarded pajamas to embarrass this crew." She smiled. "I would have thought that it'd take a lot more for you too."

"Yeah, well..." I trailed off. I didn't know how to explain it.

"It's him, isn't it? He's why you're different than a few months ago." She still studied me rather than the view from the Adirondack chairs on the porch.

"I guess so. He helped remind me who I was before all this, he broke down the walls I had in place." I sighed.

"It's more than that too." She twisted in her seat completely, one leg folded up so she could face me head on.

"I'm not out to save my own skin. I don't have to be twelve steps ahead or have my defenses up." I started listing reasons. "No one's feeding me ecstasy to make me extra crazy."

"It's a hell of a drug." She shivered, and I knew she was thinking the same thing as me. Replaying the night we'd done things to each other, remembering what a monster I'd been.

"I'm sorry for everything, I hope you know that." I hung my head, ashamed I hadn't apologized earlier.

"We're way past that." Filly laughed, an easy sound that flitted across the plateau of the house. "It was all forgiven when you helped me save Brye."

"I still owe you the words." I managed a small smile.

"Fine. Apology accepted." She raised her coffee mug toward mine and we clinked the porcelain.

Neither of us said anything else for a few minutes, instead letting the birds chatter amongst themselves. The faint tumble of the creek could still reach us in the morning when the wind was missing, and the trees stood silent.

"Brye said Niall's not going with you." Filly broke the silence, her voice softer and more sad than it had been a few minutes ago.

"He feels like he has unfinished business here." I couldn't bring myself to say he wasn't in such simple terms.

"And you're just going to let him stay?"

"Years ago I had my fortune told. She said a lot of things, but the bit that's been playing in my mind the past twenty-four hours is that she told I had to choose wisely. I had to pick the right man. One who was willing to fight through all the awful things that would happen. If I didn't, we'd both end up dead." I let out a heavy sigh. "I can't make him want to be that man. It'll kill us both."

"So you just lie down and take it?"

I cringed at her choice of words. I'd spent almost my entire life on my back taking whatever it was handed down. "That would appear to be my destiny." My voice held the same shiver of disgust.

"I didn't mean—"

"It's fine, Filly. Really it is." I smiled reassuringly. She hadn't said anything I didn't know, nor had she said it to be cruel.

"It's not fine," she said adamant. "You deserve happiness too."

"I'm going to get more of it than I deserve, Filly. I'm going to be free. That may not seem like a lot compared to a happily ever after but it's enough."

She didn't say anything though the thin, firm set of her mouth and the furrow of her brow said plenty.

"Was there more coffee in there?" I asked just as much for coffee as to change the subject.

"Yeah, help yourself." She gestured halfheartedly toward the door that lead to the kitchen as she settled back into her chair, facing out at the view.

I paused at the screen door, looking back only to see her still gnawing on my last words. I tried not to let my heart sink down to the level it wanted to.

"Hey Filly," I called. "Thanks for thinking that I deserve more. That means something to me." I flashed her a smile, albeit a weighted one, as I slipped into the kitchen.

I was filling my coffee cup back up when I felt Niall. He'd just entered the room, but I knew his footsteps, the slight limp he was battling, and my body reacted. The thrill of knowing I'd see him, touch him, smell him in my very next breaths made my heart jackknife.

"Good morning," he said as he pressed his body to mine and ran his fingers up my arms. I closed my eyes and let my senses relish each little bit of him. "I missed you in bed this morning."

"I didn't sleep real well," I confessed.

"After the orgasm I gave you? I should be offended." He carefully pressed his lips to the curve of my neck then left his chin on my shoulder, breathing in slow and deep.

"I've got a lot on my mind, cut yourself some slack." I playfully elbowed him.

"You think that's funny? Huh? Do you?" He turned me, and I fully intended to continue the volley but one look at him and I was putty in his hands.

His hair was a little disheveled, the sides a little longer and less severe then they'd been that first day, his signature curl still flopping into his face. His eyes weren't daggers anymore, just a haunting green that called to me. The smile he wore softened the sharp cut of his features.

I reached up, reminding myself to be gentle the whole way, and pulled him to my lips. I moved slowly, not just to avoid his bruises but to memorize the shape of his lips, the dance they made when they were together. He matched me as if he was doing the same. No rush. No urgency, just passion pure and simple.

Niall pulled my body closer, his big hand splaying across my back, the other wandering up and into my hair. One of mine slipped from his face to ball in his shirt.

"Nothing goes with pancakes like a porno," Conrad said from behind us, shattering the moment. Niall stepped back, his hands falling from my body. I had to talk my hand into letting go of his shirt. Conrad watched in nothing more than a towel, slung low across his tattooed waist. "Don't stop on my account. I was being serious." Conrad's gaze ran the length of Niall's body.

"Someday you're going to get shot because of that mouth." Horse walked up behind Conrad and kissed the curve of his shoulder.

"No one would dare. This thing is a national treasure." He wiped the corners of his mouth then smirked like the cat that ate the canary.

"I wouldn't say that." Horse arched an eyebrow as he reached for coffee.

"You would've last night." Conrad's smile grew.

"We have guests," Horse warned.

"And aren't we supposed to show our guests a good time?"

Horse whirled on Conrad, pinning him by the throat to the cabinets. Conrad just stretched his neck out. "You're being rude."

"So punish me," he challenged even though the words were constricted.

"Well…" Elle joined us in the kitchen, her eyes skating over Horse and Conrad frozen as they were. "Morning everyone." She walked past them as if this was her typical morning fare.

"Is Cole up?" Horse asked without loosening his grip on Conrad.

Her face darkened as she grabbed coffee. "He didn't sleep well." I noticed her quick glance at us.

"I'm sorry," I muttered.

"Don't you dare apologize." She reached over and clasped her hand around mine. "He might not look it but he's a big ole softy.

You guys remind him that all this…" she waved her hand around, "…is fragile and that we're lucky. We have each other."

I swallowed down a second apology and nodded. Niall's hand reappeared at my hip and squeezed.

"Is he okay?" Horse had let go of Conrad and stood shoulder to shoulder with Elle.

"Oh you know him." She smiled a sorrowful thing and shrugged.

"I'll go," he answered simply.

"I'll go put pants on." Conrad sighed.

We watched them walk away before I spoke again. "I should go with Niall just to get out of your hair."

"No," Elle said sharply, sharper than any other sentiment she'd shared. "You follow your heart, you hear me, wherever it leads." She turned to look Niall in the eye. "And you'd do well to do the same."

THE RYANS WERE NOTHING LIKE I EXPECTED. FIERCE BUT forgiving and all about this *follow your heart* bullshit. I was living in a damned Disney movie.

It almost made them seem naive.

They'd been out long enough that they forgot this life was about strategy and survival. Following my heart wasn't an option. Not a practical one, anyway. Not if I wanted to live long enough to do it.

I looked over at Drea and wished I was wrong. Desperately. This was all I wanted. To wake up with her naked in my arms and sip coffee in the kitchen. She looked perfect in jeans and one of those easy t-shirts, her hair in a fast braid I'd watched her deft fingers weave from the edge of our bed. She didn't have the same sadness from a week or two ago warping her features and slumping her shoulders. The thought of leaving her ripped at my insides but this was the version of herself she deserved to be.

"Let's talk," Brye said brusquely as he walked into the kitchen.

He didn't wait for my answer before turning back toward the front door. I gave Drea one more squeeze on the hip before I followed.

"You really want to do this?" He spun on me at the foot of the stairs. "You want to walk away from her."

"You sure seem to have a soft spot for her, you sure you want to fucking walk at all?"

"Come the fuck on." Brye rolled his eyes. "Filly is my whole fucking world." He sighed. "I know how that makes me sound but it's the god's honest truth. Don't get me wrong, I still want to rip people to shreds—frequently people in this house—and I take a gun or two out into the woods and shoot shit just to take the edge off on a very regular basis, but when I remember I have her, it's worth it."

"And what? You don't want me to throw that away?" I asked, skeptically.

"Yeah, you fuckhead." Brye rubbed the back of his neck. "You think people like us get a chance at a love like that more than once?"

"No, I don't think we get a chance at it at all," I said as I shrugged.

"How the fuck did someone as dumb as you almost split my stomach open?" His hand wandered aimlessly to a scar I'd given him. "She's right inside."

"She didn't pick me either. You know that right?"

"Get in the car, asshole." Brye gestured to my Range Rover.

He pressed the button to start the car as I slid into Drea's seat. That smell of vanilla and coconut still lingered, and I closed my eyes as if that would fight against it. Brye backed up a little, then turned and drove off, through the grass and past the barn toward the tree line.

There was a small gate tucked between the trees, almost hidden. He opened his window and punched a code in before starting up a rough and rutted dirt road that climbed up the mountain.

"Did you really expect her to pick you?" he asked when we reached the top of the mountain and started down the backside.

"What?" I'd had my defenses up what with being driven deep into the woods by a potentially-former, possibly-current enemy.

"Did you really think that after everything, she'd want to *stay* in the life?" he asked incredulous.

"I thought she'd want to stay with *me*."

"Do you know what Emmett did to her? He gave her to my father. You know what my father did with her? Gave her to anyone that asked." Brye had the decency to sound disgusted. "She wasn't a person. She was a thing. The things men did to her…" He shivered. "I tried to treat her better than that, but I was lost in my own shit, my own grief, so I wasn't much better."

I idly wondered if my knife was still in the SUV and whether I could get control of the vehicle back in time to not die if I plunged it into his chest.

"Despite it all, she fought for Filly and for me." He let out a heavy sigh. "So yeah, maybe I have a soft spot for her. Maybe I'm just a selfish fucking pig trying to atone for the shit I did. The shit I was."

I sat in silence as the car jostled down the hill. Each moment I had to hold back my desire to murder him. I couldn't tell if I wanted to because of what he'd done to her, or because of what he'd implied about me.

Nothing in this world—in this fucking universe—would have me sending her back to men like that. She was mine. Staying in the US did not mean she'd be doing that shit.

Did it?

"Not that I owe you an explanation but fighting for my friends does not mean I'm setting her to the wolves. She'll never do that, be that, again." I crossed my arms and glowered.

"You're delusional if you think you can be ass deep in all this and make that promise to yourself, let alone her." He pulled the car up to a beautiful vantage point, mountains spread out before us for as far as I could see. Not a house or soul in sight.

"Did you bring me out here to kill me?"

He laughed. "I know Deirdre well enough to know I'd be a dead man walking." He got out of the car and motioned for me to do the same. "I came out here to help you." He pulled a red gasoline canister from the back. "We're getting rid of this car. My guy at the DMV has a new license for you complete with driving record. We have a title and registration for you for one of the old trucks. It's not fast but it's inconspicuous." He started splashing the seats with gasoline, I grabbed my knife before he could douse it. Any trace of Drea was gone.

"One of the feds that used to be on the MacCowan payroll happened to take my call and told me where they're holding Ardan and Ailee Moore. I'm working on getting someone in there."

"Thank you." I had to bite out the words.

He just nodded as he lit the match.

"I've got a passport coming for Deirdre. Now that we know the FBI might be on their way we're going to Mexico once we have all the documentation in place."

We both stood and watched the inside of the Rover catch fire.

"We'll get her on a flight from there."

"Is that safe?" It was the gasoline choking me, not the thought of her alone on that flight. Right?

"If we have any reason to think it's not we'll get her down to Argentina."

I nodded.

"Help me with the car." He squared up to the back of the Rover and pressed his hands to it. I did the same. Step by step, we pushed the flaming SUV off the edge of the cliff. "There's a pond down there." We watched as it caught real fire a heartbeat before it splashed.

We sat there watching in silence as the vehicle bubbled and protested, sinking down into the lake. I felt like it was a reflection of my insides. Drea had lit me up and I was about to dive into the lake. It was shitty and murky, and every bit of me screamed at the prospect of diving in.

"Look, it's not any of my business," Brye finally broke the silence.

"Then don't open your mouth," I snarled.

"I've never seen her like this." He turned from the edge and started back toward the road. I watched him. "She loves you."

"She's never said that."

"She doesn't have to," he called back with a wave.

Brye kept walking. He was about halfway up the road when I realized he wasn't coming back. Nor was anyone coming to get me.

The fucker had brought me out in the middle of nowhere under the guise of helping me and hung me out to dry.

Deirdre

I heard his footsteps before I saw him, his limp was more pronounced as he neared the top of the hill. Brye hadn't beat him by much but it was enough to send me into a weird tornado of rage and worry. I'd decked Brye before running across the backyard and starting up the road to meet Niall.

"Niall!" I called as I broke the hill, finally saw him, and sprinted forward.

"I'm going to fucking kill him," he roared.

"Not if I do it first." I had to stop myself from launching my body at his. I skittered to a stop right in front of him and gently pressed up to tiptoes to wind my arms around him. "Are you okay?"

His whole body was tense beneath me but after a few deep breaths, he gathered me up and sagged against my body.

"I'm okay," he finally answered.

"Your leg…?"

"Better be good enough to get on my knees between yours." His words rumbled against my chest, and I smiled.

"Sounds lovely." I settled back onto my flat feet and brushed his curl out of his face.

His eyes drifted from mine to the world behind me. His jaw tensed again.

"I hate this, Drea. I hate them."

I slid my hands down his arms and laced my fingers in with his. "I know. I still don't know what other choice we had."

"None. And that pisses me off too." He sighed then brought our hands up between us, kissing first one set of knuckles then then other. "I feel like all my choices are being taken from me. They have been since I shot Mac."

"I'm sorry," I murmured.

"No." He shook free of my hands and cradled my face. "Do not apologize. I wouldn't take it back, I wouldn't take any of it back, I'm just saying I feel backed into a corner."

There's a way out. It was right there on the tip of my tongue. I couldn't bring myself to say it. Not when there was such little time left, I wouldn't spend it fighting.

"What can I do?" I asked.

His eyes found mine, the wide open and sorrow filled ones. They darted back and forth, and his jaw feathered as if he had something. His mouth moved just once before he snapped it shut, his eyes returned to the field beyond me. He had something but he didn't say it. It was the other side of the same coin I was flipping.

"What can I?" He finally chose his words. They hurt, not because he was being cruel but because he was being honest.

"Tell me what you guys talked about?" I had to know what I was facing.

"He already has my documents. He's getting in touch with Ardan and Ailee."

My heartbeat shot up. That meant the clock was even further along than I thought it was.

"So soon?" I tried to hide the hurt but didn't quite manage.

"He has a passport coming for you." He still couldn't meet my eyes. I nodded and slid back against his chest.

There was nothing left to say. We both knew it. Besides goodbye. There was still goodbye, but that word was going to hurt and in a way I wasn't sure how I'd recover from. Maybe I wouldn't, not really anyway. Had I ever really recovered from the first time we said it? I would just wear this wound and it's knotted up scar forever.

At least it was a way to keep him with me.

Niall knew it too. Well maybe not the sorrow and the scars, but I knew he couldn't find words. Instead he pulled me in and under his arm. He rested his temple against my forehead for a moment then left a little weight there as we walked down the hill and to the house.

Horse and Cole watched us warily as we walked up the stairs but they didn't say anything. Inside, Brye leaned against the counter with a small towel filled with ice pressed to his cheek, Filly narrowed her gaze at me.

"Say you're sorry, Brye." Elle was the only one oblivious to the tension in the room. Or maybe she was just unaffected by it as she stirred a large pot of marinara.

"He needs to test that leg. See what his limitations are considering what he's about to do," Brye replied simply, his eyes staying fixed on mine.

"That doesn't sound like sorry," Elle chided.

"Deirdre can go first." A devious little smirk pulled at his lips.

"I'm sorry that I missed your nose." I made sure to sound sickly sweet.

"Did you punch him?" Niall leaned in to murmur in my ear.

I nodded only to feel his breathy chuckle against my neck and the tightening of his hand on mine.

"You two…" Elle waved her spoon between the two of us.

"They both had their reasons. Leave them be, Ladyface," Cole said as he walked into the kitchen. The room stilled with his swagger.

"We're not savages." She shoved her hands on her hips.

"Actually, we're all exactly that," he said it with a smirk that made the scar on his cheek dance. "Ruthless, wicked monsters." He wove his hands around her waist. "I could tell them stories about *you* that would make their blood run cold." He pressed his lips to her neck, and her eyes fluttered shut.

She was always the calm and collected one. She was the one that played mediator, negotiator, and homemaker. But in his hands, she melted. She was none of those things in his arms, none of us were even here. Their world consisted of them and nothing else.

I knew the feeling and was about to lose it. I'd found myself again with Niall, I'd found home, and I wasn't exactly sure how I'd keep them after he'd gone. If only I could keep him…

Filly cleared her throat, interrupting the kisses Cole was peppering down Elle's neck. "No one wants to see that," she grumbled.

I agreed even though my reasons were different. Looking at them was like looking at the sun, it was painful and left blinding spots seared into my vision.

"We're going to excuse ourselves," Niall said. "I need to prop my knee up."

"You won't have a chance next time," Brye replied casually.

The tips of my ears heated as I lunged for Brye. Niall pulled me back and kept me tight to his chest.

"As much as I'd like to see you even him out, he's right, Drea." He laughed in my ear. "Come on." Niall pulled me out of the kitchen toward the guest room. Brye handed over his ice at the last minute.

We walked through the living room to the hallway that lead back to the guest room. He shut the door gently behind us before settling onto the bed, the ice pack at his knee.

"We should go back out there and destroy Brye's pretty boy face," I said with a huff as I plopped down on the other side of the bed.

He chuckled then trailed off with a heavy sigh. "He's right though."

"Fuck him."

"Don't you dare." He said it as a joke, but I just glowered, not finding it funny in the least. "Oh come on, Drea," he said as he reached for me. "He's a fuck head but you can't let him ruin the last few hours."

"I'm fucking furious because he took some of the last few hours." I punched the bed beside me.

Niall shifted enough to pull me down flat to the mattress. He leaned over, filling up my vision.

"Don't let him have a second more," he murmured as he bent down to kiss me.

This kiss was different than our others. Niall usually kissed me with fire enough to feel the burn but this was slow and smoldering, a little sad. The tears I'd been keeping at bay knotted in my throat. This kiss said goodbye.

I met his lips each time they moved, deepening our kiss. Heat rose in my body, my skin blanching at his touch. His tongue traced the seam of mine before I opened to let him in. My body bowed, wanting the depth of that kiss to grow, to become something deep and endless between us. He cupped my chin and shifted so the weight of his lips, his passion, could pin me to him.

He pulled back when my lips were raw and swollen.

"Don't," I said, breathless.

"I won't stop." He smiled as he began pressing the same slow-burning kisses to the line of my jaw.

I couldn't help myself when I corrected him. "Niall, don't go."

Niall

I could have asked her the same thing. I could have asked her to stay with me but for all his fucked-up traits, Brye MacCowan was right. She deserved a way out. So I simply swallowed her words with another kiss.

Another kiss. Another caress. Breathless moans as I moved her beneath me.

My knee ached when I propped myself between her legs, but I made myself stay there. I had to tolerate the pain, for Drea now, and my safety later. She could be my only weakness when I left this place, and she could only be it because she'd be far away.

It had been ages since I just kissed a girl. Over and over and over again because I couldn't stop. I wouldn't. If either of us spoke, if this moment shattered, I wouldn't get it back, so I didn't. I wouldn't let it. My lips kept hers busy. My hands began to trace her curves and the lines of her body.

I'd once told her that I wouldn't fuck her until I could wreck and ruin her and I was on the edge of taking that back. Except I wasn't going to stop this. This tender exploration of her body. This was born of the adoration I felt for her rather than the passion reignited as the flame that had made me promise her. Changing that now was… I just couldn't.

When I reached for the hem of her shirt, I didn't pull, I only pushed my hand up underneath, feeling the warmth of her skin against the palm of my hand. I moved it up to her chest. The shape of her breast and the weight of it in my hand was delicious but feeling the beat of her heart was something else entirely. I let my palm wander, heat spreading up my arm and through my heart.

After I'd felt her, all of her that I could reach anyway, I pushed the fabric of her shirt up so that her body was on display. I leaned back and looked at her, unabashed in my slow study of her skin. She blanched a perfect pink but didn't try to cover herself. She let me stare. When I'd taken my fill—at least for a little while—I bent back down to her body, my mouth replacing my hand at her breast.

Still the steady beat of her heart hit against me, the warmth of her skin spread through me. Her body bowed up toward me, and her hands found their way into my hair. I kept at my licks and flicks against her nipple only trading my moves for kisses interspersed across any swath of skin close. Her breathing became labored, her moan hitched in her throat.

My mouth moved back to hers, to swallow the sound and save it for myself. Our tongues moved against each other, teasing and tempting. My hand slid to the waist of her pants only to hesitate.

If I pressed in, I wouldn't be able to stop. And if I didn't stop, I'd take this night with me. Tasting her then turning away had already ruined me once. I'd become a monster.

I wouldn't become one again.

My hand slid back up her body and found the curve of her face. I pulled back just enough to run the pad over the plump of her bottom lip.

"Don't," she murmured again. "Please don't."

This time her plea was different. I knew what she was asking. I knew why she was asking it. We were the same her and I, cut from the same cloth woven over years of heartache and yearning. She wouldn't be able to walk away if we kept going. We'd tie ourselves to each other, ensuring the other would drown; her in regret, me in guilt.

I reached down and pulled her shirt down, covering her beautiful body once more. The tears choked in my throat, but I refused to let her see me cry. I sank down to the mattress beside her and pulled her body up against mine. She curled into my chest, her sadness not staying cemented inside like mine. I used my grip to pull her back up to my lips, kissing her just the same as before.

Kissing her through the tears of this torment.

―――

We hadn't left the room all night. We hadn't left each other's arms. I hadn't been able to sleep but Drea's soft soothing sounds told me she'd fallen asleep, but not until the deep of night swapped for the softer shades of dawn.

I brushed her beautiful hair out of her face and tucked it behind her ear, bending to press my lips to her eyelids, her nose, and then her lips. She stirred, barely murmuring my name before she snuggled back into the covers.

It took every ounce of strength I had to pull away from her in the end. As quietly as I could, I collected the few belongings I had. With each one, I reminded myself why I was doing this. I repeated Ardan and Ailee's names. Loyal. I was loyal. It was the one bit of my humanity I held on to when I'd lost all else.

I had to do this.

When there was nothing left to gather, no other reason to stall, I reached for Saint Christopher where he hung around my neck. I started rubbing him as I always did but then I stopped. I hadn't taken it off since my mother gave it to me for my confirmation. Maybe I'd been garbage at living a life of God, but I'd sworn to him plenty, and between him and the Saint, I'd been protected.

I could only pray he'd do the same for Drea.

With a hand on the mattress to brace me, I crouched down to the edge of the bed. Drea barely moved. I reached over and threaded the chain around her neck and beneath her hair. Saint Christopher hung limp on the mattress until I gently tucked it into her cleavage.

I love you was right there on the tip of my tongue but I held it back. Just in case she heard me. Like Brye had said, I hoped I didn't have to for her to know. I willed them into the last gentle brush my thumb took across her bottom lip. My prayer that I would see her again in the last whisper of my touch on Saint Christopher.

With a heavy heart and a slump to my shoulders, I slid out of the room, praying that I would find Brye or one of the Ryans. Praying they would understand.

I got my wish when I found Cole Ryan sitting in the kitchen, watching a tiny set of surveillance screens.

"Everything okay?" I asked.

He swiveled and had a gun pointed at my head before I'd taken a second breath. I held my hands up in surrender.

"Didn't hear you," he said by way of an apology.

"Didn't think I was that stealthy." I lowered my hands as he lowered his weapon.

"Brye's guy at the DMV brought your stuff up, I saw another set of headlights on the road. It's early enough that it was disconcerting."

I stepped closer, studying the frames in front of him.

"They came up the road?" I asked, remembering the drive up the day before yesterday. There was no reason to be anywhere near the Ryan's gate.

"It happens from time to time. People think it's to one of the campgrounds or trailheads. If they were behind Dexter, they might have thought he knew the way." His jaw tensed. "Brye and Horse are checking a few spots at the perimeter."

"Can you trust your DMV guy?"

"I've been able to for going on fifteen years. Dexter's the reason we know about Pyramid Peak. The reason we have this place." Cole still held the loaded gun, toying with the safety.

He flipped it suddenly and tracked the movement on the porch for a moment before the lessening gray betrayed Horse.

"They went further up the pass," Horse said, shrugging out of his coat. "It was an early two thousands Nissan Pathfinder, roof rack, stickers on the cargo box, spare tire… They went way undercover if it was the feds."

I blew out a breath I hadn't known I was holding. Cole nudged a manilla envelope next to him with the barrel of his gun.

"This is for you, McDonough."

"Thank you."

I opened the package to find a temporary license, registration, insurance card and what was probably another two thousand dollars. The guns I'd walked in here with were on the counter beneath it.

"The extraction guy's name is Dillinger. He's going to meet you in Louisville in three days, the meet info is in there. He took half payment up front, you're on your own for the other half."

I nodded.

"The truck is ready but are you?"

I glanced toward the guest bedroom. "Yeah."

"I hope I never see you again," Cole said.

"The feeling's mutual," I said with a nod. "But thank you all the same."

"You're welcome all the same." His brow furrowed, and I knew there was something else he wanted to say.

"What?" I asked.

"Look, I want you off my property and out of my life but if you were meant to be together…" He sighed. "We'll take care of her as if she was one of our own but, if she's the one, it shouldn't fall on us. If she's the one, you should hold on to her. With two hands. Trick her into fucking loving a piece of shit like you if that's what it takes."

"I want you all out of my business, but I'll tell you that *this* is what it takes." I held up the envelope in emphasis.

Cole stood and shoved his gun in the back of his waistband then held out the car keys. "Bullshit, but I'm gonna let you go anyway."

Deirdre

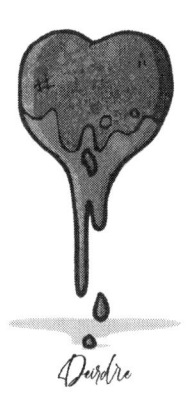

I STRETCHED MY HAND ACROSS THE EMPTY SHEETS BESIDE ME, MY other one rubbed Saint Christopher where he hung around my neck. I'd woke three days ago to find Niall gone and the amulet he'd worn every moment that I'd known him in his place. I hadn't been able to move much from this exact position since.

A soft knock at the door made me get up. Well, I knew whoever it was would come in and perch on the edge of my bed, but *I* made me get up. Everything hurt, there was a constant thump at my temple, but I had to get through this. My freedom was on the other side. Even if without Niall, I wasn't sure I wanted it.

I opened the door to find Filly standing there. With cinnamon rolls.

"How ya doing?" she asked with a half-smile.

"Better now," I answered, taking the warm treats even though I had less than zero desire to eat. "Thank you."

I turned back for the bed and folded my legs beneath me.

"Am I bothering you?" Filly asked still hovering at the door.

"No. You're welcome. I'm just not good company." I shrugged as I started picking at the warm dough.

"Well they're all fighting so…" She trailed off as she slid against the headboard.

I couldn't help but chuckle. Cole and Brye sparred like it was a sport. The house would be so quiet for a few hours then they'd erupt. Conrad seemed to have his own game going that revolved around starting them off. I kinda loved it. The sound was freedom and family incarnate.

If the pain of losing Niall wasn't the shadow of my every move, I could have been happy in Colorado.

"Love is weird." She sighed.

"Tell me about it." I wasn't sure how I managed to laugh but I did. Even if it just shook the heavy weight of my heart.

"Do you want to? Tell me about it, I mean?"

I thought about it for a moment, aimlessly picking apart my cinnamon roll. I didn't want to look too hard at it, at Niall, but I couldn't lose him. I couldn't lose any little piece of him.

"He only eats Chicago deep dish pizza," I said with a smile. "And that curl has hung in his eye every single day since I met him." I could picture brushing it out of his face as a benchmark to our lives. "He used to play lacrosse at Northwestern but that seems like a different life."

"Was he always so serious?" she asked.

I had to search for the man he'd been twelve years ago—the man he was now was all consuming. But if I looked hard enough, I could see the way he'd softened for me. He'd never been a savage, but he'd been hard to crack. He hadn't had many friends. No one fucked with him on the lacrosse field.

"He always had a soft spot for me."

"It's a heady feeling isn't it? To be the one that finds a way through their defenses." She smiled. "If he's anything like Brye, what he keeps hidden is precious and perfect."

He was. For me anyway. And remembering that made the fist that clenched my chest wrench tight. I was in a house of people who'd gotten their happily ever afters staring down the barrel of losing my happiness completely.

I'd become Deirdre of the Sorrows after all, doomed for a future filled with tragedy.

That fortune teller would be pleased wherever she was. She had predicted the death and destruction. The pain. She'd said I'd needed a solider—which I'd found in Niall after all. Now I was old enough to know that the soldier from the legend died in the end anyhow. Wasn't he dead to me like this? Honestly, the only thing left to follow the story was for me to die.

Maybe this, living without Niall every day, would do it in the end anyway.

"Thank you for the cinnamon rolls, Filly." It was the only sentence I could still verbalize for her.

She smiled a sad but knowing smile. "Of course." She leaned forward and squeezed on my arm. I knew the move was meant to spread hope—that's what she and Elle seemed to embody—but I tensed and had to fight the urge to deck her. "It'll be over soon." She chuckled. "We're leaving today."

"Oh, okay." I sounded like an idiot, but it was all I could manage.

"A few days and you'll be free of us," she added, turning at the doorframe.

"You know it's not you guys, right, Filly? Not really anyway."

She nodded and a genuine smile spread across her face. "Ride with us. We can torture Brye with a podcast or a Harry Potter audiobook or something."

My smile pulled up in the most genuine matching smile I could manage.

I SPENT TOO LONG LOOKING BACK at the massive cabin in the woods. Leaving it felt like leaving the last bit of Niall I'd been able to hold on to. When we drove away, there was nowhere that held the ghost of us. Nowhere for either of us to haunt in the hopes of a whispered or stolen touch from the other.

The afternoon wind started to pick up as I stood at the open car door, my fingers rubbing Saint Christopher where he hung at my neck. It seemed to urge us out, or maybe just onward.

"It just sits here empty?" I asked as Brye came down the steps.

"Waiting for someone else that Dexter trusts to use it." He shrugged. "He might Air B&B it."

"So I can't… We couldn't… There's no way…"

He gave me a halfhearted smile. "He's not coming back. Even if he was welcome, he didn't seem like backward was an option."

"Right," I said, trying to stay strong against each of the hits I'd been given.

Brye opened the driver's door and turned to face me. "I know how weird it is, Deirdre. I do." He laid his hand on mine. "But it's time to realize that you're free."

My eyes watered, my shoulder ached, and I was about ten seconds away from punching a hole through the nearest wall, but I wouldn't sleep. I couldn't. If I did, I dreamt of her.

This was right. Wasn't it?

No. I couldn't think about that. About her. The dream of Drea was selfish even if she was the only dream I'd ever really had. And this was right. Getting Ardan and Ailee was right.

And I'd have the details in about five minutes if Dillinger was on time.

My eyes flicked from the parking lot to the clock and back again. I was looking for a delivery van. Flowers if things went well, cakes if we needed to talk and rentals if I needed to get fuck out of town. I double checked the list one more time, trying to keep my thoughts occupied.

Just then a van with a wedding cake pulled into the motel parking lot. They pulled past the spot in front of room 118 and backed up to it, blocking my view of the door. I was supposed to be inside in one minute, but I sat watching the van instead. At the last moment, the driver got out and rather than heading to the room, he walked across the parking lot toward a diner.

"Shit."

I tucked the knife I'd been carrying into my pant leg and my gun into the waistband of my pants and shoved out of the truck door to trot across the parking lot. I leaned in to listen to the room as I knocked. A few footsteps were the only warning I got before the door whipped open.

"McDonough, get in here." A disembodied called me in.

I pulled my gun as I slid into the near-dark room. The blinds were drawn and all the lights were off.

"Put it down or I'll put you down," the same voice commanded.

I let it swivel on my finger as I held my hands up in surrender. "We needed to talk, Dillinger?"

"Payment." He came close enough that I saw the same calm, detached look on his face that Ardan got before he blew something up or cut someone's tongue out. "The Ryans said you wouldn't be able to front more cash."

"A couple thousand, tops," I answered as he took my gun and I swallowed.

I hadn't thought about this. About what I would pay. Drea had been worried, and I hadn't given it a second thought. I was an idiot.

"It's going to take me one week to get them out. I have the appropriate guards in place. A means of transport. It's just biding our time until the planets align." His voice was oily and slithered around the dark room.

"Okay." I drug out the word.

"You're going to spend that week making payments."

He stepped in front of me and I finally got a good look at him. Dillinger was almost as tall as I was with bright blue almost ghost white eyes. He'd shaved his head completely and it highlighted the scars that cut across his face and eye. He was strong but not bulky, something about the way he carried himself told me he didn't need to be.

"What kind of payments?" I wasn't sure I wanted the answer.

When his smile curled in the corners I knew. This was going to be hurt.

"I know about the Chicago families. Their penchant for filth and flesh." His hand came to my chest and I went absolutely rigid. "The Ulsters had The Pit didn't they?"

I swallowed as his hand moved lower. It took everything in me not to grab his hand and break it. Or reach for the knife in my sock and plunge it into his chest. I'd known payment was necessary. I'd chosen to ask for help. But I hadn't expected this. I had to ball my hands at my sides.

Besides, he still had my gun in his other hand.

"My line of work is lonely." He bit his lip and stepped closer.

I couldn't believe it. I mean, I could but why hadn't I planned for it? If I hadn't been fixated on Drea, maybe I would have thought this through. Bringing it back up was never a bad idea. Even just a street whore. If I'd told Drea why I needed her to come, maybe... I stopped my thoughts. Never. I would never have let her take my place. I chose this.

"Did Mac Ulster let you play?" he asked as he toyed with the edge of my shirt. "Or were you a plaything?"

Fuck. Hadn't I been just another toy regardless of which one it had felt like at the time.

"What happens if you don't get them out?"

"You get your money back." He kissed my neck as his hand pushed beneath the waistband of my pants. "I've got a big boy this time." He palmed my dick, which didn't feel particularly inspired by his touch. "Guys not your thing?" His hand moved lower as he held my balls in his hand and massaged them. My dick twitched whether I wanted it to or not. "Maybe I could be." He chuckled as he shoved my pants to the floor.

"No," I grit out.

"Getting to take my payment against your will? Even better." He fell to his knees in front of me. "And a way to get what I want from you." He shoved his thumb into the gauze covering my now exposed bullet wound.

"Ah!" I screamed.

"I'll make you scream again."

I closed my eyes and thought of Drea. I'd pushed her as far away as possible over the past few days but as Dillinger closed his mouth around me, I embraced her. The feel of her mouth. The way she sounded and smelled during sex. But more than that too. The way she made me smile, the way she'd chased all this darkness away.

The more I thought of her, the harder I got. Dillinger laughed as he swallowed me. I jerked back on instinct. His hand just above my wound tightened, making me wince. The gun he'd taken moved to an identical spot on the opposite leg.

"You're going to cum on my face then I'm going to return the favor in your ass." He squeezed one hand and flipped the safety with the other. "The longer it takes, the more *creative* I'll have to get."

I forced myself to stay still this time. To let him hollow out his cheeks on me.

Drea. Just Drea. I would think of her and only her. She lived through years of this. I could live through a week. Survive. This was what she'd done, I could do it too.

I pictured her body.

The first time she'd taken off her clothes in front of me was fucking magic. Her body was soft back then, gentle curves speaking of her naiveté. I'd been fucking floored. She wasn't the girls from porn or that showed off on Instagram accounts—she was better because she was in front of me. And vulnerable. I wanted to beat my chest, both because I had her and because I wanted to protect her.

Dillinger let my dick pop from his mouth. The sway of my now very hard, cock was almost painful. His hand started stroking on my shaft as he ducked down and sucked my balls into his mouth.

I cried out, and I hated for how much pleasure was in that sound. That pleasure belonged to Drea.

Drea. I went back to her, to her body.

That first day when Mac had her bent over the couch, before I'd known it was her, I just wanted that body. Every bit of her on display had been temptation. If Mac had asked me, I would have shoved in without hesitation. Until she moaned. Then that sound struck something deeply buried inside me.

How had I ever hated her? How had I not seen why she left?

Fucking Mac. I could have had her. I could have built a life with her. And God, that turned me on more than her body. Those few mornings I'd seen her in nothing but her pajamas, those nights eating take-out on my bed. That was a different kind of turn on.

One that wouldn't fade.

Dillinger let my balls drop and swallowed me whole. His nose brushed below my bellybutton

I shook with want. With the fury. How had I let her go?

The flashes of us since I killed Mac started flipping through my mind. Her body in the Ryan's bed. Her eyes when I shoved into her mouth. The arch of her spine when she was a goddess above me. That fucking hiss when I'd promised to destroy her so that I and I alone could pick up the pieces.

Not just those but her laughing in the passenger seat of my car. Eating Hot Tamales for dinner and her yelling at the Housewives on TV. The way she swam in my hoodie but had worn it every day since we left my house anyway. And Saint Christopher hanging between her breasts.

I gave out one haggard cry and Dillinger knew.

He pulled back and grabbed me, fisting hard on my dick and pumping twice before I shot onto his waiting face. He had his mouth open, and fuck me if I didn't feel like he was going to swallow my soul rather than my cum. Though the blood rushed from my head, I could still make out the hunger in his eyes.

It wasn't Drea's.

Fury rode the tail of my orgasm. At Mac for taking her. At Dillinger for taking this from me. But most of all, at myself for ever thinking I could fucking live without her.

"You're a beast," Dillinger said as he smoothly stood from the floor. "This is going to be a good week. I might give you back your money if your mouth is as good as that was."

Not yet I told myself. He had a gun and I needed it to level the playing field. I didn't know the layout of the room or what other weapons he had. I just knew I needed to get the fuck out of here.

I shouldn't have been here in the first place. It took a fucking bald psychopath sucking my dick to really drive that home.

"Bend over." He drove his knee into the back of my bad one and twisted my body so that my arms had to shoot out to brace myself.

He slapped my ass. Hard. A hatred and anger so real and raw roared through me. This fucker was going to die.

I thanked God himself for keeping the lights off. Dillinger couldn't see my fury, he couldn't see my wheels turning. I remembered the knife in my sock and reviewed what little I knew about Dillinger and my surroundings.

It was a basic motel, which meant that there was probably a dresser and TV against one wall and either one bed or two on this wall. There might have been a table and chair closer to the window. Maybe a dresser in between. I couldn't assume but if there was an edge to any of that...

Dillinger shoved my shirt up to my shoulders, pulling my attention back to the man himself as he pressed my face down to the bed. It was his skin against mine.

That meant he was wearing short-sleeves.

A belt buckle scraped my ass cheek as he fiddled with it. My mind wanted to wander to Drea, to the play we'd had with belts, but I focused. I fucking had to. The sound of a zipper sent shivers up my spine and he pressed his body, including his rock hard dick, against the curve of my ass.

If only I could make him suffer.

"I gotta tell you, I was nervous to accept part of the payment after but..." He bent over and slid down my body—he was wearing just a t-shirt—where he sprawled across me, "...you're the type of man that can take it the way I want to give it."

Fuck that.

I shot for my sock as fast as I could. The second my hand was around the handle I flipped the switch that set the blade free and twisted to shove it into his ribs. I got lucky when I slid in with little resistance. He bellowed as I twisted it. When I pulled it out, I acted on instinct and drove my knee up into his groin.

It was the wrong knee. I winced in pain and tried to set the leg down and couldn't without a yelp and a fresh shot of pain. Even with a gargled breath, Dillinger lunged at me, discharging a shot just as I pulled him off-kilter. The bullet lodged in one of the walls.

Shit.

That sound limited how much time I had by a long shot. I needed to finish this if I wanted to get out.

If I wanted to get back to Drea.

Each of Dillinger's breaths were raspy, and I knew he wouldn't last forever, but he came after me again, and that told me that he would last long enough. He bear hugged around me and tried to get a steady stance. I tried to do the same but we were both caught with our fucking pants down. My arms were pinned to my sides.

He kept angling for my knee, and I kept shuffling as best I could. But I used his move as inspiration, bending my arm where I could and slamming my fist into his ribs. He cried out and arched back just enough that I got my hands free.

I reached up and without much ceremony, snapped his neck.

His body went limp in my arms a moment before I dumped the fucker on the ground. I bent and pulled up my pants then flicked the curtains enough to look outside. No cops. Yet. It let in enough light that I could grab my knife, my gun and the bag of God knows what Dillinger had brought in.

I checked out the window one more time before I slid out of the hotel room. I was halfway across the parking lot when the cake van behind me revved to life. The van spun out on the dirt of the parking lot and I could tell it was coming for me.

It took every ounce of my strength left to start running toward the truck. I skittered around to the driver's side and yanked on the handle. The back door of the van whipped open and I fumbled with my gun.

But then I froze.

There was a manic ginger man with a smile that hinted at his insanity holding open the door. Ardan somehow managed to smile even wider and appear even a little more insane as he greeted me.

"Get in the goddamned van, Niall."

Deirdre

"I can't do this," I blurted out when we were only three cars back from the border patrol.

"You can and you fucking will," Brye snapped from up front. "If you bail now, it'll look suspicious as hell. We're not exactly saints up here." He grabbed Filly's hand and kissed the back of it as if that might help. "Besides, we'll have no idea if that passport works." He eyed me in the rearview mirror.

"I don't want to find out without Niall," I said with a humph, crossing my hands across my chest.

"You guys had a chance. We all tried to warn you."

"Brye, stop…" Filly tried to diffuse the tension.

"I thought I needed out more than I needed him," I grumbled.

"You did and you do. You want someone commanding you to bend over and take it in the ass in exchange for another night of protection?" His voice escalated until it drowned out the general din of the checkpoint. "That's what you're missing out on. Guarantee it."

"What do you mean guarantee it?" I grabbed the front seats and pulled myself forward.

"What currency do you think he has out there?" Brye asked as he pulled the car up to next in line.

"You didn't give him the money?" I hadn't meant to be shrill, but I wasn't mad that I'd gotten there.

"What did you do, Brye?" Filly shook loose of his hand and

leaned away from him in the front seat.

"I got him a guy that is exceptional at prison breaks and accepts alternate forms of currency," he answered with a shrug.

"I'm going to kill you," I growled as I launched at him, my arms landing around his neck so I could squeeze. And bash his head against the back of the seat.

The car in front of us pulled away but Brye only gagged rather than pull forward. Brye tried to say something about the small swatch of pavement in front of us and the guards moving closer but I gave zero fucks. Filly launched out of her seat only to crash her forearm down on mine.

"Ouch!" I yelped as my hands released Brye on instinct.

He pulled forward still gasping for air. "Lover's quarrel," he said simply in his charming voice as they took our passports. I saw him wink in the mirror at the guard standing a few feet from us. "Two chicks, one Baja hotel room. It'll be worth it in the end, am I right?"

The urge to strangle him all over again made my fingers itch.

The border agent looked at all of us again slowly and deliberately. Then he started a closer inspection of the documents. Filly shot me a look that was a scolding in and of itself.

"¿Que esta pasando aqui?" Another agent—the one Brye had winked at—barked at the man with our passports.

"Nada, pero…"

I didn't understand Spanish but the way he bowed his head said he was deferring to a supervisor.

"¿Ellos son buenos?"

"Si, pero…"

The man who'd interrupted—conveniently the one Brye had winked at grabbed our passports and shoed the agent away. He slid into the small box to double check the documents and returned a moment later.

"I'd suggest you don't draw attention to yourself next time," he said under his breath, he gestured to grease his palm. Brye pulled out a roll of cash. "Muévanse," the agent yelled louder, banging twice on the roof.

I waited a few miles down the road before the angry words dredged up from my throat. "How dare you, Brye. I've seen you do despicable things but this?"

"Come the fuck on Deirdre. If it wasn't Niall, if you didn't love him then you would find this funny too."

"I would never—" I started only for him to interrupt.

"All those years he kept girls down in those fucking cages—even the months he kept you—and now he gets the tiniest bit of payback..." His smirk spread in the rearview mirror, I thought about clawing it off. "There's a poetic justice to it."

"That's not exactly funny, Brye," Filly scolded from the front seat.

"I wasn't going for funny, I was going for what he deserves." He chuckled at himself.

"You sit there on a high horse, like all your sins have somehow been redeemed as if all your shit has been wiped clean." I sat back and crossed my arms across my chest, staring at the Mexican desert rolling by. I missed Niall, so badly it hurt, and Brye only made it worse. "He deserves a happy ending just like the one you fucking got," I said with a humph.

"No he doesn't," Brye spat.

"Hey..." Filly scolded.

"Why's that, Brye?" I asked with venom in my voice.

"Don't make me say it."

"I want to hear you say it," I bit out.

"I knew you liked pain, but this is just fucking masochistic." He rolled his eyes.

"Say it!"

"He didn't pick you, Deirdre. He didn't pick you, so he doesn't fucking deserve you."

I'd known they were coming but the weight of his words crashed on me, their sting something harsh that welted my skin and zapped my strength. I settled back into the seat, pulling Niall's sweatshirt around me. I breathed in the smell of him still lingering on the fabric and knew deep in the pit of my soul that I would never feel the same.

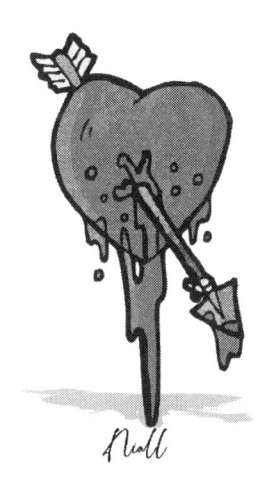

"I was a fucking fool," I said, leaning my head back against the wall in the back of the van.

"Fuck yeah, you were." Ardan laughed. "Us over pussy I *kinda* get but over your girl? Over Drea? That's bullshit and you know it."

Dillinger had broken them out that morning. His motives for lying were beyond me, unless maybe it was his way to make me feel like I had to let him fuck me. Whatever it was, he was dead, and they were out. I was grateful.

"It seemed like the right thing to do at the time." I closed my eyes and surrendered to the vision of Drea etched behind my eyelids. "It was us against the world for so long. I figured I owed you my loyalty."

"And what about what you owed her?" It was the first sentence Ailee had uttered to me in the hours she'd been driving.

I took the break in her self-imposed silence as an invitation to move forward in the van and explain myself. "She had people to help her. She had protection. I figured she would understand."

"That the man she loved picked *anything* over her." She made a sputtering sound. "Yeah she'll understand all right. She'll understand that you're a fucking prick who fed her nothing but lies, and she'll remember all men are pigs."

I raised my eyebrows and shimmied back to the seat I'd taken across from Ardan.

"Didn't get to talk to her much in there what with the separate cells and whatnot, but she was this cagey before we went in *and* after we got out." His eyes went wide and a sarcastic smile replaced his wicked one. "It's gonna be a long fucking trip."

"Cut her some slack," I offered.

"When she's about to cut my tongue out?" He chuckled. "I don't think so."

"Why don't you drive for a little while," I urged him.

"We're going to need gas soon," Ailee interjected.

"Pull over next chance you have." I pulled a roll money from my pocket. "I'm probably the least wanted felon." I tossed it up and caught it.

We drove for a little while longer, until there was a busier gas station. I made sure to scan my surroundings then managed to get gas uneventfully. When we got back in the van, Ailee settled into the back with me.

I waited until Ardan turned on the radio and let the soft whines of the country station and the rhythmic thump of the tires filled up the front seat before I spoke up.

"Wanna talk about it?"

She shook her head then let it fall in her hands.

"Come on, Ailee. I know what it's like to hurt," I said softly. I scooted across the back to sit next to her, she leaned her head against my shoulder. I blew out a deep breath and reached for her hand. "I know what you're like when you're hurt."

"This is all my fault," she murmured. "I ruined everything. Chicago, the FBI, Drea…"

"Oh, I'm pretty sure I ruined things with Drea all on my own." The sorrow swelled in my heart.

"No, it was my idea to put you two together—"

"And I'm grateful for that. I'm so grateful I got her back if only for a short time." I smiled even though it ached. Drea and all those moments with her were something I'd hold on to for a long time. Maybe forever.

"I don't know if I am yet," she said softly.

"Don't know if you're what?"

"Grateful." She sighed. "I don't know if the good can outweigh the bad."

"I'm lost, Ailee. Fill in the blanks for me." I leaned forward enough to look down on her. Her ruby red hair cascaded across her face and down my chest. It didn't cover the single tear that slid down her cheek.

"I don't know if the good memories of him outweigh his betrayal."

"What?" I pushed back to arms length.

"That guy I was screwing…?" she started only to trail off with a sigh. "It wasn't just screwing. I tried to tell myself it was but…"

I wasn't sure how my heart could hurt any worse than it already did but it ached for her.

"Can we send for him once we're somewhere safe and have some money again?"

She squeezed my hand that much tighter. "He can never know."

"What? Why?"

She hesitated for a while, but her grip didn't waver. "He's an FBI agent. *The* FBI agent. The one that put the entire family away."

"Holy fuck." I hadn't meant to say it, but I could *not* keep that shit in.

"Pretty much." She sighed.

There were a lot of things on the tip of my tongue. A million things maybe. She was the one that was always so perceptive. She was the one that saw things coming.

"Did you know?"

"Did I know? Are you stupid?" She sat up and glared at me, the fire I was familiar with lapping at her gaze. I held it, unafraid until she folded. "Yeah, I knew." She blew out a deep breath. "I didn't know he'd found something."

"Would it have changed anything?"

Her eyes searched the bottom of the van, scanning side to side. "No."

"I know that feeling." I shrugged. "Every moment with her was so good. It made me forget about the bad. Or prepared me to fight them. I don't even know."

"It was just a happiness you'd never known?" Ailee smiled but another tear streaked down her cheek.

"And a strength too."

I thought about that moment that Drea had run to me on the hill in Colorado. She'd held me with a ferocity and tenderness I hadn't known could coexist. She calmed the killing storm brewing inside me with nothing but her touch. She brought me back to myself. I'd wanted nothing more than to sit in that moment with her.

"You gotta get her back, Niall." More tears spilt down her cheeks, but she smiled at me.

"I don't know how," I said softly.

"I won't let you feel like this." She shoved at her wet cheeks.

"I don't know that it's avoidable at this point." I shrugged. "I don't know where she is."

"Well who does?" Ardan asked in his simplistic way that I realized I knew exactly who knew. And now I had a way to find them. My smile so rarely given out, spread. Ardan noticed in the rearview mirror.

"Let's go get your girl."

Deirdre

I SUPPOSE IT WAS ALL THOSE ROMANTIC MOVIES THAT HAD ME looking around the gate area, hoping that Niall would be there. The reality was that he didn't know where I was, and he didn't know where I was going.

The tidal wave of emotion slammed into me like it had been from time to time since he left. Each surge threatened to drown me. But I made myself breathe through it. I bit my trembling bottom lip and closed my eyes. Sure I saw Niall there but there was a stillness when I shuttered the world away. When it was just me and the memory.

Sorrow was a knot I could swallow down.

Hadn't I been doing that for years anyway?

Niall had always been the little piece I kept for myself. The vision behind my eyes, the person I imagined was there when things got hard. I could go back to that time. Couldn't I?

The answer was no.

Not now.

"Atencion en el area de la puerta. El vuelo número 315 a Narita ha comenzado a abordar. Si se encuentra en el grupo A, por favor haga cola detrás del podio." The voice came on over the crackling intercom.

I didn't know much Spanish, but I knew the number 315, the place Narita, and the phrase grupo A. This was me. I slung my bag over my shoulder and took one final look around. There were no piercing eyes, no muscled up man with tattooed sleeves. It was just me, with all the other random people going off to random places. So very many places. Anywhere in the globe really. Even if Niall found out where I left, where I was going…

Fucking Christ. I grabbed Saint Christopher where he hung around my neck. It was the only way I could stave off the panic when I thought about how endless the possibilities were. How impossible it all seemed.

My hands shook as I took out the English book I'd been lucky enough to find in the airport and stored a few treats in the seat pocket in front of me. I took a deep breath, then another. My hands stilled, and I turned my attention to the people filing onto the plane. Face after face until they blurred together.

I settled back against my seat, letting the world turn to mush. Maybe I would sleep. Maybe this would eventually feel like normal rather than numbing.

Just when I was fading out completely, a thickly tattooed arm appeared on the seatback in front of me. My heartbeat sped up, and my mouth went dry. Everything inside me swelled—lust, love and hope in crushing amounts. I looked up almost expectantly.

"There's nowhere else on this plane that I'd rather be," a dark, honied voice said as he pointed to the open seat beside me.

But it wasn't the one I wanted to hear.

I got up with a small smile and let him shuffle in. He was built like Niall but in even just a few seconds I found all the ways he didn't measure up.

"Where you headed?" He leaned over.

His eyes were green but they just reminded me of a sweater I used to wear. His hair was cut like a hipster but it was a few greasy, straight strands that hung in his eyes. All of his tattoos were cheap.

I forced a smile as I said nothing, and I grabbed my book.

"A mysterious minx." He leaned in and started reading over my shoulder somehow thinking it was cute.

"A wanted FBI felon fleeing North America for a non-extradition country if you must know," I corrected him as I smiled and batted my eyelashes.

He laughed but it was shaky and fell short as he debated whether I was telling the truth. If I wasn't mistaken, he was a little scared. Niall would have laughed. Loud and big and brash.

This time it wasn't sorrow but a longing so deep it gnawed on my bones. I had a feeling the wicked dog of fate would do that to me from time to time. It could have my bones. I didn't really want them anymore.

"Were you... uh... serious?" The wannabe next to me asked.

"Hit on me again and maybe you'll find out." I winked then opened the cover of the book I'd bought.

Of course it read *Once upon a time...*

"IF I HAVE ONE REGRET IN THIS ENTIRE LIFE, IT'S THAT I DIDN'T cut Brye MacCowan deeper and watch his guts spill out onto the fucking floor," I roared as I slammed Dillinger's phone down on the hot asphalt of the Mexican highway. It shattered.

"He didn't give you any info?" Ardan asked from where he leaned against the Chevy we'd stolen once we walked across the border in Nogales.

"They dropped her off at the Mexico City Airport two days ago with enough money to go anywhere. They didn't ask questions." Something jagged ripped at my heart. It felt a lot like loss but it was honed and sharpened in the shape of a knife.

"Those fuckers," Ardan agreed

"Stop and think, Niall," Ailee said in her steady voice. "You know her. Where would she go?"

"I don't know this." I kicked the shattered phone.

Ailee stepped in front of me and crossed her arms on her chest with an exasperated sigh. "Don't even feed me that bullshit. Think, Niall."

What did I know about Drea that was soul deep? What would she make decisions based on? I played all our conversations over again in my mind while the wind whipped sand from the roadside into my face. It was grit peeling at my skin as the heat baked it. I turned my back into the wind to protect myself…

That was it.

Drea had, for as long as I had known her, acted on the desire to be safe. Even that stupid fucking prophecy that had caused us trouble before Mac was about a savior.

"She's a survivor," I blurted. Ailee smiled.

"Then she'll know to get somewhere they can't drag her back from," Ailee answered, her eyes sparking. "Non-extradition narrows it considerably. Think of that list, which of those countries would she go to?"

"Something familiar." I knew she wouldn't go somewhere where she'd stick out, or somewhere that had customs that made her uncomfortable.

"What's familiar?"

"Dubai, Marrakesh or Bali," Ardan said with certainty.

"What?" Ailee and I said in unison.

"Housewives." He shrugged. "Beverly Hills went to Dubai in season six, New York went to Marrakesh in season four and Orange County went to Bali in season nine."

"Are you serious?"

"Yeah they're always the most epic fight episodes. You know what they say about traveling with people."

I blinked a few times at him. It was the most outrageous and quite possibly the most logical argument I'd ever heard Ardan make all at once.

But it sounded like Drea.

It sounded like those few nights where my best friend and my girlfriend filled my house with laughter. It sounded like the precious moments I hadn't meant to keep but was incredibly grateful I had. I mean, honestly, it made me sound like a pussy and I'd never been so fucking grateful to be one.

"Bali," I said, knowing.

It was the cheapest of the three. The safest. She'd blend right in with the abundance of tourists. She'd survive there.

Not to mention she'd had that massive beach photo on her wall at the MacCowans place.

"You're sure?" Ailee asked.

A smile—another real fucking smile—pulled at my cheek. "The only thing I'm more sure of is that I can't live without her.."

Deirdre

Bali was not what I expected. After over twenty-eight hours of flying, I'd been craving pristine beaches and tranquility. From the air, it seemed bustling and beautiful but when I landed, I had to take a deep breath to stave off the panic.

Denpasar was hot and crowded. Sweat dripped down my back almost immediately. Cars, busses, and motorcycles all shoved into the wrong lanes of traffic. Horns sounded regularly and there were offers in kind but broken English every few feet for tours, taxis. No one was rude, I never felt unsafe, but I felt alone.

This wasn't just missing Niall—though that pain had become my very shadow—this was knowing that there was no one. No one was coming. I had no help, no companionship, no confidant. Freedom and independence looked a lot like isolation on the other side of the world.

Tears burned at the corners of my eyes and a knot built in my throat.

With another deep breath I realized something though. I was free. I didn't have to look over my shoulder to see if Mac was there. Or a MacCowan. No one would use me for my body again. A smile spread across my face. There was no FBI on my tail and even if they were, they could go fuck themselves.

I was free.

A giggle bubbled up in my throat on the street, mixing up with the tears that had threatened to fall. Niall had fought for me and given me this gift. He'd been my soldier, my savior, my everything even if we were something twisted too.

I sagged against the shop next to me and tried to wade through the mix of emotions barreling through me. What I needed was to sleep. Without Niall I doubted it would be a blissful respite but it had to give me enough of a recharge to make a plan.

To make a new life.

I was going to drown in the wave of overwhelming that sentence became. I didn't have a formal education to get a job, I didn't have the slightest idea of how to find a place to live, I knew no one and had nowhere to start. I didn't even have a phone to start researching.

If only I could curl up under the covers and forget that any of this had happened.

A tear rolled down my cheek as I looked around the Denpasar street. As if someone still bothered to look out for me, my answer lay just a little ways ahead.

I stepped into the internet cafe to find cheap plastic furniture, an ancient computer, and a man with a genuine smile. He immediately came out and started helping me, his exuberance obvious in each of his wild gestures he used to communicate. There was something reassuring about him, his willingness to help. His genuine gratitude that I was in his cafe.

When the internet was up and running, I stared at the screen for a second. What did I Google? How to start your life over? That yielded a lot of results that made a case for some serious soul searching and therapy. I tried *moving to Bali* only to find I'd already screwed up on the visas and wasn't exactly set up for any kind of success when it came to working or living here. The only thing I'd managed to feel confident was printing off a few pages of common Balinese phrases so I could say *please* and *thank you* without sounding like a complete jackass.

On everything else I felt like a failure. An idiot. Even helpless.

The tears threatened to come back and it was only the kind cafe owner that kept me from falling to bits at the keyboard.

One more deep breath. I knew that I could get through

anything, I'd done it for years. I just needed to compartmentalize and move forward. If I ate a good meal and slept in a comfortable bed, tomorrow I could figure out the visas. Once I figured out the visas, I could find a job. Then a house. I had enough money to stay in a hotel while that happened. Unless of course…

I stopped myself.

Find a fucking hotel.

What did I know about the island? Or about choosing a place to stay? *Nothing,* the angry and scared voice inside of me reminded.

Well nothing outside of The Real Housewives trip. I smiled. Those episodes were a blow out. Beautiful though. I Googled the hotel they'd stayed in and found it really wasn't far from where I was now. It was expensive but Brye and Filly had taken good care of me. I could do it for a few nights. As a treat. Well that's how I justified it anyway.

"Matur suksma," I said practicing my new thank you very much as I paid and left the cafe.

I hailed a cab and gave them the address, following the advice of one of the Google articles and asking for the meter to go on.

The Mulia was everything I remember from the episodes. It was grandeur tucked among the palm trees. It was a treat I'd never had, sure as hell never given myself. Some of the fear broke free, and I finally felt the excitement. Even if I was bone tired, this was bucket list sort of stuff.

In my room I tossed my single bag on the giant bed and watched the plush bedding poof up around it. I walked into the bathroom, flipped on the warm water to fill the bathtub, then pressed against the floor to ceiling window. The pools of the resort rippled thanks to the graceful fountains adorned in lotus flowers, the ocean rolled against the sand just beyond. Everything was vibrant and alive.

Maybe even me.

But as I slid into the tub, I knew that wasn't quite right. Maybe it never would be.

Not without Niall.

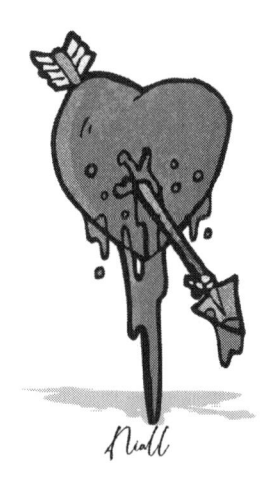

TWENTY-EIGHT HOURS ON A PLANE WAS ENOUGH TO MAKE ANYONE want to murder. Me? I had plotted the death of at least fifteen different people on the plane, figured out how to kill most of them with items within reach, and there were even a few different ways to hide bodies.

But then I stepped out of the plane and into the Bali heat.

It was the kind of heat that pressed on my chest and choked my throat, but I welcomed it. Drea was here and here was a fresh start.

Ardan had told me the hotel the Housewives had stayed in before he chose to stay with his sister. She was going to find some way to do what I was doing. She was going to win her happily ever after. None of us deserved them but I finally wanted to be the soldier that trudged through the muck and mire to fight for mine. In her own way, she wanted that too.

I flagged a taxi down and told him the hotel. We haggled over the price, and I finally rolled my eyes and caved. We drove through Denpasar and I barely noticed. I just kept looking for her. On street corners, at shops, in the food stalls. Every tall, remotely attractive brunette became Drea, my fantasies compounded by anticipation.

But when we pulled up to the hotel, I got nervous.

What if she wasn't here? What if she wasn't in Indonesia at

all? God, my chest went tight, and my hand went to where Saint Christopher should have been.

What if she didn't want to see me? I hadn't said goodbye…

"Niall?"

That voice, that utter siren song, was for me. It was mine. Every dulcet, butter note stilled my heart and stole my breath.

"Drea?"

I looked up to find her framed by the lush palms of the courtyard growing into the open walkways. She wore a bikini that had soaked through a drapey gauze-like cover up. The faint lines of her body were visible beneath it. Shock colored her face even beneath the big sunglasses she wore.

"Are you real?" Her voice barely reached across the lobby.

"A real asshole for not coming with you in the first place." I drifted closer to her.

"But you're here now?" She tried to smile but she choked on a sob instead.

I didn't answer her this time. There was nothing to say, I just walked straight to her and gathered her up in my arms. She wrapped her arms around my neck and hugged me fiercely, burying her face in my neck.

"I didn't know… I didn't think…" Her tears were warm against the curve of my neck. "How did you find me?"

"Did you know in season nine of The Real Housewives of Orange County they came to this exact hotel?"

She laughed even though it still had the cadence of her tears.

"Ardan told me I could choose Dubai, Marrakesh, or Bali."

That made her laugh even a little harder. "I love you," she whispered.

"I love you." I turned just enough to press a kiss to her head. "And I'll never leave you again. Not ever. Not for anything."

She settled back onto flat feet. "You mean it?" Her bottom lip trembled.

I lifted her sunglasses up and pressed them to hold her hair back. Tears had started down her cheeks, and I lifted my big hands to wipe them away.

"I knew the moment I was going to get what I wanted that it was nothing compared to what I'd had." I leaned my forehead to hers. "I know what you went through, more intimately than I could have ever imagined, and there was no other choice for you. You should have been the only choice for me."

"I made that mistake once too." Her voice was as uneven as it was soft.

"I'm going to make some more, but I'm going to make them with you." I kissed her forehead gently.

She finally unwound from my neck, but the contentment and strength stayed, pressing against me like the tropical heat. It was new and a hair bit uncomfortable, but I craved it. I craved her.

"And speaking of other things I'd like to do with you…" I bent down and nibbled on her ear before pulling back and devouring her whole, flicking my lip ring as I did.

She was still a mix of laughter and tears, but her smile spread. "I seem to recall a promise being made…"

I reached down and snatched her into my arms. When she was tight to my chest, I arched an eyebrow and dropped my voice down lower.

"Not the last one of those I'm going to make to you either."

Deirdre

How? How? How? My heart beat out the question over and over as Niall carried me to the room. How was he here? How did he find me? How did we get this fucking lucky?

He shifted and it was just enough to press Saint Christopher into my skin. It was a reminder that I didn't need to ask, I could just relish his presence. This moment.

"Here?" Niall set me down and pressed me up against the door.

I glanced over just enough to see the room number. "Yes." My word jackknifed with my heart.

"Get in there and get fucking naked." He raised one hand to the doorframe and smacked my ass when I turned to slide my key in the door.

I walked in and waited until the metal clink of the lock latched in place. I didn't need to turn to find his eyes on me. My skin blanched the way it always did when he stared.

"Drea." My name on his lips made my insides flip. "Any last requests?"

"Anything. You can have anything as long as you take it," I said as I pulled the linen cover up over my shoulders.

"I'll make you regret that," he growled from behind me. Goose bumps spread across my skin.

"Try," I whispered as I pulled the string of my bikini loose.

"I promise," he said with a wicked lilt.

Without warning he came up behind me and shoved my

bottoms to the floor. A moment later he wrapped his hand around my middle and carried me the few steps to the bed only to unceremoniously drop me and pin my chest to the mattress with his knee. I couldn't be smothered, not even by Niall, but the weight of him like this was blissful. He had a way of knowing what the line between too much and just enough was.

He left me to wait beneath him until I had to fidget. I couldn't help it. The jolt of pain from his hand landing hard and fast across my ass came just a moment before the snap of his spank rang out. My hands flew to cover up. He batted them away and landed another before pushing two fingers into my sex.

"Fuck," he hissed. "You just drip for me."

He thrust leisurely into me once, twice, three times then kept going. He managed to move slowly, unwavering in the deep but long drawn out path of his fingers. His restraint seemed unending. So much so that I melted into the mattress, lost control of my limbs. The weight of his body just held me still. My breathing started to match his movements, and I couldn't find a way back to myself.

Niall knew. Somehow, he fucking knew, and another *swack* rang out across my ass. I jerked wildly this time, jolted from pleasure to the pain. When I settled back beneath him, he pressed his thumb against the pucker of my backside. I tensed against his touch, but he'd managed to lube his finger somehow. I couldn't resist as he pressed in.

"Fuck me." I bit my lip and my hands clenched the comforter beneath me.

"Oh, I am, and I will be for quite some time today."

He picked up the same slow thrust as he'd had a few moments ago, his movements synchronized both back and front. Slow and torturous all over again. Over and over and over he worked until I thought I might fall off the edge. Only the way he dug into my back kept me anchored.

That singular spanking between his moves slowed my ascent. My body was even more desperate for him, but I wasn't ready to come. Good fuck, I wasn't anywhere close, I was just a puddle of want and need and *please keep going* and *end this* all at once.

Niall changed his tactic, so subtle at first I didn't notice but his thrusts changed, becoming a massage. His two fingers split to rub on either side of his thumb through the thin skin of me between them. This wasn't in and out, this was an exploration. It made me groan and roll my forehead flat against the mattress.

He stretched me, pressed and circled on the spots that drove me insane, then pulled out just as quickly as he'd pushed in. His knee disappeared from my back and my knees knocked together. I sagged into the mattress, my body already Jell-O.

But then the two fingers that had been in my sex reappeared at my flesh. Higher. He pressed into my backside the way he did everything else. Confident and unabashed.

His fingers split into a V a moment before the soft sound of fabric hit the floor behind me. *Fuck, fuck, fuck.* I knew what was coming and I wasn't sure how I'd survive.

Niall's dick pressed against my sex. Even I couldn't deny I was dripping for him, begging him to shove in. Begging him to take me completely.

The bastard moved just as slowly into me as his fingers had before.

I let out a low moan as each bit of him filled me. I was damn near delusional, but I swore I could fill the ridges of him as he pressed in. The feel of him, of Niall McDonough, of *my* Niall buried inside me was...

God almighty, I couldn't describe it, so I grabbed Saint Christopher where he hung around my neck and just prayed. I had no idea whether I was praying for this to end or continue forever—maybe just to make it through.

His fingers massaged on either side of his cock, drawing a hitch from his body and a guttural cry from his lips. I shuddered at the sound.

He managed to find his rhythm again. His discipline in torturous thrusts was unwavering once more. That tell-tale feeling built up in my stomach, molten, bone obliterating flame.

Niall knew.

Again.

He pulled out the exact moment and another severe spank snapped across my ass. It was the match that struck, leaving my orgasm to burn me to the ground.

"You're fucking mine," Niall snarled as he swiftly bent and pressed his lips to my quaking sex. "I own you." He moved over and pressed his lips to my still singing ass cheek. "And that was just the foreplay."

I had to show her that I loved her, cherished her, and put her first in my own special way. Now I was going to ruin her in the same fucking fashion. Mine.

Her body had barely stopped trembling when I pressed my dick to her ass and gracelessly shoved in. She started to scream but I wrapped my hands around her throat and stopped it. Her hands flew to my wrists, but she didn't pull at my hands. She came along for the ride as I pulled her from the mattress to have my way with her.

My tattoos contrasted against her unmarred skin as I held her firmly in place. My hips hit against her as I forced her body to swallow me whole over and over again.

I dropped her throat just to spank her again, relishing the bright red blooming on her ass that likely matched the color her face was turning. She gasped only for one of my hands to crush against her throat again. The other laced into her hair and pulled her head back. The brutal curve of her spine was one of the most beautiful shapes I'd ever seen.

She tried to whimper but her sounds were garbled. Her hand came back to mine, but she could barely manage to find her grip again. The one that stayed on the bed faltered, her motor skills failing too.

When I knew she needed a breath, I let her go. I didn't stop though. No, the way her ass gripped me was too good. The fine line of her ass and the purely sexual shape it made was intoxicating. I couldn't stop.

And even if I could, I wouldn't.

I drug my fingers down the raw curve of her ass before grabbing the fold of her hips. I pulled her back onto me and held her there as I grabbed her knee and slid it onto the bed, first one side then the other. I followed her, kneeling beneath where I kept her perched on my lap. One quick slap to the side of her hip and she started sliding up and down on me.

She sagged back against my chest, draping her body across mine. It was a view I relished and a body I'd destroy. She kept up her movements, the gentle sway of her hips when I bit down on the curve of her neck. She moaned, and I mimicked even though her skin stayed in my mouth.

My hands went to her nipple and her clit. She arched her body into them. I rubbed her clit in small circles and gently flicked her nipple with the pad of my thumb. She moaned again. Just like before, I practiced all the self-restraint I had, making the movement slow and steady. Drea trembled when I just kept at it.

Just like I had before, I suddenly stopped my ministrations and traded them for slaps. First between her legs then up across her breast.

Drea cried out.

I went back to the gentle circles and flicks I'd maintained a minute ago. Deliberate and delicious until her body sank back into the rhythm. She whimpered as she rode me, as I fondled her. The slight tremble of her body started up again, so I stopped only to land three more solid *swacks*. Two on her pert breast separated by one on her clit.

Her sob was some twisted-up combination of agony and ecstasy. I wanted to keep at this for however long I could manage to hold back, but she was breaking. I could hear it in her voice.

I shoved her away from my chest so her face was buried in the comforter. I held her between her shoulder blades with one outstretched hand and landed a few brutal spanks against her already brilliant ass before hammering into it.

Drea's sounds digressed into wild, wounded, and wonderful sobs and screams. She didn't ask to stop, she didn't ask for anything, so I kept going. My thrusts unrelenting. Until I got close.

I pulled out, wincing the moment I dropped out of her. The moment we weren't connected anymore. I pawed at the side of her body and flipped her. She sat gasping for air, her eyes vacant as they stared up at the ceiling. Her whole body shook with the slam of her heart against her chest.

My smile spread despite my heavy breathing as I left her for the bathroom. I threw one towel over my shoulder as I reached for a washcloth. A warm, soapy cloth on my dick was almost painful. I jerked away from my own hand.

But I made myself do it.

When I returned to Drea, her legs spread open, her pussy dripping, I knew it was worth it. All of it was worth it.

I took the towel from my shoulder and folded it beneath her. My hands couldn't stay away, skating across her warm skin before pressing gently against her thigh. I slid my fingers into her and let her have it.

Drea had always been so responsive to my touch, I should have known it wouldn't take my brutal assault on her G-spot too long to yield results. She jerked and writhed against my touch. Her body shook with the ferocity of my strokes. Her eyes found mine, wide and panicked, her mouth open in a silent scream and then she splashed against my hand.

"Fuck," she whimpered, making the word twenty-some-odd syllables, each marked by a jagged shallow breath.

Every inch of skin between her thighs glistened, an invitation to finish what I'd started. I edged slowly back onto the bed.

"I can't," she whimpered.

"Do you trust me?" I asked softly.

"With whatever is left of my very soul." She shook in turn with unshed tears.

I bent to kiss her. One small kiss on each eyelid, one on the tip of her nose before I surrendered to her lips. "Same, Drea." I pulled back and murmured against her lips as I pushed her hand away and slid into her.

Into the only real home I'd ever need.

EPILOGUE

I forgot how crowded Denpasar was. Drea and I had left the beach a few months ago, choosing the quieter forests of Ubud instead. I hadn't been around this many people in three weeks. Crowds somehow made the air thicker, the humidity press in on my chest.

Then I saw the flaming red hair.

Even in the crowded arrivals hall he stood out. The porters shoved for him, yanking on his backpack, and pulling him toward the taxis. He turned toward them and started saying no but they just pulled harder. I shoved through the crowd to get to him.

"Tidak, terima kasi," I said *no, thank you,* as I pushed past the porters and into Ardan's arm. "How are you, ya crazy fucker?"

"Better now. That's a long fucking flight." He stretched, trying to crack his back even though I was still hugging the moron.

"It takes a lot of work to get lost." I chuckled as I patted his shoulder and pulled away. "It's good to see you."

"You too." He smiled and another piece of my heart settled back into place. We started walking out of the airport in easy companionship. "You can ask me, ya know." He chuckled.

"I care about more than the ring." I laughed. "I'm really glad to see you."

"Bullshit." His piercing crazy laugh rang out, making a few of the closest people turn.

I smiled. I couldn't help myself. That laugh meant that I had my batshit crazy friend back. For however long it lasted, I would be grateful.

"Oh come on," Ardan whined. "Ask me!"

"How's your sister?" I took my lip ring into my mouth to keep from laughing harder.

"How's my sister?" He threw his arms up, exasperated. It took everything I had not to lose it. My smiles came so much easier these days. "She's an idiot but she's great." He rolled his eyes.

"Not a fan of the suit?" I asked.

He grunted and waved me off. "Since you're so freaking curious, about *everything* but the reason I came here..." he sighed dramatically, "...yes. I have the ring."

"I never doubted you."

We broke free of the airport turmoil and started walking toward my shitty little half car, half truck half breed. Neither of us fit real well in the cab.

As soon as the doors snapped shut, I folded. "Let me see it."

"I worked really hard to find the perfect one. Though I don't understand why you didn't just get it yourself." He materialized a small black velvet box.

"I can't exactly get it shipped via Amazon Prime. It's Bali, and I'm a wanted felon." I took the box from him and rubbed my finger across the fine fabric. "Plus, I wanted someone to put eyes on it. It had to be perfect."

"And you couldn't?"

"The nearest place that sells Claddagh rings is probably a thirty-three hour flight." And it had to be a Claddagh ring.

"Fuck. You're telling me."

I took a deep breath before I popped the box open. The thin silver band sat on the satin pillow. Delicate hands held a perfect heart topped with an intricate and elegant crown. It was polished but showed the signs of being worn over many, many years. An engraving on the inside read *mo ghrá 1911*.

"Ardan…"

"Yeah, I know." Ardan sagged back against the car seat with a huge smile. "Deirdre's gonna love it. And speaking of Deirdre…"

"She's got stuff planned for you." I couldn't help but shake my head. The next couple of days with Ardan were going to be ridiculous, nothing like our new normal. But that kind of made them perfect for what I was planning.

"What? She's the one getting engaged." He shot me a look.

"Yeah, well, she doesn't know that, and she's not going to learn it from you either, is she?" I growled as I reached over and poked him in the chest.

He shrunk back as I pinned him with a look, proving that I still had that fearsome edge if I needed, but I couldn't hold it. My laugh broke out and coaxed Ardan's wild one to match as I started the car and pulled out of the airport.

"You're different, man." Ardan eyed me as I navigated traffic.

"I am and I'm not." I blew out a breath. "This man, the one who's fucking head over heels was always there, I just buried him under hurt and hate. Those things fed off life with Mac and it was easy to forget. She helped me find myself in the end."

"You don't have to propose to me." Ardan snorted.

I slugged him. Hard. But we both digressed into laughter as I wove through the streets of Denpasar. Scooters flew by, busses ambled until they shot forward, and cars chose their lanes with little care. It took a little while to get comfortable driving, and Drea and I preferred scooters usually, but it felt different having a friend beside me. It felt good.

Bali was starting to feel like home.

We turned and Ardan sucked in a deep breath. The tall wood entryway made me smile too. The Mulia hotel was another type of homecoming. I could still picture her staring at me in disbelief from across the lobby. I could still feel the way my heart raced when I realized I found her. When I found her and got to keep her.

It did the same now just knowing that she was here.

"This is the Housewives hotel isn't it?" Ardan said, shoving his head out of the window to look around.

"I told you Deirdre had something planned."

As soon as I said her name, she seemed to materialize. Her dark hair had lightened here but still fell in easy chocolate waves around her face and down her back. She was wearing a dusty rose dress that hinted at the perfect body beneath and seemed to fade into her darkly tanned skin. My dick twitched as I thought about how perfectly the color matched her nipples.

But it was the smile that broke as she waved at us that I found sexiest of all.

She was happy. The hard and harsh, the sadness and anger of the years we'd spent apart had started to wash away in the turquoise waters of Bali. I rushed to get out, even throwing my keys at the valet a little too hard.

"Hi you." Drea shielded her eyes from the sun, her eyes that were fixated on me.

Ardan didn't exist. At least not for this moment. Nothing but her and I did. The rest of the world fell away. Bali cut through the bullshit and all that was left was us.

I wrapped my arm around her low back and shoved the other into her hair to pull her to me. Her lips hit mine and what was left of me disintegrated. I couldn't feel anything but her lips against mine, the gentle sweep of her tongue across the seam of mine.

"If I wanted to watch two people make out, I would have stayed with Ailee and that fuckhead," Ardan whined. "Or I'd go watch porn."

"There's not much kissing in porn," Drea said as she pulled away and finally smiled at Ardan.

I barely let her go so she could hug him.

"It's good to see you Ardan."

And the longer they squeezed the more I realized I didn't care. There was no jealousy raging in my chest. There was just my heartbeat that said *mine, mine, mine, mine.*

Deirdre

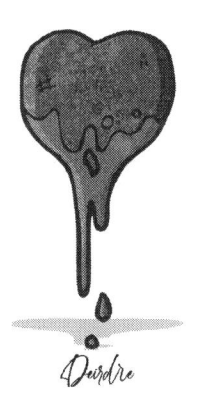

Niall was acting weird. I'd planned a mini Housewives tour for Ardan complete with a few nights at the Mulia, elephant rides, a bike ride to the terraced rice paddies and feeding monkeys. Niall came with us on all of it.

And he didn't complain.

He didn't even roll his eyes.

"Okay, what's going on?" I asked softly as I settled onto the edge of the pool that night. The moon and the firelight reflected off the dark of the water.

Niall slid between my legs, wrapping his big hands around my calves and leaning his head against my knee.

"Nothing," he said with a shrug.

I chuckled. "Liar."

"I mean it, Drea." He rubbed his thumb along my leg.

"But you're so… patient." I suppose that was the word for being a doting boyfriend rather than a stone cold killer. "I mean you rode an elephant today. By yourself. While I giggled with Ardan."

"I know. It was pretty cute." He chuckled.

"Cute?" I asked, my eyebrow arching wildly. "I'm cute?"

"Are you kidding me?" His face fell into its familiar serious lines as he pulled me into his arms. I barely sank into the water as my legs wrapped around his torso.

"You're fucking gorgeous. Every moment of every goddamn day I wonder how you're more beautiful than the day before. How I could love you more than I already do. But every fucking day you are and damn do I." He reached up and pushed some of my hair behind my ear.

"Who are you?" I said softly, leaning into his hand.

"The man madly in love with you," he answered simply.

"You never talk like this." I pulled myself in closer.

"I fucking think like this. Every minute of every day."

How? How could this man build up every little broken bit of me? I knew I loved him. I knew I'd never stopped and seeing him show up for me had solidified it. But this… My heart was going to split.

"I love being back here," I said, looking around at the hotel.

"I had the best sex of my life in this hotel," Niall muttered all seriously sexy.

Warmth pooled in the pit of my stomach and my body bowed toward him. "I got you back here."

"Forever." He leaned into the curve of my neck.

This. This was the better than anything physical. The way his body folded into mine. The peace in this kind of intimacy was indescribable.

"Let's go upstairs," he murmured against my skin. I giggled because *that* kind of intimacy wasn't that bad either.

All I had to do was nod. Niall waded over to the edge of the pool and pushed me up to the edge of our cabana. I twisted and pushed up, scratching Ardan's toes as I went.

"Get up, sleepyhead. We're going to bed."

Ardan grumbled as he stumbled up to standing and started blindly out of the cabana. I let him go with a laugh, knowing that I could wrangle him later if he fell asleep in a hallway.

"Well that was easy." Niall got out of the pool and wrapped himself around me. "This next part is not going to be. It's going to be very, very hard." He drug out the word as he whispered against my skin and pressed his erection against me. When he nipped at my ear my knees knocked together. Those big, tattooed arms caught me. "I want you upstairs. Now."

He slapped my ass and I skittered to my cover up. I whipped it over my shoulders and skipped out of the cabana. Niall's whispered touch tickled up the back of my thighs. With a playful shriek, I took off running. He stayed right behind me until just before the elevator when he grabbed me around the middle and spun me.

I couldn't stop laughing.

I wouldn't let him go.

Life was everything wonderful and different than it had been a year ago. The sob choked in my throat and tears pricked the corners of my eyes even though laughter was still on my lips. He set me down gently in the elevator, and I sagged against the wall before wiping away a tear with the back of my hand.

"What's wrong?" he asked as he boxed me, a hand pressed to the wall on either side of my head.

"Nothing." I could barely breathe. "For the first time, absolutely nothing."

The elevator dinged before Niall could answer, his hand slipped down the wall to mine and pulled me from the elevator. Then wordlessly toward our room. My heart still pounded when I knew he was going to touch me. I could taste anticipation.

I got butterflies.

After everything I'd been through, all the things I'd seen and done and been forced to do, I wanted him. I wanted to see what he would do to me. I trusted him to do it. He excited me.

Niall pulled me into the room and pressed me up against the hotel door. He looked at me like he was going to say something but just leaned in and pressed a single kiss to the sensitive spot beneath my ear. His kisses trailed down the curve of my neck, so painfully slow.

When he got to my bikini, he turned me and stroked down my back, stopping only to untie my string. His kisses followed his hands down the valley of my spine then his teeth scratched along the edge of my bottoms. He pushed them just enough that they fell to my ankles by themselves. His knees hit the floor a moment later.

And turned me.

His kisses were flutter soft against my skin as he worked his way from one hip to the other. Then down. His tongue slid out as he kissed squarely between my thighs. My body thumped as I sagged back against the door, and my eyes fluttered shut.

Niall lapped at me until the ball in his lip ring stroked the perfect spot on my clit. I jerked and my knees spasmed inward. He didn't stop. Big broad strokes of his tongue lead to that parting kiss with the twist of his lip ring every time.

Slow. Steady. Controlled.

He added two fingers that moved at the same mind-numbing pace. My breathing hitched up and *please* dripped from my lips. Niall stayed steady. Unwavering in his assault.

My leg started to quake, and my moan trickled to a whisper.

"With or without?" Niall asked in a growl from between my legs.

"With," I said breathlessly.

He stopped without warning and grabbed me roughly as he stood. I couldn't get my legs wrapped around him, let alone catch my breath before we fell to the mattress.

With me on top.

I'd never quite been able to stomach being pinned completely. Not even by something as delectable as Niall. He always remembered.

He shoved at his pants and guided me onto him in one swift move. I arched back as I slid onto him. His hand splayed across my stomach, tattoos showing against my tanned skin as he coaxed me to ride him.

I did until my thighs burned. Until my ragged breathing hurt.

His thumb found my clit and started rubbing in small circles on that electric nub inside of me. I arched backward, bracing my hands on his thighs. My fingers dug into him as I threw my head back in surrender.

Niall knew. He always knew. His hand fell away just as the

wave of my orgasm crashed through me. Instead his hands came to my hips and held me down. I felt my body grip him, drawing him in, and judging by Niall's sharp intake of breath, he could too.

He shot into me a moment later. Each small throb of his orgasm made me twitch, each harsh flex of his hands into my flesh renewed my goose bumps.

I trembled on top of him for just a moment before he grabbed me and folded me into his chest. He ran his hands through my hair.

"It's never enough. I never get enough of you." His lips brushed against my ear.

"Me neither." I pressed my kiss to the curve of his jaw and let my entire body relax into his hold.

I closed my eyes and nuzzled into his neck. He traced lazy circles on my shoulder blade.

"You know I looked up that legend once?" His voice had a slight edge that I wasn't sure how he could still have.

"What?" I pushed up just enough to look him full in the face. I wasn't sure where this had come from.

"The one the fortune teller mentioned all those years ago."

"Yeah?" I quirked my eyebrow as I slid off of him. He winced. I was still a little disoriented.

"Yeah," he answered. "And I figured out where they went wrong."

"Oh?" I decided to just go with it and slid down into bed beside him, our faces so close where we cuddled on the pillows.

"They were happy in Scotland. They were happy with each other." He brushed a few rogue hairs behind my ear.

"Yeah, I guess they were, weren't they?" I smiled and let my eyes flutter shut at the whisper of his touch.

"I don't know why they wanted more. I know I don't." He pulled away and reached for something in the bedside table. He rolled back toward me only to set a black velvet ring box between us. "I just want you."

"I…" Didn't know what to say. Yes, I had Niall. Yes, I was happy. No, I'd never need anything else. But I'd never given a second thought to marriage.

Could I be married? Someone like me, who had done what I'd done and been what I'd been? How could anyone—even Niall—want that?

And where had all this come from in the first place?

"Open it, Drea," he said roughly, somehow both stern and fraying at the edges.

The voices quieted and I realized I couldn't deny that man, that voice, anything.

The boxed opened with a soft pop and I gasped. The silver Claddagh ring was beautiful. It was slim and delicate, small hands holding a perfect heart adorned with an exquisite and intricate crown. I picked it up and studied it closer. The silver had the rounded edges and slight tarnish of something old. The engraving inside confirmed it. Mo ghrá was carved in tiny letters in the band. *My love.*

It was perfect.

"I don't… Is this… Niall…" I could barely breathe.

"I don't know what I did to deserve you but I'm not going to question it. And I'm not going to let you go." He took it the ring from me. "I would have married you then but now… now I know what good times and bad really are. I know that I will love you through them all because I already have. I can promise you so much more with so much less now, Drea." He slid the ring onto my left ring finger, the crown first, moving slowly toward my knuckle. My heart fluttered. "With this crown I give you my loyalty. With these hands I offer my service. With this heart I give you mine." Niall pressed his lips to my fingers over top of the ring.

I couldn't think straight. Not like this. Not after words like those. Of course I could give him those things, they were already his. But it wasn't enough. How could I ever repay the man for building back up my broken soul?

"I don't have anything to give you in return." My words were choked and teary.

"Say yes."

"Yes," I said. Unequivocally. "It's still not enough."

"It's more than enough." He smiled and ran his fingers through my hair again. "You've already given me everything else."

And I knew right then that Niall McDonough, the man who'd be my husband, had given me everything and then some. He'd given me freedom, he'd given me myself. And he still wanted to give me the gift of him.

ACKNOWLEDGMENTS

Let me tell you, I can write a kiss a thousand different ways. Sex at least a hundred, but I'm never really sure how to write my acknowledgements differently. I always want to pour my heart into them but they always sound the same. I hope, as similar as they may be, you all know how genuine they are.

My crew means absolutely everything to me and my heartfelt (though oh so similar) thank yous are below.

The Twisted books are, at their very core, books for my readers. What started out as just a chapter in my newsletter is now five full length books with a sixth in process and it's all because of you my loves. My readers are not my fans, I consider you all my friends, and I will write absolutely anything for my friends. If that is a whole bunch of tattooed up, sexy bad boys, well then just twist my arm. Honestly, every time I dip my toe into the Twisted pool, it just feels great. Every time you guys shout about the books or call them your favorite dark romance series, my heart damn near explodes. Thank you from the bottom of my heart for loving these characters the way I do.

This book more than other, my husband deserves a thank you. When it wouldn't go live, he brainstormed off the wall and weird things to promote it. He kept hope when I couldn't. He believed in me when I didn't. He tells me to spend the money even if it means sacrificing or wracking up credit card debt. He's never read a word of my books, but his belief in me is unwavering. I'm not sure if a book written about a boy like that would sell real well but a life lived like that is a pretty damn good one.

Courtney, you're my rock babes. A wife, a life partner and a fellow creative and I'm not sure how I got lucky enough to find you but you keep me strong. You keep me going. Thank you for being unabashedly you and sharing that with me.

Dyllan, every single cell in your body is a good one. I would write my books just for you if I had to. Sharing chapters with you is one of the greatest joys in my life. Thank you for how you help me. Thank you for loving my words.

Harloe, your friendship and guidance is invaluable. Thank you for your support always. It's pretty cool that the Twisted books brought us together and there's yet another one out in the world.

Brenda, Jill, Júlia, Sarah and Wendy you five are the most amazing beta team I could have asked for. Your feedback was invaluable and this book is better because of each of you. I hope you know you're stuck with me now. Forever. We're friends whether you like it or not.

Amanda and Morgen thank you for all that you do. Your love and support are unwavering and never ending. Not a moment of it goes unnoticed.

Kathleen… I'm not sure how I got so lucky to meet you all those years ago in Seattle but I thank the universe every day. There's no one else I could trust with my words and vulnerability the way I trust you. Your attention to detail is just as important to me as your sense of humor and friendship. You always make me better and you're accomplishing things my AP English could only have wished for.

Talia at Book Cover Kingdom, girl, you are an artist and I'm so grateful that you share your gifts with me. You bring my books to life. I am eternally grateful that you share your talent and artwork with me. Each book I put out is better for it.

There is a very long list of author friends that need to be thanked too. Each of you that shares my work, that lets me into my group, comes to my parties and inspires me are absolutely invaluable. There's at least thirty badass babes that I could list here that always have my back. I hope you lovelies know I always have yours. It is an amazing thing to be able to call thirty of my peers my friends, my tribe. You all inspire me, you act as mentors to me, and it's a privilege to share this strange journey with you.

ABOUT THE AUTHOR

Ace Gray is a best selling author, self-proclaimed troublemaker and connoisseur of both the good life and fairy tales. After a life-long love affair with both books, she undertook writing the novel she wanted to read. Ten books later, she's gotten to live in the world of billionaires, twisted murders, and sweet small towns. She's made her heart race both with suspense and serious swoon and wouldn't trade one minute, one word of it.

When she's not writing, she owns a taco truck in a ski town in Colorado even though she can't cook a lick (that's all her husband). She loves paddle boarding, snowboarding, camping, basically anything outside... and hosting dinner parties (though she's only in it for the drinks). Oh, and of course, writing more words.

Ace is the author of Strictly Business, Bad For Business, Family Business, Twisted Fate, Twisted Death, A Twisted Love Story, Twisted Secrets, Something Twisted, Of Smoke & Cinnamon: A Christmas Story, Pretty Young Things, All The Letters I'll Never Send You and All The Letters I've Ever Read. These titles are available on Amazon.

OTHER BOOKS BY ACE GRAY

IN THE TWISTED WORLD

Twisted Fate (A Twisted Fairy Tale Duet book 1)

Twisted Death (A Twisted Fairy Tale Duet book 2)

A Twisted Love Story

Twisted Secrets

Something Twisted

Twisted Loyalties (Coming Fall 2020)

Pretty Young Things

All The Letters I'll Never Send You (Handwritten & Heartbroken Duet book 1)

All The Letters I've Ever Read (Handwritten & Heartbroken Duet book 2)

Strictly Business (Mixing Business with Pleasure book 1)

Bad For Business (Mixing Business with Pleasure book 2)

Family Business (Mixing Business with Pleasure book 3)

Of Smoke & Cinnamon: A Christmas Story

Anthologies Author Credits

Brothel: The Magnolia Diaries

Because Beards

Made in the USA
Columbia, SC
05 June 2020